The Dreamfighter and Other Creation Tales
TED HUGHES

Ted Hughes (1930–1998) was born in Yorkshire. His first book *The Hawk in the Rain* was published in 1957 by Faber and Faber and was followed by many volumes of poetry and prose for adults and children. He received the Whitbread Book of the Year for two consecutive years for his last published collections of poetry, *Tales from Ovid* (1997) and *Birthday Letters* (1998). He was Poet Laureate from 1984, and in 1998 he was appointed to the Order of Merit.

THE DREAMFIGHTER
and Other Creation Tales
TED HUGHES

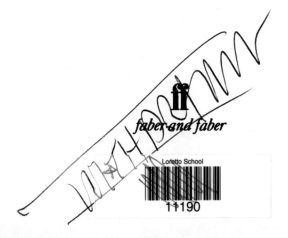

faber and faber

This collection first published in 2003
by Faber and Faber Limited
3 Queen Square London WC1N 3AU

Typeset by RefineCatch Limited, Bungay, Suffolk
Printed in England by Mackays of Chatham plc, Chatham, Kent

How the Whale Became first published in 1963
Tales of the Early World first published in 1988
The Dreamfighter and Other Creation Tales first published in 1995
Where is the Key to the Universe and Spider first published in 2003

A CIP record for this book
is available from the British Library

ISBN 0–571–21435–5

2 4 6 8 10 9 7 5 3 1

Contents

BOOK ONE

How the Whale Became

Illustrated by George Adamson

The stories in 'How the Whale Became'
are particularly suitable for children of 5+,
to read aloud or for reading alone.

For Frieda and Nicholas

Contents

Long ago when the world was brand new, before animals or birds, the sun rose into the sky and brought the first day.

The flowers jumped up and stared round astonished. Then from every side, from under leaves and from behind rocks, creatures began to appear.

In those days the colours were much better than they are now, much brighter. And the air sparkled because it had never been used.

But don't think everything was so easy.

To begin with, all the creatures were pretty much alike – very different from what they are now. They had no idea what they were going to become. Some wanted to become linnets, some wanted to become lions, some wanted to become other things. The ones that wanted to become lions practised at being lions – and by and by, sure enough, they began to turn into lions. So, the ones that wanted to become linnets practised at being linnets, and slowly they turned into linnets. And so on.

But there were other creatures that came about in other ways . . .

Why the Owl Behaves as it does

When Owl became an Owl, the first thing he discovered was that he could see by night. The next thing he discovered was that none of the other birds could.

They could see only by day. They knew it was no use trying to see by dark night, so at every grey dusk they closed their eyes and slept until the grey dawn. They had been doing this for so long, they had forgotten what the dark was.

Owl thought about this. Then he went to the other birds and said: 'I know a country where there are farms, but no farmers. You may eat when and where you please. There are no guns, no bird-scarers, no men. I will take you there if you like.'

Every day, Man killed large numbers of the birds as they were feeding in the fields. They said:

'This sounds like a safe, peaceful country, made for birds. Let us go with Owl.'

Owl smiled to himself.

'Good,' he said. 'Now, as we have no passports, we shall have to cross the frontier by night, when no one can see us. We shall leave at dusk and should be there by dawn.'

When dusk came, Owl led all the birds to a rabbit hole on the hill.

'Hold each other's hands,' he cried. 'I will lead you.'

All the rabbits that lived on the hill ran up to see what new game the birds were playing. Owl led the way down into the dark hole.

'Is this night, then?' whispered the linnets in the pitchy darkness of the hole.

'Hmm,' said the crows. 'So this is night.'

It was so dark down the hole that the birds couldn't even

see their own beaks. Each one clung to the wing of the bird in front and followed blindly. Owl led them to and fro in the loops and twists of the hole for about five minutes. By that time, the birds, who were not at all used to walking, felt as if they had been travelling for hours.

'Is it much further?' cried the swallows. 'Oh, our poor little feet!'

At last Owl shouted:

'Halt, while I see if it's all clear up ahead.'

He popped his head out of the rabbit hole and looked around. It was darker than when they had entered the hole a few minutes before, but it was not yet quite night. There was still a pale light in the west.

'Here we are!' he cried then. 'Over the border, just as dawn is breaking.'

And he led the birds out into the open. All the rabbits ran up again and sat, one ear up and one ear down, watching the birds with very puzzled expressions.

'Is this the new country?' asked the birds, and they crept close together, looking round at the almost dark landscape.

'This is it,' said Owl. 'And that is dawn you can see breaking in the east.'

The birds had quite lost their bearings in the dark underground, and the landscape was now too dark to recognize as the one they knew so well by day. They believed everything that Owl said.

Owl led them off the hill and down towards a farm.

'But it seems to be getting darker,' said the doves suddenly.

'Ah, I am glad you noticed that,' said Owl. 'That is something I forgot to tell you. In this country, day is darker than dawn.'

He smiled to himself, but the birds looked at each other in dismay.

8

'But what about the nights?' they cried. 'If day is darker than dawn, how dark are the nights?'

Owl stopped and looked at them. They couldn't see his face, but they could tell that he was very serious.

'Night here,' he said, 'is so dark, so terribly dark, that it is impossible for a mere bird to survive one glimpse of it. There is only one thing to do if you want to keep alive. You must close your eyes as tight as you can as soon as the dark of the day begins to turn grey. You must keep them closed until I awake you at grey dawn. One peep at the dark, and you are dead birds.'

Then, without another word, he led them into the stack-yard of the farm.

The farm lights were out. The farmer was sleeping. The farm was silent.

'Here you are,' said Owl. 'Just as I promised. Now feed.'

The birds scratched and pecked, but by now it was too dark to see a thing. At last they learned to find the grains by feeling with their feet. But it was slow work.

Meanwhile Owl sat on the corner of the barn, overlooking the stackyard. Whenever he felt like it, he dropped down and snatched up a nightingale or a willow-warbler. In the pitch dark, the rest of the birds were no wiser. 'This is better than rats and mice and beetles,' said Owl, as he cleaned the blood from his beak. By the time the first grey light showed in the sky, Owl was fuller than he had ever been in his life.

He gave a shout:

'Here comes the grey of dusk. Hurry, hurry! We must get to our beds and close our eyes before the terrible dark comes.'

Tumbling over each other and bumping into things, the birds ran towards his voice. When they were all gathered, he led them to a nearby copse which was full of brambles.

'Here is good roosting,' said Owl. 'I will awaken you at dawn.'

And so, in the grey of dawn, which Owl had told them was the grey of dusk, the birds closed their eyes. All that bright day they stood in groups under the brambles, their eyes tightly closed. Some of them were too frightened to fall asleep. Not one of them dared to open an eye. One look at that darkness, Owl had said, and you are dead birds.

Owl dozed happily in the dark hollow of a tree. His trick was working perfectly. He was very pleased with himself. No more mice and rats and beetles for him.

At dusk he gave a shout.

'Here is dawn,' he told the birds. 'Back to our feeding.'

And he led them back to the farm where everything happened as the night before.

In this way, Owl grew fat and contented, while the other birds grew wretched.

They grew tired of scraping in the dark stackyard. Sometimes they swallowed a grain, but as often it was a cinder. The farm cocks and hens that picked the stackyard over from end to end all day long had not left much for the birds.

And when they fell asleep, they were terrified lest they have a dream, open their eyes without thinking, and catch a glimpse of the deadly darkness. It was a great strain. Owl was continually warning them of the danger.

'One peep at that darkness,' he kept saying, 'and you are dead birds.'

If only one little bird had peeped, for only one second, with only one eye, he would have seen that there was no such thing as deadly darkness. He would have seen the sun, and the countryside he knew so well. But Owl made sure that none ever did.

10

The birds grew thin. Their feathers began to fall out. Their feet ached with stumbling about in the darkness, and their wings ached with never being used. They did not like the new country.

They complained among themselves.

At last one dusk, when Owl awoke them with his usual cry: 'Dawn!' they all went up to him and told him they could stand it no longer.

'Please lead us back to our own country,' said the birds.

Owl was worried. He wanted to keep the birds in his power. He didn't want to go back to eating rats, mice and beetles.

Then he had an idea.

'Yes,' he said. 'You are right. This is a fine country, and not dangerous. But, as you say, it is hard to make a living here. Let us find the hole by which we came and return to our own country.'

He led them up to the rabbit warren on the hill. It was almost dark.

'Here are the birds playing that game again,' said the rabbits, and they all ran up to stare.

'Now,' said Owl to the birds. 'It was one of these holes, but just which one I cannot remember. Can any of you remember?'

'I think it might have been this one,' said Cuckoo.

'Or perhaps this one,' said Jenny Wren.

'Let us try them all,' said Owl.

Most of the birds didn't dare to enter the holes lest they get lost. The ones that did were soon up again saying:

'This one comes out here.'

And:

'This one comes out here.'

11

Owl pretended to be distressed.

'We have lost our way back, and it is all my fault. Oh dear!' he cried. Then he made his voice sound very brave, as he said:

'As we are here for good, let us make the best of it.'

And he led them down to the stackyard for the night's feeding.

So it went on, for almost a year.

At last the birds decided they had had enough. They were too unhappy to go on living.

'This is no life whatsoever,' they said to each other.

'Let us all die bravely, and at once,' said Robin, 'rather than go on dying slowly in this miserable way.'

'We will do that!' cried the storm-cocks. 'Let us all die bravely together, rather than live like this.'

'But how?' said Little Gold-Crested Wren. 'How can we die?'

'Let us open our eyes,' said Robin, 'to the deadly darkness. Owl said that will kill us all.'

The unhappy birds went out with Owl that night for the last time. He led them to the stackyard as usual, and took up his post. But instead of trying to find food, the birds all sat down together in a big close group in the middle of the yard. They had decided what to do. But Owl knew nothing of it. He stared down. Softly, the birds began to sing their old songs.

'What's the matter with you?' cried Owl. 'You'll starve if you don't eat!'

But the birds took no notice of him. They went on singing, in their thin, hungry voices. It was a long time since they had sung. Now they sang very low, and very sadly.

It was a bright night, with a full moon, but Owl couldn't catch a single one of those birds. They were pressed far too closely one against another. He couldn't even pick one from the edge of the group. And they sang all night long.

By dawn Owl was furious.

'Dusk!' he cried. 'Back to the copse! Here comes the deadly dark.'

He was very hungry. But he knew what he would do. He would sneak down on them by broad day, when they were standing under the brambles with their eyes tight shut. Then he would eat his fill. He would have a song-thrush, a yellow-hammer, a greenfinch, and five bluetits –

'Where are you going?' he cried.

Instead of following him back to the copse, the birds had turned up the hill. Following the rising ground, they came at last to the very top. All around them lay the dark landscape. They gathered under the three elm trees there and faced the first grey line that was showing in the East. Then, once more, they began to sing their old songs.

Soon the deadly darkness would begin to spread through the sky. Or so they thought. They stared into the brightening dawn and sang, holding their eyes as wide as they could to catch the first rays of deadly darkness.

Oh, they were so tired of their lives.

To die like this was better than to live as they had been doing, going nowhere but where Owl led them, always in darkness, scraping their feet raw for a few grains.

They sang, and stared into the dawn. Every moment they expected the first killing ray of black to shoot out of the bright east.

At the edge of the field Owl was beating his head with his wings. He knew what the result would be. In a few minutes the sun would rise, and the birds would recognize the landscape round them.

'Come home!' he cried. 'You sillies! You'll all be killed dead as stones. Come home and close your eyes!'

But the birds had no more interest in anything that Owl said. They only wanted to die.

Slowly the sun put its burning red edge into the sky.

Lark gave a shriek. He sprang up into the air.

'It's the sun!' he cried. 'It's real day!'

Slowly the sun rose.

As it rose, the birds flew up into the branches of the elms, dancing on the twigs, and singing till their heads rang.

'It's the sun!' they sang. 'It's real day!'

From under a blackthorn bush at the field's edge, Owl stared in rage. Then he ducked his head, and flew away down the hedge, low over the ground. Even so, the birds saw him.

'He tricked us!' they cried. 'And there he goes! There goes the trickster!'

In a shouting mob, all the birds flocked after Owl. All the way back to his tree they beat him with their wings, and pulled out his feathers. He buried himself deep in his hollow tree.

The birds flew up into the tree top and sang on.

And so it is still.

Every morning the birds sing, and the Owl flies back to his dark hole. When the birds see him, they mob him, remembering his trick. He dare come out only at night, to scrape a bare living on rats, mice and beetles.

How the Whale Became

Now God had a little back-garden. In this garden he grew carrots, onions, beans and whatever else he needed for his dinner. It was a fine little garden. The plants were in neat rows, and a tidy fence kept out the animals. God was pleased with it.

One day as he was weeding the carrots he saw a strange thing between the rows. It was no more than an inch long, and it was black. It was like a black shiny bean. At one end it had a little root going into the ground.

'That's very odd,' said God. 'I've never seen one of these before. I wonder what it will grow into.'

So he left it growing.

Next day, as he was gardening, he remembered the little shiny black thing. He went to see how it was getting on. He was surprised. During the night it had doubled its length. It was now two inches long, like a shiny black egg.

Every day God went to look at it, and every day it was bigger. Every morning, in fact, it was just twice as long as it had been the morning before.

When it was six feet long, God said:

'It's getting too big. I must pull it up and cook it.'

But he left it a day.

Next day it was twelve feet long and far too big to go into any of God's pans.

God stood scratching his head and looking at it. Already it had crushed most of his carrots out of sight. If it went on growing at this rate it would soon be pushing his house over.

Suddenly, as he looked at it, it opened an eye and looked at him.

God was amazed.

The eye was quite small and round. It was near the thickest end, and farthest from the root. He walked round to the other side, and there was another eye, also looking at him.

'Well!' said God. 'And how do you do?'

The round eye blinked, and the smooth glossy skin under it wrinkled slightly, as if the thing were smiling. But there was no mouth, so God wasn't sure.

Next morning God rose early and went out into his garden.

Sure enough, during the night his new black plant with eyes had doubled its length again. It had pushed down part of his fence, so that its head was sticking out into the road, one eye looking up it, and one down. Its side was pressed against the kitchen wall.

God walked round to its front and looked it in the eye.

'You are too big,' he said sternly. 'Please stop growing before you push my house down.'

To his surprise, the plant opened a mouth. A long slit of a mouth, which ran back on either side under the eyes.

'I can't,' said the mouth.

God didn't know what to say. At last he said:

'Well then, can you tell me what sort of a thing you are? Do you know?'

'I,' said the thing, 'am Whale-Wort. You have heard of Egg-Plant, and Buck-Wheat, and Dog-Daisy. Well, I am Whale-Wort.'

There was nothing God could do about that.

By next morning, Whale-Wort stretched right across the road, and his side had pushed the kitchen wall into the kitchen. He was now longer and fatter than a bus.

When God saw this, he called the creatures together.

'Here's a strange thing,' he said. 'Look at it. What are we going to do with it?'

16

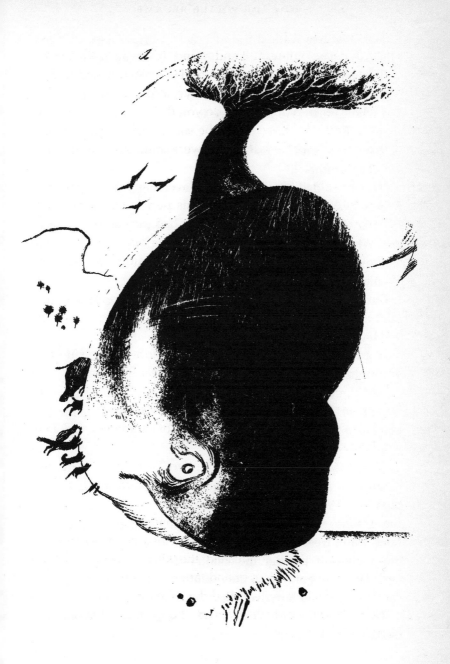

The creatures walked round Whale-Wort, looking at him. His skin was so shiny they could see their faces in it.

'Leave it,' suggested Ostrich. 'And wait till it dies down.'

'But it might go on growing,' said God. 'Until it covers the whole earth. We shall have to live on its back. Think of that.'

'I suggest,' said Mouse, 'that we throw it into the sea.'

God thought.

'No,' he said at last. 'That's too severe. Let's just leave it for a few days.'

After three more days, God's house was completely flat, and Whale-Wort was as long as a street.

'Now,' said Mouse, 'it is too late to throw it into the sea. Whale-Wort is too big to move.'

But God fastened long thick ropes round him and called up all the creatures to help haul on the ends.

'Hey!' cried Whale-Wort. 'Leave me alone.'

'You are going into the sea,' cried Mouse. 'And it serves you right. Taking up all this space.'

'But I'm happy!' cried Whale-Wort again. 'I'm happy just lying here. Leave me and let me sleep. I was made just to lie and sleep.'

'Into the sea!' cried Mouse.

'No!' cried Whale-Wort.

'Into the sea!' cried all the creatures. And they hauled on the ropes. With a great groan, Whale-Wort's root came out of the ground. He began to thresh and twist, beating down houses and trees with his long root, as the creatures dragged him willy-nilly through the countryside.

At last they got him to the top of a high cliff. With a great shout they rolled him over the edge and into the sea.

'Help! Help!' cried Whale-Wort. 'I shall drown! Please let me come back on land where I can sleep.'

'Not until you're smaller!' shouted God. 'Then you can come back.'

'But how am I to get smaller?' wept Whale-Wort, as he rolled to and fro in the sea. 'Please show me how to get smaller so that I can live on land.'

God bent down from the high cliff and poked Whale-Wort on the top of his head with his finger.

'Ow!' cried Whale-Wort. 'What was that for? You've made a hole. The water will come in.'

'No it won't,' said God. 'But some of you will come out. Now just you start blowing some of yourself out through that hole.'

Whale-Wort blew, and a high jet of spray shot up out of the hole that God had made.

'Now go on blowing,' said God.

Whale-Wort blew and blew. Soon he was quite a bit smaller. As he shrunk, his skin, that had been so tight and glossy, became covered with tiny wrinkles. At last God said to him:

'When you're as small as a cucumber, just give a shout. Then you can come back into my garden. But until then, you shall stay in the sea.'

And God walked away with all his creatures, leaving Whale-Wort rolling and blowing in the sea.

Soon Whale-Wort was down to the size of a bus. But blowing was hard work, and by this time he felt like a sleep. He took a deep breath and sank down to the bottom of the sea for a sleep. Above all, he loved to sleep.

When he awoke he gave a roar of dismay. While he was asleep he had grown back to the length of a street and the fatness of a ship with two funnels.

He rose to the surface as fast as he could and began to blow. Soon he was back down to the size of a lorry. But soon, too, he felt like another sleep. He took a deep breath and sank to the bottom.

When he awoke he was back to the length of a street.

This went on for years. It is still going on.

As fast as Whale-Wort shrinks with blowing, he grows with sleeping. Sometimes, when he is feeling very strong, he gets himself down to the size of a motor-car. But always, before he gets himself down to the size of a cucumber, he remembers how nice it is to sleep. When he wakes, he has grown again.

He longs to come back on land and sleep in the sun, with his root in the earth. But instead of that, he must roll and blow, out on the wild sea. And until he is allowed to come back on land, the creatures call him just Whale.

How the Fox Came to be where it is

Now there were two creatures that were very much alike. But one was rusty-red, with a thick tail, neat legs, and black pricking ears, while the other was just plain shaggy black and white. They were both rivals for the job of guarding Man's farm from the other animals.

The shaggy black and white one was called Foursquare, and he wanted the job because he longed to lie beside Man's fire on the cold nights. The rusty-red one was called Slylooking, and he wanted the job for a very different reason. He loved cabbages, and the only way to get near Man's cabbages was by pretending to guard them.

This rivalry went on for a long time, and still neither of them had got the job. At last Man told them to settle the matter between themselves, within a week, or else he would have to employ a bird.

'It is plain,' said Slylooking, 'that we must put our problem before a committee.'

'Very well,' said Foursquare. 'I'm glad to see you so fair-minded. I suggest that we let the cows decide it. They ponder a great deal.'

'But about what?' cried Slylooking, pretending to be alarmed. 'Scenery! That's what they ponder about. They gaze at the scenery and it looks as if they're pondering, and so they get a great name as thinkers. They're no use for important, deep problems such as ours.'

'Then whom do you suggest?'

Now Slylooking had a secret plan. 'I suggest,' he said with a sly look, 'I suggest the hens. They sit on their perches, without a move, and in the dark and all night long – they have nothing else to do but think. They have no scenery to distract them. Besides, they have a fine chairman, the cock, who keeps them in very good order.'

'Then hens it is,' said Foursquare generously.

The hens listened carefully to the problem and promised to give their answer by eleven o'clock next morning.

Foursquare found a soft warm place between hay-ricks and settled down for the night. But Slylooking could not sleep. He had much too much to do.

First of all he went to Rabbit-becomer. He said that he had discovered a whole store of cabbages which, he knew, Rabbit loved as much as he himself did.

'Where? Where?' cried Rabbit, hopping from one leg to the other.

'Well,' said Slylooking with a sly look, 'they're in the garden inside Man's farm. If only I could dig a hole as well as you can, I'd have them in a jiffy. Now if you . . .'

His voice sank to a whisper.

Away went Rabbit with Slylooking to dig the hole. After an hour's hard digging, under Slylooking's directions, Rabbit burst up through the floor of the hen-house. In a flash, Slylooking slipped past him. The hens shouted and flapped in the darkness for a moment – then snickity-snackity! Fox had gobbled the lot.

'These are lively cabbages,' said Rabbit, blinking in the darkness.

'They're the wrong ones!' cried Slylooking, pretending to be very alarmed. 'Run for your life, they don't taste like cabbages at all. I think they're cocks and hens.'

At this, Rabbit ran, and behind him, laughing silently, ran Slylooking, away down the long burrow.

Next morning Slylooking roused Foursquare, and together they went along to the hen-house to hear the decision.

Slylooking kept his head turned so that Foursquare should not see his smile. He knocked loudly on the hen-house door. When there was no answer, he pretended to look very surprised.

'They must be still deep in thought,' he said, as he knocked again. Still there was no answer, and with a puzzled frown at Foursquare, he opened the door.

And immediately jumped back.

'Murder! Murder!' he cried. 'Oh, look at the poor hens!'

Foursquare ran in. Nothing was to be seen but piles of feathers and a fresh rabbit hole in the middle of the floor.

'Who's been here?' cried Slylooking, pointing at the burrow.

'Well, that looks like Rabbit's work,' said Foursquare.

'The villain!' cried Slylooking. 'Does he hope to get away with this?'

And away he went down the long burrow, almost choking with laughter.

He found Rabbit crouched in the end of a side-shoot, still trembling, terrified by what Slylooking had persuaded him to do. Without a word, Slylooking bundled him into a sack and carried him back to Man.

'Here's the villain who murdered all your poor chickens,' he said. 'Put him in your pot.'

Man was delighted. He was so pleased, in fact, that he employed Slylooking on the spot to guard his farm, and told him to go and tell Foursquare the decision.

And so Slylooking became the sentry at the farm and was happy among the cabbages. But not for long. He could not get out of his head the way those hens had tasted. One night, as he patrolled the farm, chewing a cabbage leaf, he thought and thought of those hens until he could bear it no longer. There were new hens in the hen-house and Slylooking went straight there.

23

'Good evening, ladies,' he said as he entered. 'Is everything all right?' Once he had the door closed behind him he chose the fattest hen and snap! she was gone. The others looked at him in alarm.

'What will Man say when we tell him?' they cried.

Slylooking smiled, and snuppity, snippity, snoppity, snap! There was nothing left but a pile of feathers.

Next morning, Man just couldn't understand it. But he put new hens in the hen-house. Slylooking swore he had never heard a thing.

That night he visited the hen-house again.

And so every night for a week. He couldn't resist it. And each time he had to gobble up every single hen lest any be left to tell Man what he had been up to. He quite lost his taste for cabbage leaves.

One evening, as he was going for a stroll in the fields, he met Foursquare.

'What are you doing, still snooping round here? Away with you!' he cried. 'I've to guard the farm against such creatures as you.'

Foursquare looked at him steadily and said, 'You have a hen feather in the corner of your mouth.'

Slylooking was furious, but before he could say anything Foursquare had walked away.

Slylooking didn't like Foursquare's remark at all. It looked as if he suspected the truth. So Slylooking decided to play a trick on Foursquare and get rid of him. He went straight to Man.

'I have an idea,' he said, with a sly look, 'that Foursquare is at the bottom of this hen mystery. He is taking his revenge on you for employing me instead of him.'

'Why,' said Man, 'that seems very likely. Certainly he has very fierce teeth. But how are we to catch him?'

'Leave it to me,' said Slylooking. He had another plan already worked out.

Away he went, and finally he found Foursquare sitting on a green hill watching the river.

'Someone is still eating Man's hens,' said Slylooking. 'Will you help us to catch him?'

Now Foursquare was a very honest creature, and when he heard this he was quite ready to believe that Slylooking was not the culprit as he had suspected.

'How are we to do it?' he asked.

'Well,' said Slylooking, 'it isn't clear whether the murderer comes up through the floor of the hen-house, or whether he comes over the farmyard gate and in at the hen-house door. So tonight, while I watch the farm gate, I want you to hide in the hen-house and keep an eye on the floor.'

'Well, that should catch him, whoever it is,' said Foursquare. 'What time shall I come?'

'Come about midnight. I'll let you in,' said Slylooking with a sly look.

A quarter of an hour before midnight Slylooking slipped into the hen-house and had a banquet of hens. Then he went off to meet Foursquare. Foursquare was waiting under the hedge.

'Quickly, quickly!' said Slylooking. 'The murderer may be here any minute. Hurry. Into the hen-house.'

As soon as Foursquare was in the hen-house with the pile of feathers, Slylooking bolted the door and ran for Man.

'I've trapped the murderer!' he cried. 'I've got him!'

Man came running to see who it was.

'Why it's Foursquare. Just as you said. Well done, Slylooking.' Man dragged Foursquare out of the hen-house, tied him to the fence, and ran to fetch his gun.

Slylooking danced round poor Foursquare, looking at him merrily out of his eye-corner and singing:

'This is the end of this stor-ee,
Bullets for you and chickens for me.'

'Oh, is that so!' roared Man's voice. He had returned more quickly than Slylooking had expected. Bang! went his gun, and Bang! But Slylooking was over the wall and three fields away and still running.

There and then Man untied Foursquare and led him into the farm kitchen. He gave him a great bowlful of food and after that a rug to stretch out on at the fireside.

But that night, and every night after it, Slylooking had to sleep in the wet wood. And whenever he came sneaking back to the farm, sniffing for hens, Foursquare would hear him. He would jump up from his rug, barking at the top of his voice, and Man would be out through the door with his gun.

But Slylooking was too foxy to be caught. In fact, he was so foxy that pretty soon nobody called him Slylooking any more. They called him what we call him – plain Fox.

How the Polar Bear Became

When the animals had been on earth for some time they grew tired of admiring the trees, the flowers and the sun. They began to admire each other. Every animal was eager to be admired, and spent a part of each day making itself look more beautiful.

Soon they began to hold beauty contests.

Sometimes Tiger won the prize, sometimes Eagle, and sometimes Ladybird. Every animal tried hard.

One animal in particular won the prize almost every time. This was Polar Bear.

Polar Bear was white. Not quite snowy white, but much whiter than any of the other creatures. Everyone admired her. In secret, too, everyone was envious of her. But however much they wished that she wasn't quite so beautiful, they couldn't help giving her the prize.

'Polar Bear,' they said, 'with your white fur, you are almost too beautiful.'

All this went to Polar Bear's head. In fact, she became vain. She was always washing and polishing her fur, trying to make it still whiter. After a while she was winning the prize every time. The only times any other creature got a chance to win was when it rained. On those days Polar Bear would say:

'I shall not go out in the wet. The other creatures will be muddy, and my white fur may get splashed.'

Then, perhaps, Frog or Duck would win for a change.

She had a crowd of young admirers who were always hanging around her cave. They were mainly Seals, all very giddy. Whenever she came out they made a loud shrieking roar:

'Ooooooh! How beautiful she is!'

Before long, her white fur was more important to Polar Bear than anything. Whenever a single speck of dust landed on the tip of one hair of it – she was furious.

'How can I be expected to keep beautiful in this country!' she cried then. 'None of you have ever seen me at my best, because of the dirt here. I am really much whiter than any of you have ever seen me. I think I shall have to go into another country. A country where there is none of this dust. Which country would be best?'

She used to talk in this way because then the Seals would cry:

'Oh, please don't leave us. Please don't take your beauty away from us. We will do anything for you.'

And she loved to hear this.

Soon animals were coming from all over the world to look at her. They stared and stared as Polar Bear stretched out on her rock in the sun. Then they went off home and tried to make themselves look like her. But it was no use. They were all the wrong colour. They were black, or brown, or yellow, or ginger, or fawn, or speckled, but not one of them was white. Soon most of them gave up trying to look beautiful. But they still came every day to gaze enviously at Polar Bear. Some brought picnics. They sat in a vast crowd among the trees in front of her cave.

'Just look at her,' said Mother Hippo to her children. 'Now see that you grow up like that.'

But nothing pleased Polar Bear.

'The dust these crowds raise!' she sighed. 'Why can't I ever get away from them? If only there were some spotless, shining country, all for me . . .'

Now pretty well all the creatures were tired of her being so

much more admired than they were. But one creature more so than the rest. He was Peregrine Falcon.

He was a beautiful bird, all right. But he was not white. Time and again in the beauty contests he was runner-up to Polar Bear.

'If it were not for her,' he raged to himself, 'I should be first every time.'

He thought and thought for a plan to get rid of her. How? How? How? At last he had it.

One day he went up to Polar Bear.

Now Peregrine Falcon had been to every country in the world. He was a great traveller, as all the creatures well knew.

'I know a country,' he said to Polar Bear, 'which is so clean it is even whiter than you are. Yes, yes, I know, you are beautifully white, but this country is even whiter. The rocks are clear glass and the earth is frozen ice-cream. There is no dirt there, no dust, no mud. You would become whiter than ever in that country. And no one lives there. You could be queen of it.'

Polar Bear tried to hide her excitement.

'I could be queen of it, you say?' she cried. 'This country sounds made for me. No crowds, no dirt? And the rocks, you say, are glass?'

'The rocks,' said Peregrine Falcon, 'are mirrors.'

'Wonderful!' cried Polar Bear.

'And the rain,' he said, 'is white face powder.'

'Better than ever!' she cried. 'How quickly can I be there, away from all these staring crowds and all this dirt?'

'I am going to another country,' she told the other animals. 'It is too dirty here to live.'

Peregrine Falcon hired Whale to carry his passenger. He sat on Whale's forehead, calling out the directions. Polar Bear sat on the shoulder, gazing at the sea. The Seals, who had begged to go with her, sat on the tail.

After some days, they came to the North Pole, where it is all snow and ice.

'Here you are,' cried Peregrine Falcon. 'Everything just as I said. No crowds, no dirt, nothing but beautiful clean whiteness.'

'And the rocks actually are mirrors!' cried Polar Bear, and she ran to the nearest iceberg to repair her beauty after the long trip.

Every day now, she sat on one iceberg or another, making herself beautiful in the mirror of the ice. Always, near her, sat the Seals. Her fur became whiter and whiter in this new clean country. And as it became whiter, the Seals praised her beauty more and more. When she herself saw the improvement in her looks she said:

'I shall never go back to that dirty old country again.'

And there she is still, with all her admirers around her.

Peregrine Falcon flew back to the other creatures and told them that Polar Bear had gone for ever. They were all very glad, and set about making themselves beautiful at once. Every single one was saying to himself:

'Now that Polar Bear is out of the way, perhaps I shall have a chance of the prize at the beauty contest.'

And Peregrine Falcon was saying to himself:

'Surely, now, I am the most beautiful of all creatures.'

But that first contest was won by Little Brown Mouse for her pink feet.

How the Hyena Became

One creature, a Wild-Dog-Becomer called Hyena, copied Leopard-Becomer in everything he did.

Leopard-Becomer was already one of the most respected creatures on the plains. He was strong, swift, fierce, graceful, and had the most beautiful spotted skin.

Hyena longed to be like this. He practised walking like him, crouching like him, pouncing like him. He studied his every move. 'I must get it perfect,' he kept saying to himself.

He followed Leopard-Becomer so closely, in fact, that he never had time to go off and kill his own game. So he had to eat what Leopard left. Leopard didn't take at all kindly to Hyena, and often made him wait a long time for the leftovers. In this way Hyena grew used to eating meat that was none too fresh.

Nevertheless, so long as he could keep near Leopard he was satisfied.

Only one thing could take him from Leopard's track, and that was a chance to boast to the wild-dogs.

'You're nothing but a Wild-Dog yourself,' they said. 'Who do you think you are? Putting on all these Leopard airs?'

'Ha ha,' he replied. 'You wait. Watch me and wait. You're in for a surprise. I'll be a leopard yet.'

One morning he awoke to find his skin covered with big spots, almost like a leopard's.

'Joy! Joy!' he cried, and danced about till he was sodden with dew. He ran off to show himself to the wild-dogs. When they saw his spots they all fled, looking back over their shoulders fearfully.

'Ha ha!' cried Hyena. 'So you thought I was Leopard, did you?'

It was a long time before he could persuade them that he really was Hyena. Even so, they never quite trusted him again.

They began to move away quietly whenever they saw him coming.

As for Hyena, he returned to his Leopard-Becoming with a renewed zest.

This went on for many years.

At last, Hyena began to feel impatient.

'Shall I never be a leopard?' he asked himself. 'I'm still not anywhere near as good as Leopard-Becomer. In fact, he picks up new tricks faster than I learn his old ones.'

He ran to the Wild-Dog-Becomers.

'Am I Leopard yet?' he asked.

They peeped back over the skyline behind which they had run at the first sight of him.

'You are not,' they said. 'But you are not Wild-Dog either, not any more. The Lord knows what sort of a thing you are now.'

Hyena went back to Leopard. For some years he went about in a very disgruntled condition, but still following Leopard. One day he came as close to Leopard as he dared and said:

'Shall I never become a leopard, Leopard?'

Leopard looked at him in disgust.

'You,' he said, 'have already become what you are going to become.'

'And what is that, please?' asked Hyena politely.

'You have become,' said Leopard, 'a Leopard-Follower.'

Hyena retired to a safe distance and thought about this. He became very embittered.

33

'Very well,' he said at last. 'If I cannot ever be a leopard, that's finished it. I shall go back to being a wild-dog. Leopard is a stupid creature anyway, calling me a Leopard-Follower.'

And he ran back to the wild-dogs. He knew they would run away when they caught sight of him, so while he was still in the distance he began to shout:

'It's me, Hyena. I'm coming back to be one of you. I've finished with Leopard.'

But it was no use. The wild-dogs ran, and faster than Hyena they ran. He chased them as far as he could move, shouting till his throat ached. At last he stood alone, panting, in the middle of a flat, empty, silent plain.

Sadly, he drooped his tail and turned back. He was feeling hungry. Then he remembered that he didn't know how to kill anything. He walked on and on, getting hungrier and hungrier.

Suddenly he stopped, and sniffed. A leopard had killed a gazelle near there a week ago. He found the bones, cracked them, and sucked them. Then, sniffing, he followed the track of the leopard.

This leopard lived under a rock on top of a hill. Hyena made his bed at the bottom of the hill. Whenever Leopard went out hunting Hyena followed him and ate what he left. In this way he lived.

But he was deeply ashamed. He now saw that he was nothing but a Leopard-Follower after all. He became more bitter than ever. He no longer imitated Leopard. His greatest pleasure now was to sit at a safe distance, when Leopard was eating, and make critical remarks in a loud clear voice:

'What a stupid animal you are! How gluttonously you eat! How boorishly you tear the meat! How disgustingly you growl as you chew!'

And between each comment he gave a laugh, a loud

mocking laugh, so that all the other animals within hearing would think he was getting the better of Leopard in some way.

'If I cannot be a leopard,' he said to himself, 'then you shall be ashamed of being a leopard.'

Leopard, of course, was much too fine a beast ever to be ashamed of being what he was.

That was as far as Hyena ever got. He is the same still. He follows Leopard from meal to meal, and laughs and laughs, while Leopard gorges himself on the choicest portions of the meat.

Afterwards, when Leopard has eaten his fill and strolled off to sleep, Hyena stops laughing. Then, at dusk, and on bent legs so as not to be seen, he runs in and tears and gulps all night long at the bones and scraps and rags of meat that are left.

How the Tortoise Became

When God made a creature, he first of all shaped it in clay. Then he baked it in the ovens of the sun until it was hard. Then he took it out of the oven and, when it was cool, breathed life into it. Last of all, he pulled its skin on to it like a tight jersey.

All the animals got different skins. If it was a cold day, God would give to the animals he made on that day a dense, woolly skin. Snow was falling heavily when he made the sheep and the bears.

If it was a hot day, the new animals got a thin skin. On the day he made greyhounds and dachshunds and boys and girls, the weather was so hot God had to wear a sun hat and was calling endlessly for iced drinks.

Now on the day he made Torto, God was so hot the sweat was running down on to the tips of his fingers.

After baking Torto in the oven, God took him out to cool. Then he flopped back in his chair and ordered Elephant to fan him with its ears. He had made Elephant only a few days before and was very pleased with its big flapping ears. At last he thought that Torto must surely be cool.

'He's had as long as I usually give a little thing like him,' he said, and picking up Torto, he breathed life into him. As he did so, he found out his mistake.

Torto was not cool. Far from it. On that hot day, with no cooling breezes, Torto had remained scorching hot. Just as he was when he came out of the oven.

'Ow!' roared God. He dropped Torto and went hopping

away on one leg to the other end of his workshop, shaking his burnt fingers.

'Ow, ow, ow!' he roared again, and plunged his hand into a dish of butter to cure the burns.

Torto meanwhile lay on the floor, just alive, groaning with the heat.

'Oh, I'm so hot!' he moaned. 'So hot! The heat. Oh, the heat!'

God was alarmed that he had given Torto life before he was properly cooled.

'Just a minute, Torto,' he said. 'I'll have a nice, thin, cooling skin on you in a jiffy. Then you'll feel better.'

But Torto wanted no skin. He was too hot as it was.

'No, no!' he cried. 'I shall stifle. Let me go without a skin for a few days. Let me cool off first.'

'That's impossible,' said God. 'All creatures must have skins.'

'No, no!' cried Torto, wiping the sweat from his little brow. 'No skin!'

'Yes!' cried God.

'No!' cried Torto.

'Yes!'

'No!'

God made a grab at Torto, who ducked and ran like lightning under a cupboard. Without any skin to cumber his movements, Torto felt very light and agile.

'Come out!' roared God, and got down on his knees to grope under the cupboard for Torto.

In a flash, Torto was out from under the other end of the cupboard, and while God was still struggling to his feet, he ran out through the door and into the world, without a skin.

The first thing he did was to go to a cool pond and plunge straight into it. There he lay, for several days, just cooling off.

Then he came out and began to live among the other creatures. But he was still very hot. Whenever he felt his own heat getting too much for him, he retired to his pond to cool off in the water. In this way, he found life pleasant enough.

Except for one thing. The other creatures didn't approve of Torto.

They all had skins. When they saw Torto without a skin, they were horrified.

'But he has no skin!' cried Porcupine.

'It's disgusting!' cried Yak. 'It's indecent!'

'He's not normal. Leave him to himself,' said Sloth.

So all the animals began to ignore Torto. But they couldn't ignore him completely, because he was a wonderfully swift runner, and whenever they held a race, he won it. He was so nimble without a skin that none of the other creatures could hope to keep up with him.

'I'm a genius-runner,' he said. 'You should respect me. I am faster than the lot of you put together. I was made different.'

But the animals still ignored him. Even when they had to give him the prizes for winning all the races, they still ignored him.

'Torto is a very swift mover,' they said. 'And perhaps swifter than any of us. But what sort of a creature is he? No skin!'

And they all turned up their noses.

At first, Torto didn't care at all. When the animals collected together, with all their fur brushed and combed and set neatly, he strolled among them, smiling happily, naked.

'When will this disgusting creature learn to behave?' cried Turkey, loudly enough for everyone to hear.

'Just take no notice of him,' said Alligator, and lumbered round, in his heavy armour, to face in the opposite direction.

All the animals turned round to face in the opposite direction.

When Torto went up to Grizzly Bear to ask what everyone was looking at, Grizzly Bear pretended to have a fly in his ear. When he went to Armadillo, Armadillo gathered up all his sons and daughters and led them off without a word or a look.

'So that's your game, is it?' said Torto to himself. Then aloud, he said: 'Never mind. Wait till it comes to the races.'

When the races came, later in the afternoon, Torto won them all. But nobody cheered. He collected the prizes and went off to his pond alone.

'They're jealous of me,' he said. 'That's why they ignore me. But I'll punish them: I'll go on winning all the races.'

That night, God came to Torto and begged him to take a proper skin before it was too late. Torto shook his head:

'The other animals are snobs,' he said. 'Just because they are covered with a skin, they think everyone else should be covered with one too. That's snobbery. But I shall teach them not to be snobs by making them respect me. I shall go on winning all the races.'

And so he did. But still the animals didn't respect him. In fact, they grew to dislike him more and more.

One day there was a very important race-meeting, and all the animals collected at the usual place. But the minute Torto arrived they simply walked away. Simply got up and walked away. Torto sat on the race-track and stared after them. He felt really left out.

'Perhaps,' he thought sadly, 'it would be better if I had a skin. I mightn't be able to run then, but at least I would have friends. I have no friends. Besides, after all this practice, I would still be able to run quite fast.'

But as soon as he said that he felt angry with himself.

'No!' he cried. 'They are snobs. I shall go on winning their races in spite of them. I shall teach them a lesson.'

And he got up from where he was sitting and followed them. He found them all in one place, under a tree. And the races were being run.

'Hey!' he called as he came up to them. 'What about me?'

But at that moment, Tiger held up a sign in front of him. On the sign, Torto read: 'Creatures without skins are not allowed to enter.'

Torto went home and brooded. God came up to him.

'Well, Torto,' said God kindly, 'would you like a skin yet?'

Torto thought deeply.

'Yes,' he said at last, 'I would like a skin. But only a very special sort of skin.'

'And what sort of a skin is that?' asked God.

'I would like,' said Torto, 'a skin that I can put on, or take off, just whenever I please.'

God frowned.

'I'm afraid,' he said, 'I have none like that.'

'Then make one,' replied Torto. 'You're God.'

God went away and came back within an hour.

'Do you want a beautiful skin?' he asked. 'Or do you mind if it's very ugly?'

'I don't care what sort of a skin it is,' said Torto, 'so long as I can take it off and put it back on again just whenever I please.'

God went away again, and again came back within an hour.

'Here it is. That's the best I can do.'

'What's this!' cried Torto. 'But it's horrible!'

'Take it or leave it,' said God, and walked away.

Torto examined the skin. It was tough, rough, and stiff.

'It's like a coconut,' he said. 'With holes in it.'

And so it was. Only it was shiny. When he tried it on, he found it quite snug. It had only one disadvantage. He could move only very slowly in it.

'What's the hurry?' he said to himself then. 'When it comes to moving, who can move faster than me?'

And he laughed. Suddenly he felt delighted. Away he went to where the animals were still running their races.

As he came near to them, he began to think that perhaps his skin was a little rough and ready. But he checked himself:

'Why should I dress up for them?' he said. 'This rough old thing will do. The races are the important thing.'

Tiger lowered his notice and stared in dismay as Torto swaggered past him. All the animals were now turning and staring, nudging each other, and turning and staring.

'That's a change, anyway,' thought Torto.

Then, as usual, he entered for all the races.

The animals began to talk and laugh among themselves as they pictured Torto trying to run in his heavy new clumsy skin.

'He'll look silly, and then how we'll laugh.' And they all laughed.

But when he took his skin off at the starting-post, their laughs turned to frowns.

He won all the races, then climbed back into his skin to collect the prizes. He strutted in front of all the animals.

'Now it's my turn to be snobbish,' he said to himself.

Then he went home, took off his skin, and slept sweetly. Life was perfect for him.

This went on for many years. But though the animals would now speak to him, they remembered what he had been. That didn't worry Torto, however. He became very fond of his skin. He began to keep it on at night when he came home after the races. He began to do everything in it, except actually race. He crept around slowly, smiling at the leaves, letting the days pass.

There came a time when there were no races for several weeks. During all this time Torto never took his skin off once. Until, when the first race came round at last, he found he could not take his skin off at all, no matter how he pushed and pulled. He was stuck inside it. He strained and squeezed and gasped, but it was no use. He was stuck.

However, he had already entered for all the races, so he had to run.

He lined up, in his skin, at the start, alongside Hare, Greyhound, Cheetah and Ostrich. They were all great runners, but usually he could beat the lot of them easily. The crowd stood agog.

'Perhaps,' Torto was thinking, 'my skin won't make much difference. I've never really tried to run my very fastest in it.'

The starter's pistol cracked, and away went Greyhound, Hare, Cheetah and Ostrich, neck and neck. Where was Torto?

The crowd roared with laughter.

Torto had fallen on his face and had not moved an inch. At his first step, cumbered by his stiff, heavy skin, he had fallen on his face. But he tried. He climbed back on to his feet and made one stride, slowly, then a second stride, and was just about to make a third when the race was over and Cheetah had won. Torto had moved not quite three paces. How the crowd laughed!

And so it was with all the races. In not one race did Torto manage to make more than three steps, before it was over.

The crowd was enjoying itself. Torto was weeping with shame.

After the last race, he turned to crawl home. He only wanted to hide. But though the other animals had let him go off alone when he had the prizes, now they came alongside him, in a laughing, mocking crowd.

'Who's the slowest of all the creatures?' they shouted.

'Torto is!'

'Who's the slowest of all the creatures?'

'Torto is!' – all the way home.

After that, Torto tried to keep himself out of sight, but the other animals never let him rest. Whenever any of them chanced to see him, they would shout at the tops of their voices:

'Who's the slowest of all the creatures?'

And all the other creatures within hearing would answer, at the tops of their voices:

'Torto is!'

And that is how Torto came to be known as 'Tortoise'.

How the Bee Became

Now in the middle of the earth lived a demon. This demon spent all his time groping about in the dark tunnels, searching for precious metals and gems.

He was hunch-backed and knobbly-armed. His ears draped over his shoulders like a wrinkly cloak. These kept him safe from the bits of rock that were always falling from the ceilings of his caves. He had only one eye, which was a fire. To keep this fire alive he had to feed it with gold and silver. Over this eye he cooked his supper every night. It is hard to say what he ate. All kinds of fungus that grew in the airless dark on the rocks. His drink was mostly tar and oil, which he loved. There is no end of tar and oil in the middle of the earth.

He rarely came up to the light. Once, when he did, he saw the creatures that God was making.

'What's this?' he cried, when a grasshopper landed on his clawed, horny foot. Then he saw Lion. Then Cobra. Then, far above him, Eagle.

'My word!' he said, and hurried back down into his dark caves to think about what he had seen.

He was jealous of the beautiful things that God was making.

'I will make something,' he said at last, 'which will be far more beautiful than any of God's creatures.'

But he had no idea how to set about it.

So one day he crept up to God's workshop and watched God at work. He peeped from behind the door. He saw him model the clay, bake it in the sun's fire, then breathe life into it. So that was it!

Away he dived, back down into the centre of the earth.

At the centre of the earth it was too hot for clay. Everything was already baked hard. He set about trying to make his own clay.

First, he ground up stones between his palms. That was powder. But how was he to make it into clay? He needed water, and there in the centre of the earth it was too hot for water.

He searched and he searched, but there was none. At last he sat down. He felt so sad he began to cry. Big tears rolled down his nose.

'If only I had water,' he sobbed, 'this clay could become a real living creature. Why do I have to live where there is no water?'

He looked at the powder in his palm, and began to cry afresh. As he looked and wept, and looked and wept, a tear fell off the end of his nose straight into the powder.

But he was too late. A demon's tears are no ordinary tears. There was a red flash, a fizz, a bubbling, and where the powder had been was nothing but a dark stain on his palm.

He felt like weeping again. Now he had water, but no powder.

'So much for stone-powder,' he said. 'I need something stronger.'

Then quickly, before his tears dried, he ground some of the precious metal that he used to feed the fire of his eye. As soon as it was powder he wetted it with a tear off his cheek. But it was no better than the stone-powder had been. There was a flash, a fizz, a bubbling, and nothing.

'Well,' he said. 'What now?'

At last he thought of it – he would make a powder of precious gems. It was hard work grinding these, but at last he had finished. Now for a tear. But he was too excited to cry.

He struggled to bring up a single tear. It was no good. His eye was dry as an oven. He struggled and he struggled. Nothing! All at once he sat down and burst into tears.

'It's no good!' he cried. 'I can't cry!' Then he felt his tears wet on his cheeks.

'I'm crying!' he cried joyfully. 'Quick, quick!' And he splashed a tear on to the powder of the precious gems. The result was perfect. He had made a tiny piece of beautiful clay. Only tiny, because his tears had been few. But it was big enough.

'Now,' he said, 'what kind of creature shall I make?'

The jewel-clay was very hard to work into shape. It was tough as red-hot iron.

So he laid the clay on his anvil and began to beat it into shape with his great hammer.

He beat and beat and beat that clay for a thousand years.

And at last it was shaped. Now it needed baking. Very carefully, because the thing he had made was very frail, he put it into the fire of his eye to bake.

Then, beside a great heap of small pieces of gold and silver, for another thousand years he sat, feeding the fire of his eye with the precious metal. All this time, in the depths of his eye glowed his little creature, baking slowly.

At last it was baked.

Now came the real problem. How was he going to breathe life into it?

He puffed and he blew, but it was no good.

'It is so beautiful!' he cried. 'I must give it life!'

It certainly was beautiful. All the precious gems of which it was made mingled their colours. And from the flames in which it had been baked, it had taken a dark fire. It gleamed and flashed: red, blue, orange, green, purple, no bigger than your finger-nail.

But it had no life.

There was only one thing to do. He must go to God and ask him to breathe life into it.

When God saw the demon he was amazed. He had no idea that such a creature existed.

'Who are you?' he asked. 'Where have you come from?'

The demon hung his head. 'Now,' he thought, 'I will use a trick.'

'I'm a jewel-smith,' he said humbly. 'And I live in the centre of the earth. I have brought you a present, to show my respect for you.'

He showed God the little creature that he had made. God was amazed again.

'How beautiful!' he kept saying as he turned it over and over on his hand. 'How beautiful! What a wonderfully clever smith you are.'

'Ah!' said the demon. 'But not so clever as you. I could never breathe life into it. If you had made it, it would be alive. As it is, it is beautiful, but dead.'

God was flattered. 'That's soon altered,' he said. He raised the demon's gift to his lips and breathed life into it.

Then he held it out. It crawled on to the end of his finger.

'Buzz!' it went, and whirred its thin, beautiful wings. Like a flash, the demon snatched it from God's finger-tip and plunged back down into the centre of the earth.

There, for another thousand years, he lay, letting the little creature crawl over his fingers and make short flights from one hand to the other. It glittered all its colours in the light of his eye's fire. The demon was very happy.

'You are more beautiful than any of God's creatures,' he crooned.

But life was hard for the little creature down in the centre of the earth, with no one to play with but the demon. He had God's breath in him, and he longed to be among the other creatures under the sun.

And he was sad for another reason. In his veins ran not blood, but the tears with which the demon had mixed his clay. And what is sadder than a tear? Feeling the sadness in all his veins, he moved restlessly over the demon's hands.

One day the demon went up to the light to compare his little creature with the ones God had made.

'Buzz!' went his pet, and was away over a mountain.

'Come back!' roared the demon, then quickly covered his mouth with his hands, frightened that God would hear him. He began to search for his creature, but soon, frightened that God would see him, he crept back into the earth.

Still his little creature was not happy.

The sadness of the demon's tears was always in him. It was part of him. It was what flowed in his veins.

'If I gather everything that is sweet and bright and happy,' he said to himself, 'that should make me feel better. Here there are plenty of wonderfully sweet bright happy things.'

And he began to fly from flower to flower, collecting the bright sunny sweetness out of their cups.

'Ah!' he cried. 'Wonderful!'

The sweetness lit up his body. He felt the sun glowing through him from what he drank. For the first time in his life he felt happy.

But the moment he stopped drinking from the flowers, the sadness came creeping back along his veins and the gloom into his thoughts.

'That demon made me of tears,' he said. 'How can I ever hope to get away from the sadness of tears? Unless I never leave these flowers.'

And he hurried from flower to flower.

49

He could never stop, and it was too good to stop.

Soon, he had drunk so much, the sweetness began to ooze out of his pores. He was so full of it, he was brimming over with it. And every second he drank more.

At last he had to pause.

'I must store all this somewhere,' he said.

So he made a hive, and all the sweetness that oozed from him he stored in that hive. Man found it and called it honey. God saw what the little creature was doing, and blessed him, and called him Bee.

But Bee must still go from flower to flower, seeking sweetness. The tears of the demon are still in his veins ready to make him gloomy the moment he stops drinking from the flowers. When he is angry and stings, the smart of his sting is the tear of the demon. If he has to keep that sweet, it is no wonder that he drinks sweetness until he brims over.

How the Cat Became

Things were running very smoothly and most of the creatures were highly pleased with themselves. Lion was already famous. Even the little shrews and moles and spiders were pretty well known.

But among all these busy creatures there was one who seemed to be getting nowhere. It was Cat.

Cat was a real oddity. The others didn't know what to make of him at all.

He lived in a hollow tree in the wood. Every night, when the rest of the creatures were sound asleep, he retired to the depths of his tree – then such sounds, such screechings, yowlings, wailings! The bats that slept upside-down all day long in the hollows of the tree branches awoke with a start and fled with their wing-tips stuffed into their ears. It seemed to them that Cat was having the worst nightmares ever – ten at a time.

But no. Cat was tuning his violin.

If only you could have seen him! Curled in the warm smooth hollow of his tree, gazing up through the hole at the top of the trunk, smiling at the stars, winking at the moon – his violin tucked under his chin. Ah, Cat was a happy one.

And all night long he sat there composing his tunes.

Now the creatures didn't like this at all. They saw no use in his music, it made no food, it built no nest, it didn't even keep him warm. And the way Cat lounged around all day, sleeping in the sun, was just more than they could stand.

'He's a bad example,' said Beaver, 'he never does a stroke of work! What if our children think they can live as idly as he does?'

'It's time,' said Weasel, 'that Cat had a job like everybody else in the world.'

So the creatures of the wood formed a Committee to persuade Cat to take a job.

Jay, Magpie, and Parrot went along at dawn and sat in the topmost twigs of Cat's old tree. As soon as Cat poked his head out, they all began together:

'You've to get a job. Get a job! Get a job!'

That was only the beginning of it. All day long, everywhere he went, those birds were at him:

'Get a job! Get a job!'

And try as he would, Cat could not get one wink of sleep.

That night he went back to his tree early. He was far too tired to practise on his violin and fell fast asleep in a few minutes. Next morning, when he poked his head out of the tree at first light, the three birds of the Committee were there again, loud as ever:

'Get a job!'

Cat ducked back down into his tree and began to think. He wasn't going to start grubbing around in the wet woods all day, as they wanted him to. Oh no. He wouldn't have any time to play his violin if he did that. There was only one thing to do and he did it.

He tucked his violin under his arm and suddenly jumped out at the top of the tree and set off through the woods at a run. Behind him, shouting and calling, came Jay, Magpie, and Parrot.

Other creatures that were about their daily work in the undergrowth looked up when Cat ran past. No one had ever seen Cat run before.

'Cat's up to something,' they called to each other. 'Maybe he's going to get a job at last.'

Deer, Wild Boar, Bear, Ferret, Mongoose, Porcupine, and a cloud of birds set off after Cat to see where he was going.

After a great deal of running they came to the edge of the forest. There they stopped. As they peered through the leaves they looked sideways at each other and trembled. Ahead of them, across an open field covered with haycocks, was Man's farm.

But Cat wasn't afraid. He went straight on, over the field, and up to Man's door. He raised his paw and banged as hard as he could in the middle of the door.

Man was so surprised to see Cat that at first he just stood, eyes wide, mouth open. No creature ever dared to come on to his fields, let alone knock at his door. Cat spoke first.

'I've come for a job,' he said.

'A job?' asked Man, hardly able to believe his ears.

'Work,' said Cat. 'I want to earn my living.'

Man looked him up and down, then saw his long claws.

'You look as if you'd make a fine rat-catcher,' said Man.

Cat was surprised to hear that. He wondered what it was about him that made him look like a rat-catcher. Still, he wasn't going to miss the chance of a job. So he stuck out his chest and said: 'Been doing it for years.'

'Well then, I've a job for you,' said Man. 'My farm's swarming with rats and mice. They're in my haystacks, they're in my corn sacks, and they're all over the pantry.'

So before Cat knew where he was, he had been signed on as a Rat-and-Mouse-Catcher. His pay was milk, and meat, and a place at the fireside. He slept all day and worked all night.

At first he had a terrible time. The rats pulled his tail, the mice nipped his ears. They climbed on to rafters above him and dropped down – thump! on to him in the dark. They teased the life out of him.

54

But Cat was a quick learner. At the end of the week he could lay out a dozen rats and twice as many mice within half an hour. If he'd gone on laying them out all night there would pretty soon have been none left, and Cat would have been out of a job. So he just caught a few each night – in the first ten minutes or so. Then he retired into the barn and played his violin till morning. This was just the job he had been looking for.

Man was delighted with him. And Mrs Man thought he was beautiful. She took him on to her lap and stroked him for hours on end. What a life! thought Cat. If only those silly creatures in the dripping wet woods could see him now!

Well, when the other farmers saw what a fine rat-and-mouse-catcher Cat was, they all wanted cats too. Soon there were so many cats that our Cat decided to form a string band. Oh yes, they were all great violinists. Every night, after making one pile of rats and another of mice, each cat left his farm and was away over the fields to a little dark spinney.

Then what tunes! All night long . . .

Pretty soon lady cats began to arrive. Now, every night, instead of just music, there was dancing too. And what dances! If only you could have crept up there and peeped into the glade from behind a tree and seen the cats dancing – the glossy furred ladies and the tomcats, some pearly grey, some ginger red, and all with wonderful green flashing eyes. Up and down the glade, with the music flying out all over the night.

At dawn they hung their violins in the larch trees, dashed back to the farms, and pretended they had been working all night among the rats and mice. They lapped their milk hungrily, stretched out at the fireside, and fell asleep with smiles on their faces.

How the Donkey Became

There was one creature that never seemed to change at all. This didn't worry him, though. He hated the thought of becoming any single creature. Oh no, he wanted to become all creatures together, all at once. He used to practise them all in turn – first a lion, then an eagle, then a bull, then a cockatoo, and so on – five minutes each.

He was a strange-looking beast in those days. A kind of no-shape-in-particular. He had legs, sure enough, and eyes and ears and all the rest. But there was something vague about him. He really did look as if he might suddenly turn into anything.

He was called Donkey, which in the language of that time meant 'unable to stick to one thing'.

'You'll never become anything,' the other creatures said, 'until you stick to one thing and that thing alone.'

'Become a lion with us,' the Lion-Becomers said. 'You're so good at lioning it's a pity to waste your time eagling.'

And the eagles said: 'Never mind lioning. You should concentrate on becoming an eagle. You have a gift for it.'

All the different creatures spoke to him in this way, which made him very proud. So proud, in fact, that he became boastful.

'I'm going to be an Everykind,' Donkey cried, kicking up his heels. 'I'm going to be a Lionocerangoutangadinf.'

Half the day he spent on a high exposed part of the plain practising at his creatures where everyone could see him. The other half he spent sleeping in the long grass. 'I'm growing so fast,' he used to say, 'I need all the sleep I can get.'

But Donkey had a secret worry. He had no means of

earning his living. He couldn't earn his living as a lion – not when he only practised at lion five minutes a day. He couldn't earn his living as any other creature either – for the same reason.

So he had to beg.

'When you see me grow up into a Lionocerangoutang-adinf,' he said, as he begged a mouthful of fish from Otter, 'you'll be glad you helped me when I was only learning.'

And he went off kicking up his heels.

Before long the animals grew tired of his begging. It took them all day to find food enough for themselves. So whenever Donkey came up to them to beg they began to tease him:

'What?' they cried. 'Aren't you the finest, greatest creature in the world yet? What have you been doing with your time?'

This made Donkey furious. He galloped off to a high hill, and there he sat, brooding.

'The trouble is,' he said, 'there's no place among these creatures for somebody with real ambition. But one day – I'll make them stare! I'll be a better lion than lion, a better eagle than eagle, and a better kangaroo than kangaroo – and all at the same time. Then they'll be sorry.'

All the same, he wished he could earn his living without having to beg.

As he sat, he heard a long sigh. He looked around. He hadn't noticed that he was so near Man's farm. He looked over the fence and saw Man sitting beside a well, with his head resting in his hands. As he looked, Man gave another sigh.

'What's the matter?' asked Donkey.

Man looked up.

'I'm weary,' he said. 'Drawing water from this well is hard work.'

'Hard?' Donkey cried. 'If it's strength you're wanting, here I am. I'm the strongest creature on these plains.'

'But still not strong enough to draw water,' sighed Man.

'Just watch this.' Donkey marched across, took hold of the long pole that stuck out over the well, and began to drag it round. He had often seen Man doing this, so he knew how. Water gushed out of a pipe on to Man's field of corn.

'Wonderful!' cried Man. 'Wonderful!'

Donkey flattened back his ears and pulled all the harder. Man danced around him, crying:

'You're a marvel. Oh, what I wouldn't give to have you working for me.'

As he said that, Donkey got an idea. He stopped.

'If you'll give me food,' he said, 'I'll do this every day for you.'

'It's a bargain!' said Man.

So Donkey started to work for Man.

Only a little bit each morning, mind you. He still spent most of the day out on the plains practising at all his creatures. Then he retired early to sleep in the little shed that Man had made for him – it was dark, out of the wind, and the floor was covered with deep straw. Lovely! There he would lie till it was time for work next morning.

One day Man said to him:

'If you'll work twice as long for me, I'll give you twice as much food.'

Donkey thought:

'Twice as much food means twice as much strength. And if I'm going to be a Lionocerangoutangadinf – well – I shall need all the strength that's going.'

So he agreed to work twice as long.

Next day, Man asked him the same again. Donkey agreed. And the next day, and again Donkey agreed. He was now working from dawn to dusk. But the pile of food that Man gave him at the day's end! Well, after eating it, Donkey could do nothing but lie down on his straw and snore.

After about a week of this he suddenly thought:

'Here I am, being gloriously fed. Getting stronger and stronger. But I never have time to practise at my creatures. How can I hope to become a Lionocerangoutangadinf if I never practise my creatures?'

So what did he do? He couldn't very well practise while he was working. The sight and sound of it would have terrified Man, and Donkey didn't want to lose his job. So he did the only thing he could. He began to practise in his head.

Soon he got to be wonderfully good at this. He could fancy himself any creature he wished – a mountain goat, for instance, leaping among the clouds from crag to crag, or a salmon, climbing a swift fierce torrent – for hours at a time, all in his head. He would quite forget that he was only walking round a well.

Once or twice Man removed him from the well and set him to draw a plough. But donkey was so absorbed in practising at his creatures inside his head that he forgot to turn at the end of the furrow. He went ploughing straight on, through the hedge and into the next field. After this, Man never asked him to do anything but walk around the well, and Donkey was quite contented.

So it went on for several years, and Donkey fancied that he was becoming more and more skilful at his creatures. 'I mustn't be in too great a hurry,' he said to himself. 'I want to be better at everything than every other creature – so a little bit more practice won't hurt.'

So he went on. Always staying on with Man for just a little bit more practice inside his head.

'Soon,' he kept saying, 'soon I shall be perfect.'

At last it seemed to Donkey he was nearly perfect. 'A few more days, just a few more days!' Then he would burst out on to the plains, the first Lionocerangoutangadinf. Within three days, perhaps even within two, the animals would crown him their king – he was sure of that. Just as he was thinking these lovely thoughts he heard a sudden cry. He looked up and saw Man running towards his house, his arms in the air.

At the same moment, over the high fence, came Lion.

Donkey stood, and watched Lion out of the corner of his eye. He tilted one fore-foot carelessly.

Lion stared at him.

At last, making his voice sound as friendly as he could, Donkey said: 'My word, Lion-Becomer, you've changed. Are you Lion yet?'

Lion turned away from him without a word and walked up the path. When he reached Man's house, he stood up on his hind legs and, lifting one paw, like a lion in a coat of arms, began to beat upon the door.

'Throw out your wife and children, Man!' he roared.

Man was crouching under the table inside the house, trembling all over, not daring to breathe.

Finally Lion got tired of beating the door, which was of thick wood and studded with big bolts. He turned round and began to sniff among the outhouses and gardens. He came to Donkey again, who was still propped idly on one foreleg beside the well.

'Hello again, Lion,' said Donkey, and he let his voice be ever such a little bit scornful. 'Your hunting isn't so good, is it? I think I could give you a lesson or two in lioning.'

Lion stared, amazed.

'Now,' thought Donkey, 'now to reveal my true self. Now to reveal what I have made myself after all these years of hard practice.'

60

And he gave a great leap and roared.

'See!' he cried. 'This is the way!'

And again he leapt and roared, leapt and roared. He became so taken up with his lioning that he completely forgot about Lion.

Now it was years since Donkey had actually tried to leap or roar. He was far too stiff with his years of hard work to leap, and his voice had become stiff as his muscles.

So, though it seemed to him he was doing a wonderful lion, he was really only kicking out his heels stiffly, and sending up a harsh bray.

But he was delighted with himself. He went on, leaping and roaring, as he thought, leaping and roaring, so that his harness clattered, the long pole bounced and banged, and Lion screwed up his eyes in the dust from the kicking-out feet.

At last Lion could stand it no longer. He raised his paw, and with one blow knocked donkey clean into the well. He then jumped back over the fence and returned to his wife, who was waiting on the skyline.

Poor Donkey! When Man hauled him out of the well he was in a sorry state. But he was a wiser Donkey. That night he ate his oats and lay down with a new feeling. No more Lionocerangoutangadinf for him. No more pretending to be every creature.

'It's best to face the truth,' he said to himself, 'and the truth is I'm neither a lion nor an eagle. I am a well-fed, comfortable, hard-working Donkey.'

He could hear the lions roaring hungrily out on the plains, and he thought of the antelopes running hither and thither looking for a safe corner and a place out of the wind. He pushed his head under the warm straw, and smiled into the darkness, and fell into a deep sleep.

How the Hare Became

Now Hare was a real dandy. He was about the vainest creature on the whole earth.

Every morning he spent one hour smartening his fur, another hour smoothing his whiskers, and another cleaning his paws. Then the rest of the day he strutted up and down, admiring his shadow, and saying:

'How handsome I am! How amazingly handsome! Surely some great princess will want to marry me soon.'

The other creatures grew so tired of his vain ways that they decided to teach him a lesson. Now they knew that he would believe any story so long as it made him think he was handsome. So this is what they did:

One morning Gazelle went up to Hare and said:

'Good morning, Hare. How handsome you look. No wonder we've been hearing such stories about you.'

'Stories?' asked Hare. 'What stories?'

'Haven't you heard the news?' cried Gazelle. 'It's about you.'

'News? News? What news?' cried Hare, jumping up and down in excitement.

'Why, the moon wants to marry you,' said Gazelle. 'The beautiful moon, the queen of the night sky. She wants to marry you because she says you're the handsomest creature in the whole world. Oh yes. You should just have heard a few of the things she was saying about you last night.'

'Such as?' cried Hare. 'Such as?' He could hardly wait to hear what fine things moon had said about him.

'Never mind now,' said Gazelle. 'But she'll be walking up

that hill tonight, and if you want to marry her you're to be there to meet her. Lucky man!'

Gazelle pointed to a hill on the Eastern skyline. It was not yet midday, but Hare was up on top of that hill in one flash, looking down eagerly on the other side. There was no sign of a palace anywhere where the moon might live. He could see nothing but plains rolling up to the farther skyline. He sat down to wait, getting up every few minutes to take another look round. He certainly was excited.

At last the sky grew dark and a few stars lit up. Hare began to strut about so that the moon should see what a fine figure of a creature was waiting for her. He looked first down one side of the hill, then down the other. But she was still nowhere in sight.

Suddenly he saw her – but not coming up his hill. No. There was a black hill on the skyline, much farther to the East, and she was just peeping silver over the top of that.

'Ah!' cried Hare. 'I've been waiting on the wrong hill. I'll miss her if I don't hurry.'

He set off towards her at a run. How he ran. Down into the dark valley, and up the hill to the top. But what a surprise he got there! The moon had gone. Ahead of him, across another valley, was another skyline, another black hill – and that was the hill the moon was climbing.

'Wait for me! Wait!' Hare cried, and set off again down into the valley.

When he got to the top of that hill he groaned. And no wonder. Far ahead of him was another dark skyline, and another hill – and on top of that hill was the moon standing tiptoe, ready to fly off up the sky.

Without a pause he set off again. His paws were like wings. He ran on the tops of the grass, he ran so fast.

By the time he got to the top of this hill, he saw he was too late. The moon was well up into the sky above him.

'I've missed her!' he cried. 'I'm too late! Oh, what will she think of me!'

And he began leaping up towards her, calling:

'Moon! Moon! I'm here! I've come to marry you.'

But she sailed on up the black sky, round and bright, much too far away to hear. Hare jumped a somersault in pure vexation. Then he began to listen – he stretched up his ears. Perhaps she was saying terrible things about him – or perhaps, yes, perhaps flattering things. Perhaps she wanted to marry him much too much ever to think badly of him. After all, he was so handsome.

All that night he gazed up at the moon and listened. Every minute she seemed more and more beautiful. He dreamed how it would be, living in her palace. He would become a king, of course, if she were a queen.

All at once he noticed that she was beginning to come down the other side of the sky, towards a black hill in the West.

'This time I'll be waiting for her,' he cried, and set off.

But it was just the same. When he got to the top of the hill she was no longer there, but on the farther hill. And when he got to the top of that, she was on the next. And when he got to that, she had gone down behind the farthest hills.

Hare was furious with himself.

'It's my own fault,' he cried. 'It's because I'm so slow. I must be there on time, then I shan't have to run after her. To miss the chance of marrying the moon, and becoming a king, all out of pure slowness!'

That day he told the animals that he was courting the moon, but that the marriage day was not fixed yet. He strutted in front of them, and stroked his fur – after all, he was the creature who was going to marry the moon.

He was so busy being vain, he never noticed how the other creatures smiled as they turned away. Hare had fallen for their trick completely.

That night Hare was out early, but it was just the same. Again he found himself waiting on the wrong hill. The moon came over the black crest of a hill on the skyline far to the East of him. Hill by hill, he chased her into the East over four hills, but at last she was alone in the sky above him. Then, no matter how he leapt and called after her, she went sailing on up the sky. So he sat and listened and listened to hear what she was saying about him. He could hear nothing.

'Her voice is so soft,' Hare told himself.

He set off in good time for the hill in the West where she had gone down the night before, but again he seemed to have misjudged it. She came down on the hilly skyline that was further again to the West of him, and again he was too late.

Oh, how he longed to marry the moon. Night after night he waited for her, but never once could he hit on the right hill.

Poor Hare! He didn't know that when the moon seemed to be rising from the nearest hill in the East or falling on to the nearest hill in the West, she was really rising and falling over the far, far edge of the world, beyond all hills. Such a trick the creatures had played on him, saying the moon wanted to marry him.

But he didn't give up.

Soon he began to change. With endlessly gazing at the moon he began to get the moonlight in his eyes, giving him a wild, startled look. And with racing from hill to hill he grew to be a wonderful runner. Especially up the hills – he just shot up them. And from leaping to reach her when he was too late, he came to be a great leaper. And from listening and listening, all through the night, for what the moon was saying high in the sky, he got his long, long ears.

How the Elephant Became

The unhappiest of all the creatures was Bombo. Bombo didn't know what to become. At one time he thought he might make a fairly good horse. At another time he thought that perhaps he was meant to be a kind of bull. But it was no good. Not only the horses, but all the other creatures too, gathered to laugh at him when he tried to be a horse. And when he tried to be a bull, the bulls just walked away shaking their heads.

'Be yourself,' they all said.

Bombo sighed. That's all he ever heard: 'Be yourself. Be yourself.' What was himself? That's what he wanted to know.

So most of the time he just stood, with sad eyes, letting the wind blow his ears this way and that, while the other creatures raced around him and above him, perfecting themselves.

'I'm just stupid,' he said to himself. 'Just stupid and slow and I shall never become anything.'

That was his main trouble, he felt sure. He was much too slow and clumsy – and so big! None of the other creatures were anywhere near so big. He searched hard to find another creature as big as he was, but there was not one. This made him feel all the more silly and in the way.

But this was not all. He had great ears that flapped and hung, and a long, long nose. His nose was useful. He could pick things up with it. But none of the other creatures had a nose anything like it. They all had small neat noses, and they laughed at his. In fact, with that, and his ears, and his long white sticking-out tusks, he was a sight.

As he stood, there was a sudden thunder of hooves. Bombo looked up in alarm.

'Aside, aside, aside!' roared a huge voice. 'We're going down to drink.'

Bombo managed to force his way backwards into a painful clump of thorn-bushes, just in time to let Buffalo charge past with all his family. Their long black bodies shone, their curved horns tossed, their tails screwed and curled, as they pounded down towards the water in a cloud of dust. The earth shook under them.

'There's no doubt,' said Bombo, 'who they are. If only I could be as sure of what I am as Buffalo is of what he is.'

Then he pulled himself together.

'To be myself,' he said aloud, 'I shall have to do something that no other creature does. Lion roars and pounces, and Buffalo charges up and down bellowing. Each of these creatures does something that no other creature does. So. What shall I do?'

He thought hard for a minute.

Then he lay down, rolled over on to his back, and waved his four great legs in the air. After that he stood on his head and lifted his hind legs straight up as if he were going to sunburn the soles of his feet. From this position, he lowered himself back on to his four feet, stood up and looked round. The others should soon get to know me by that, he thought.

Nobody was in sight, so he waited until a pack of wolves appeared on the horizon. Then he began again. On to his back, his legs in the air, then on to his head, and his hind legs straight up.

'Phew!' he grunted, as he lowered himself. 'I shall need some practice before I can keep this up for long.'

When he stood up and looked round him this second time, he got a shock. All the animals were round him in a ring, rolling on their sides with laughter.

'Do it again! Oh, do it again!' they were crying, as they rolled and laughed. 'Do it again. Oh, I shall die with laughter. Oh, my sides, my sides!'

Bombo stared at them in horror.

After a few minutes the laughter died down.

'Come on!' roared Lion. 'Do it again and make us laugh. You look so silly when you do it.'

But Bombo just stood. This was much worse than imitating some other animal. He had never made them laugh so much before.

He sat down and pretended to be inspecting one of his feet, as if he were alone. And, one by one, now that there was nothing to laugh at, the other animals walked away, still chuckling over what they had seen.

'Next show same time tomorrow!' shouted Fox, and they all burst out laughing again.

Bombo sat, playing with his foot, letting the tears trickle down his long nose.

Well, he'd had enough. He'd tried to be himself, and all the animals had laughed at him.

That night he waded out to a small island in the middle of the great river that ran through the forest. And there, from then on, Bombo lived alone, seen by nobody but the little birds and a few beetles.

One night, many years later, Parrot suddenly screamed and flew up into the air above the trees. All his feathers were singed. The forest was on fire.

Within a few minutes, the animals were running for their lives. Jaguar, Wolf, Stag, Cow, Bear, Sheep, Cockerel, Mouse, Giraffe – all were running side by side and jumping over each other to get away from the flames. Behind them, the fire came through the tree-tops like a terrific red wind.

'Oh dear! Oh dear! Our houses, our children!' cried the animals.

Lion and Buffalo were running along with the rest.

'The fire will go as far as the forest goes, and the forest goes on for ever,' they cried, and ran with sparks falling into their hair. On and on they ran, hour after hour, and all they could hear was the thunder of the fire at their tails.

On into the middle of the next day, and still they were running.

At last they came to the wide, deep, swift river. They could go no further. Behind them the fire boomed as it leapt from tree to tree. Smoke lay so thickly over the forest and the river that the sun could not be seen. The animals floundered in the shallows at the river's edge, trampling the banks to mud, treading on each other, coughing and sneezing in the white ashes that were falling thicker than thick snow out of the cloud of smoke. Fox sat on Sheep and Sheep sat on Rhinoceros.

They all set up a terrible roaring, wailing, crying, howling, moaning sound. It seemed like the end of the animals. The fire came nearer, bending over them like a thundering roof, while the black river swirled and rumbled beside them.

Out on his island stood Bombo, admiring the fire which made a fine sight through the smoke with its high spikes of red flame. He knew he was quite safe on his island. The fire couldn't cross that great stretch of water very easily.

At first he didn't see the animals crowding low by the edge of the water. The smoke and ash were too thick in the air. But soon he heard them. He recognized Lion's voice shouting:

'Keep ducking yourselves in the water. Keep your fur wet and the sparks will not burn you.'

And the voice of Sheep crying:

'If we duck ourselves we're swept away by the river.'

And the other creatures – Gnu, Ferret, Cobra, Partridge, crying:

'We must drown or burn. Goodbye, brothers and sisters!'

It certainly did seem like the end of the animals.

Without a pause, Bombo pushed his way into the water. The river was deep, the current heavy and fierce, but Bombo's legs were both long and strong. Burnt trees, that had fallen into the river higher up and were drifting down, banged against him, but he hardly felt them.

In a few minutes he was coming up into shallow water towards the animals. He was almost too late. The flames were forcing them, step by step, into the river, where the current was snatching them away.

Lion was sitting on Buffalo, Wolf was sitting on Lion, Wildcat on Wolf, Badger on Wildcat, Cockerel on Badger, Rat on Cockerel, Weasel on Rat, Lizard on Weasel, Tree-Creeper on Lizard, Harvest Mouse on Tree-Creeper, Beetle on Harvest Mouse, Wasp on Beetle, and on top of Wasp, Ant, gazing at the raging flames through his spectacles and covering his ears from their roar.

When the animals saw Bombo looming through the smoke, a great shout went up:

'It's Bombo! It's Bombo!'

All the animals took up the cry:

'Bombo! Bombo!'

Bombo kept coming closer. As he came, he sucked up water in his long silly nose and squirted it over his back, to protect himself from the heat and the sparks. Then, with the same long, silly nose he reached out and began to pick up the animals, one by one, and seat them on his back.

'Take us!' cried Mole.

'Take us!' cried Monkey.

He loaded his back with the creatures that had hooves

71

and big feet; then he told the little clinging things to cling on to the great folds of his ears. Soon he had every single creature aboard. Then he turned and began to wade back across the river, carrying all the animals of the forest towards safety.

Once they were safe on the island they danced for joy. Then they sat down to watch the fire. Suddenly Mouse gave a shout:

'Look! The wind is bringing sparks across the river. The sparks are blowing into the island trees. We shall burn here too.'

As he spoke, one of the trees on the edge of the island crackled into flame. The animals set up a great cry and began to run in all directions.

'Help! Help! Help! We shall burn here too!'

But Bombo was ready. He put those long silly tusks of his, that he had once been so ashamed of, under the roots of the burning tree and heaved it into the river. He threw every tree into the river till the island was bare. The sparks now fell on to the bare torn ground, where the animals trod them out easily. Bombo had saved them again.

Next morning the fire had died out at the river's edge. The animals on the island looked across at the smoking, blackened plain where the forest had been. Then they looked round for Bombo.

He was nowhere to be seen.

'Bombo!' they shouted. 'Bombo!' And listened to the echo. But he had gone.

He is still very hard to find. Though he is huge and strong, he is very quiet.

But what did become of him in the end? Where is he now?

Ask any of the animals, and they will tell you:

'Though he is shy, he is the strongest, the cleverest, and the kindest of all the animals. He can carry anything and he can push anything down. He can pick you up in his nose and wave you in the air. We would make him our king if we could get him to wear a crown.'

BOOK TWO

Tales of the Early World

Illustrated by Andrew Davidson

The stories in 'Tales of the Early World'
are particularly suitable for children of 8+.

For Carol

Contents

How Sparrow Saved the Birds

Of all the birds, Sparrow was one of the first to be invented. Plain little Sparrow. He lived with his wife in a hole in a tree, and sometimes sat in his doorway singing his plain little song – which isn't really a song at all.

Sparrow and his wife had no children. 'It's God's fault,' cried his wife. 'Go to God and tell him so. Tell him to do something about it.' And she burst into tears. 'Surely he'll help us.'

Instead, Sparrow went to the Toad. The Toad was already making a name for herself as a witch. From her, he bought a powerful spell.

'When this spell fails to bring twins,' said the Toad, 'it brings triplets.'

Then she blinked her great, brilliant, golden eyes and added: 'Octuplets have been known.'

But it didn't work.

Sparrow's wife wept a lot, in her dark hole in the tree. 'Go to God,' she sobbed. 'Simply go to God. That's all there is to it. Why not? Go and ask him for help.'

Sparrow glared at his wife, frowning under his black thinking-cap. He was actually quite a fierce-looking little bird. His wife was right. Why not go to the top?

So he filled his knapsack with seeds, food for a very long journey, and he set off.

God was still making birds. Since making Sparrow, he'd enlarged his designs a good deal, and brought in some new

79

ideas. He'd built a new workshop too, on stilts, on top of a hill, so the new birds would get a good take-off.

And at last Sparrow was climbing the rickety ladder to the workshop. As he got to the top rung, and peered in through the open door, a great flurry of white cloud came out. He glimpsed a small, round, black eye, then he was knocked backwards. He fell five rungs and clung there, while the giant form of a white Swan laboured out into the air, with its weird, slow wingbeats – each wingbeat giving the yelp of a hound. Sparrow stared at the whiteness, the slowness, the long neck. 'And probably,' he thought, 'it has a beautiful song too!'

He climbed back to the top, but again as he lifted his head to peer into the workshop another Swan came hurtling out. This time he ducked, then watched as the two Swans together side by side circled the tower, on their yelping wings. He watched, until they turned and flew out over the deep green valleys towards the blue curve of the world's edge. What flyers! And where were they going? What adventure!

He suddenly remembered where he was. Bracing himself, he stepped into the workshop where God was bent over his workbench.

'Hello, God,' called Sparrow, and stood.

God went on working. He was concentrating deeply on a very tricky job. Under his hands lay the first Curlew, and he was trying to adjust its voice-box so the song would go up at the end.

Sparrow scraped his clawy foot on the floor and coughed. Then again he shouted: 'Hello, God, it's me, your old Sparrow!'

God uttered a cry, and jerked his hands up as if his fingers had been stung. Then he grabbed his hair in his fists.

'No!' he roared. 'Oh no!'

Sparrow coughed, and again shouted: 'God!'

God turned sharply and glared at him.

'You!' he suddenly bellowed. 'You made me do it. I thought I was hearing voices but it was you! I've snapped it. Now it will never be right! Oh no!'

And he turned back to peer into the throat of the Curlew.

'God,' shouted Sparrow again, 'I've come – '

'What do you want?' God was glaring at him angrily.

Sparrow took a deep breath. 'Well, God, we're only Sparrows, I know, but my wife and I would like a nestling or two or even three if it's possible because – '

'Go away!' shouted God. 'Not today. Some other time. Sparrows! I can't think about Sparrows. I'm on Curlews! And Sanderlings are coming up any minute. Go away.'

And he bent low over the Curlew with the damaged voice-box.

Sparrow didn't move. He didn't know what to do. If he went home, what would his wife feel? At the same time, he didn't dare to ask God again.

'I'll stand here,' he thought, 'until he's finished. However long that maybe.'

But at that very moment, a rushing wall of twigs hit him. God's mother was tidying and her broom swept Sparrow straight out through the doorway.

He flew down and landed on a rock, blinking the dust out of his eyes. What now?

Well, maybe he would wait here. One thing was sure: he wasn't going to give up, till God had listened to him in a patient, thoughtful way.

A Curlew swooped out of the workshop and then climbed

away. Its wobbling, thin, whistling cry trailed away downward at the end, broken.

Sparrow sat on, through that day. He watched Sanderlings fling out of God's workshop, in twos, followed by Golden Plover, followed by Snipe. Then a Gannet, with funny, stiff-looking wings, like boards, and horrible pale little eyes at the corners of its mouth. The eye pupils were tiny as pinpricks.

The world was filling up with birds. Already, the motes tossing in clouds from hill to hill, over the valleys, were birds. The deep throbbing and thrilling voice of the forests was actually birds. The lakes were sprinkled and dimpled with birds. The edge of the sea, where the breakers tore into blowing tatters, was a lifting and falling commotion of birds. And high above, suspended from the blue, the slow, dark, circling crosses were birds.

And still God went on creating more. And more. And more.

He had a passion for birds!

Then towards the evening, as the sun lowered its red ball towards the cold Western sea, God came out on to his veranda, at the top of his ladder, and held up his hands, cupped together. Sparrow had been dozing, but now he woke with a jerk, and watched closely. What was God up to?

God threw up his hands gently and opened them. A peculiar black shape whizzed out of them. Sparrow blinked. He thought God had thrown a boomerang at him. It seemed to be black spinning blades going at terrific speed, and it dived down straight at Sparrow, then:

Fffffwwwt!

It whacked past his head and shot up into the sky – just like a boomerang. But it wasn't a boomerang. It was a real bird.

God stood laughing softly with joy, as the bird spun away into the world. Sparrow could see he was almost weeping, his eyes were moist, as if he could hardly believe what he saw.

'I did it!' cried God. And he looked down at Sparrow and pointed at the vanishing marvel. 'I did it! I made a Swift!'

'Now,' thought Sparrow, 'now is my moment. He's in a joyful mood. He's just brought off a winner. He'll be feeling easy-going and generous. I'll land on his shoulder and nibble his ear, and make my request.'

And he flew up off the rock.

But at that instant, the sun touched the Western sea. A strange, rumbling quake spread over the waters, and came across the lands, and above it a darkness, full of lightnings. Sparrow checked his flight and hovered in mid-air, amazed to see the forests swirling like water. Then he saw God clutch his doorpost, while his tower swayed like a palm tree.

That was the last thing Sparrow saw, before the blackness snatched him up.

Then he was whirling in a blackness. All round him he could hear birds, crying and screeching, the frightcries of the birds! He was no longer trying to fly. He folded his wings tightly, and tucked up his feet, and squeezed his head down between his shoulders, and peered out over his eyelids. Now and again a feathery body struck him. He knew he was whirling in a cloud of birds, a black bagful of birds. Were they all in a sack? Were they all being carried off in a great bag?

Something God had never heard about, a Black Hole in space, had lowered its whirling snout to the earth, like an Elephant's trunk. First it had blown all the birds off their

perches, and out of their bushes, then it had sucked them up in one whoosh – a spinning whoosh. Like water going out of a plug-hole downwards, all the birds of the world were whirling into the Black Hole upwards. They were being hoovered up.

And in a few minutes they were gone. The world was emptied of birds.

God wandered over the hills, calling to the birds. Every single one had gone. Or so it seemed to God. He just couldn't believe it. Actually, one bird was left. The Burrow Owl. Two big yellow eyes stared upwards from the bottom of its black burrow. But it wouldn't come out. No, not even to comfort God. It stayed where it was, waiting for the next terrible blast of black wind.

God sat down on a ridge, his elbows on his knees, clutching the roots of his hair in his hands, and watching the tears splash into the dust between his feet as he sobbed. He really felt his heart was broken this time.

How could he begin again? How could he ever create a Hummingbird again? Or a Sparrow-hawk? Or a Skylark? Or a Wren? Or a Kingfisher? Or a Snow Bunting?

As he recited their names, new sobs shook him. The animals gazed at him in fear and went past softly. The worms drew back into their holes. The flies crept under leaves.

And in the lakes, and in the rivers, and in the sea, the fish hung motionless, listening round-eyed, hearing through all the shaking curtains of water the heartbroken sobbing of God.

'Where are they?' he suddenly roared. 'Who has stolen my birds?'

But God knew nothing about the Black Hole. So he never guessed where they might have gone. It was a total mystery. He wandered about, stunned. He stopped making things. He lay full length beside the sea, his forearm over his eyes, and he looked as if he'd died of grief, except that his fists were tightly clenched, and tears crept back into his ears, while all over the world the eggs in the nests went cold.

Meanwhile, the birds huddled together in the darkness. Now it had stolen them, the Black Hole seemed quite satisfied. They seemed to be in some sort of pit. The various Owls glared, trying to give a little light with their eyes. But it wasn't the sort of light any other bird could see by.

'We are in a deep, deep pit,' said the Snowy Owl. 'Don't you see?'

'It looks pretty hopeless,' said the Barn Owl.

They knew they were a vast distance from the world. But they had no idea where.

The Homing Pigeons were baffled. They turned their heads this way and that.

'Our compasses don't work,' they whimpered. 'We must be somewhere beyond the stars.'

Hearing this, many of the birds began to cry again. Then, from far above, came a laugh. A long, rippling, eerie laugh! The birds felt their feathers stick up on end and they all went dead silent.

'Who's that?' whispered a Coot.

'Now you're mine, pretty birds. My mother wanted a pretty bird. So now you all belong to my mother.'

And from high up there, somewhere in the dark, the peculiar laugh came again. The birds would have liked to look at each other. Instead, even though they were huddled together so tightly, they just stared horrified into the utter black, each on his own, each by herself.

'Sing for my mother,' said the voice then. 'Come on, let's have a cheery morning chorus.'

The birds listened in horror. Suddenly there came a bang, and all the birds crashed together in a heap, their ears ringing. The voice seemed to have slapped the pit with its hand, or maybe kicked it.

'Sing, you brats,' it screeched. And again there came a bang, and again they all turned somersaults and landed on top of each other.

'Are you going to sing?' came the screech.

Then the Crow, very quick, shouted in his worst voice:

'You've broken our voices, you big idiot. Just listen. You've broken our glottals.'

Hearing the Crow, the Black Hole thought it was true, it had broken their voices. It didn't know anything about birds.

It howled a great curse, up in the black, and fell silent. What next? What was it thinking now? All the birds waited for it to play its next dreadful trick.

And in the silence, very quietly at first, the birds began to cry again.

It was in this crying that Sparrow heard his wife. He pushed through the crush, and found her. They put their wings around each other, and sat there in the dark.

'If only God knew!' whispered his wife. 'Surely he'd help us!' But God did not know. God lay in the world, beside the booming surf, and his mind, too, was simply one big blackness.

Quite soon, the birds began to feel hungry. The Sparrow undid his knapsack, and shared his seeds. He worked his way among the tightly packed birds, and asked each one:

'Can you eat seeds?'

And in the pitch dark, the birds would answer. Sparrow gave one seed to each seed-eater. He couldn't help the insect-eaters, and the grub-eaters, such as the Wrens and the

87

Woodpeckers. Once, coming up against a very horny, unbird-like body, he asked: 'Do you eat seeds?' And a voice from far above his head replied, in a deep, drum-like rumble:

'I am the Monkey-eating Eagle.'

Sparrow realized he was leaning on the Eagle's ankle, and he got clear fast.

He knew this couldn't go on very long. Pretty soon, the Eagles and Owls and Hawks and Gulls would begin to eat the others. If they were all to get back to earth, it would have to be quick. Otherwise – he couldn't bear to think about it. It would be awful. It might be happening already. The sly Owls, with their night sight, were probably at it already – snatching up the nearest small bird with such a savage, sudden grip there wasn't even a gasp.

Sparrow gave out every seed except for two. One for his wife, and one for himself.

'That's it,' he whispered to her, then. 'No more seeds.'

'Are you sure?' she asked. She always wanted to make sure. So she opened his knapsack, and stuck her head inside. She pulled her head out quickly and listened.

'Do you hear the sea?' she asked.

'What?' said her husband. 'What do you mean, hear the sea?'

'Inside your bag,' she said. 'I heard the sea.'

Sparrow stuck his head inside the knapsack. And there it was. The strong, crumpling boom of heavy surf, falling on a shingly beach.

He listened, amazed. Then he realized it was coming from one corner of the knapsack. He poked down there, with his beak, and found a seed. One seed. And the sound of the sea was coming out of the seed.

He brought it out, nipped in his bill. The sound of the surf filled his head.

A sudden wild clamour went up from the Gulls somewhere in the dark. 'It's the sea!' they cried. 'The sea! Listen! It's the sea!'

All the birds shouted excitedly. And the voice of the Loon cried above them all:

'The earth is coming, the earth is looking for us! That's its panting breath, as it climbs through space!'

Sparrow turned his head this way and that. Although the sea-sound came out of the seed, he felt it was coming from one direction only. He turned towards the sound. And as he did so, a strange thing happened. He saw the sea! Tiny and far off, as if he were looking through the wrong end of a telescope.

With the seed in his bill, and the sound of the surf in his ears, he saw the long shore, and the great slow combers crumbling to whiteness.

He took the seed out of his bill, and was going to tell his wife to look at the sea, but the moment he took the seed from his bill everything went dark. And though he could still hear the surf, the sea had vanished.

He put the seed back in his bill, and after twisting his head this way and that, he found the sea again. It was just as if his brain was a telescope – but only if he held the seed in his bill.

'I see the sea!' he shouted. 'I see the earth and the sea!'

As he shouted the seed fell from his beak. But he found it again, between his wife's toes, because of the noise of the surf coming out of it. He put it back in his beak, to make sure it wasn't broken. And this time he saw more. He saw the sea, the surf, and the long beach. And lying along the beach – God!

He took the seed in his claw.

'I see God!' he yelled.

All the birds went silent, listening to the sea, and hearing Sparrow's words, and trying to see something in the perfect blackness.

'Come on,' cried Sparrow. 'Follow me! Follow me! Follow the sea-sound!'

And he gripped the seed in his bill, and flew up, flying towards that vision of the sea and of God lying beside it.

It was easy to keep his direction. It was exactly like following a compass. As long as he held the seed, he simply flew towards the bright little picture of God lying beside the surf.

And with a dull roar, like another sea, all the birds flew up into the dark, and followed him. They couldn't see the picture. And in that blank dark they couldn't see Sparrow. But they could hear the sea, booming out of the seed in Sparrow's bill.

So all the birds of the world set off, a rustling, immense cloud, flying through the great darkness of space, following the sound of the surf.

Far above, a voice howled: 'Come back!'

But the birds flew on, blindly. Only Sparrow could see anything. And what he saw seemed to be both very far off, and inside his head, as he held the seed. The rest flew into the pitch dark, as if their eyes were closed.

'Come back!' screeched the thin, terrible voice again, growing closer.

The Black Hole was coming after them, with its sucker.

Then it swirled in among them. It was like the nozzle of a vacuum cleaner whirling about in a dense cloud of flies. The birds felt themselves caught in the whirlwind and snatched away.

Soon, Sparrow was flying alone. He didn't know it. He thought they were all following him. He didn't dare take the seed from his bill, because he thought he might drop it into empty space. And the sound of the surf in his head made it impossible to hear the little cries of the birds as they were sucked away once again into the Black Hole.

For some reason the Black Hole couldn't get a grip on Sparrow. It tore off some of his tail feathers, but as long as he held the seed, and kept his eyes on his bright picture, it couldn't suck him in. Finally, it coiled up and whipped away with a howl, and Sparrow flew on into a faint growing light like dawn.

Now he saw he was alone. But there was nothing he could do about it. Now his only hope was to tell God. He kept going. And the light brightened.

And at last, worn out, with frayed feathers, he fell on to God's chest, swallowed the seed, and lay panting.

Imagine God's joy, when he looked down at what had dropped on his chest, and found Sparrow.

'Look!' he shouted to his mother. 'Look! Sparrow! Where have you been?'

She gave Sparrow a drink and God listened to his tale. As he listened, his frown darkened. And when Sparrow had finished, God stood up.

'An oversight,' he said grimly. 'That Black Hole has made its nest in the stars. Once it was only a little dust-devil, playing in the ashes of volcanoes. Now it's eating the stars and growing. Yes, that's what must be happening. Something I never expected! Well, we'll soon fix it, now we know what it is.'

And with those words God leaped upwards. 'Be careful!' shouted his mother. But the heavens were already rumbling. A few stars fell, in broad daylight.

God tied the Black Hole and its mother into a tight knot, and fed them to the constellation of Capricorn. Then he brought the birds home. And they spread out over the world, a thousand times more joyful than before.

God nodded and smiled. 'A very good thing!' he said. 'Some of them used to moan and grumble a lot. But after a spell in the Black Hole, now they know better.'

Then he saw Sparrow, sitting on the veranda rail of his workshop, with his wife beside him.

'As for you,' said God, 'for you there is a reward. To tell you the truth, Sparrow, I wasn't too sure about you. I thought you had it in you to be a real pest. But you've proved your quality. And this is your reward: your children shall inherit the whole earth.'

Then Sparrow put back his head and let out a song of joy, a psalm to God. And his wife, too, she lifted her beak and sang out beside him.

It sounded the same as ever. A few raspy chirrups, like a Stone-Age man trying to strike a spark between two flints, and not having much success.

But God was pleased.

Then Sparrow and his wife flew off, back to their hole in the tree, in the middle of the forest from which the singing of all the birds rose like the sound of surf.

The Guardian

Man was easy to create. God simply shaped the clay, breathed life into it, and up jumped Man, ready to go.

God smiled. 'Now,' he said, 'I'll make your better half. Then you'll be complete.'

So then God shaped Woman. He took great care, and she turned out perfect. God was pleased. But when he tried to breathe life into her – nothing happened. He tried again, breathing the life in very gently. She just lay there, lifeless clay. He shook her slightly, and frowned.

Man was watching anxiously. 'What's wrong?' he cried. God didn't answer. He only rolled Woman up into a ball between his palms, and started all over again.

This time he took even more care. And pretty soon, there she lay, more perfect than ever. So once again, God kneeled forward, and breathed life into her, more warmly and gently even than before.

Still nothing happened.

There she lay, warm from God's hands, perfectly shaped. Much more perfect than Man. But lifeless.

Man couldn't hold back any longer. 'Let me have a go!' he cried, and almost pushed God aside. He grabbed Woman by the shoulders and began to shake her. 'Wakey wakey!' he called. 'Come on! Time to go!'

Her limp body shook like a rag doll, but her eyes stayed shut.

All at once he seemed to grow angry. His hair began to fly, he ground his teeth, his eyes blazed, and God was suddenly afraid what might happen as Woman's arms flapped and flopped, and her head joggled and rolled. He caught Man's arm and jerked him away. 'Steady on!' God shouted. 'She's fragile!'

But Man began to pound the earth with his fists. 'I can't bear it!' he cried. 'Do something. She's my other half. You can't just leave her lying there on the cold ground.'

God stared at him hard. Easy enough to say 'Do something', but if life wouldn't go into this marvellous new creation of his, then it wouldn't go, and that was that. He didn't know what else he could do.

At that moment, a small bird flew down and landed on Woman's left big toe. 'Let me have a try,' said the bird. 'I have magic.'

It was the Nightingale. Nightingale had a most peculiar voice. God looked at this slim, brown, tiny creature and remembered all the trouble he'd had with the voice-box. Nightingale's voice-box was incredibly complicated. God had been struggling to get this voice-box right. And then, one night, it had come to him in a dream. The perfect voice-box! And it solved one of his toughest problems: how to get the voice of the seven seas into an organ the size of a common House-Fly. And there it was in his dream. He'd woken up with a jolt, and snatched it out of the air before it could vanish. He got it – but grabbing it like that, half asleep, he'd broken it.

And what a job that had been, trying to start it up again inside the bird's tiny throat. Still, it just about worked, finally. But the voice, wonderful as it sounded, was obviously only the bits and pieces of something much more tremendous.

'Try if you like,' sighed God, and he watched gloomily as Nightingale perched on Woman's nose and began to sing.

Man had never heard the Nightingale sing. And now it really let itself go, he couldn't believe his ears. As it sang, his eyes grew very large and round. Suddenly they closed, his head dropped forward on his chest, and he was in a trance.

And a row of eight Monkeys, sitting on the branch of a tree above him, fell to the ground, bounced once, and lay still, eyes closed, in a trance.

What singing!

But Woman never stirred. And though Nightingale flung out his chest, and fluttered his wings, and though his throat was a blur of throbbing song, Woman simply went on lying there, like a heap of clay.

'No good!' cried God. He clapped his hands and Nightingale flew startled into a bush.

As God clapped his hands, something else moved. A snake, the deadly Puff-Adder, lifted his head. He had actually been lying tucked in under Woman's side for the warmth of God's hands that was still in the clay. And now he peered over her waist, his forked tongue dancing, and said:

'I think I can solve your problem. I think I can awaken this perfect person.' And his long mouth seemed to smile.

God eyed the Puff-Adder anxiously. He didn't trust this snake at all, with its eye-chips of granite. He was almost sorry he'd made him. When he'd pressed those eyes into place one had cut his thumb, and the wound had festered for days.

'Under Woman's heart', said Puff-Adder, 'lives a Frog. It got in there with the clay you used. You didn't notice.'

God was surprised to hear that.

'I can smell it', said Puff-Adder, 'through her ribs.' And he flickered his dancing thread of a tongue over Woman's chest. 'Here it is.' He tapped with his nose to show the exact spot.

'This Frog', he went on, 'simply sucks up all the life you breathe into her. As you breathe the life in, the Frog swells up. Look.'

And it did seem to God, as he looked more closely, that Woman's stomach was slightly swollen there, under her heart.

The Puff-Adder laughed. 'Now,' he said, 'watch me extract it.'

And he began to glide up beside Woman's throat, and over her chin and was just about to slide his blunt strange head between her parted lips when God caught his tail and threw him into a stiff little thorn-bush nearby.

The Puff-Adder yelped with pain. 'You'll pay for this!' he cried. 'I would have picked that Frog out in no time. Then you could have breathed life into Woman and she would have lived. But now – now – now – '

'Well?' roared God. 'Now what?'

The snake was silent.

'I know you,' God shouted angrily. 'You'd have got in there, and eaten the Frog, if there is a Frog, and then just curled up in its place. That's what you'd have done. And you'd never have come out again. You'd have been a thousand times worse than any Frog.'

The Puff-Adder gave a wild laugh. Then he hissed: 'You're right. I would. But at least Woman would have come to life. And what a life! She and I together – we'd have conquered the world! We'd have driven you out among the furthest stars. Man would have crawled after us in the dust.'

God was furious. He didn't know what to think. Had the snake told the truth? Was there truly a Frog under Woman's heart? A Frog that sucked up the breath of life as he breathed it into her?

He stared at Man, lying there in a trance among the Monkeys. And he stared at the faint bulge under Woman's beautiful, lifeless ribs, and he gnawed the soft inside of his lower lip.

God advertised for help. 'Divine Rewards for whoever can make Woman live.' The creatures talked about little else. Every day, somebody came with an idea. None worked. And Woman went on lying there, perfect and lifeless.

Till one day, as God sat in his workshop, with his head in his hands, pondering this great problem, he heard a rustling voice.

A familiar voice!

He lifted his head. Whose voice was it? And what was it saying? Surely he knew that voice! Then a strange expression came over his face and his heart began to thump. He twisted round, and now he heard the voice clearly. It was coming from under a dusty heap of workshop rubbish, in that far corner.

'I can help you,' it whispered. 'I have the answer.'

In two strides he was across the room and lifting the rubbish aside, carefully, piece by piece. The dust rose and the gloom was thick. But at last he saw. He put one hand flat on the ground, and bent even lower, and peered. Yes, there she was – embedded in rubbish, like a Crab under a flat rock – his own little mother!

He'd completely forgotten her!

Gently he lifted her, and carried her out into the middle of the room. She was a great knot of doubled-up arms and legs, like a big, dry, dusty Spider. And almost weightless! He set her down, ran out and came back with a glass of brandy. She smacked her wet, blackened lips, and her eyes glittered. She smiled up at him, easing her joints slowly.

'I know your problem,' she said. She half closed her eyes, and seemed to rest a little. Then she said: 'First, bring me the new moon.'

That was easy for God. He reached down the new moon.

He watched as she half crawled over the floor, lifted the cellar hatch, and disappeared down the dark hole, with the new moon cupped in her hand. He peered after her. He'd never dared lower himself into that place. But it had always been his mother's favourite den, in the old days. And now, suddenly, her skinny hand rose up out of it again, holding the new moon like a bowl – a bowl that was brimful of dark liquid.

'Take this,' said her voice out of the darkness. 'Put it in your kiln. Just as it is. And stoke it very hot. The hotter the better.'

As God took the new moon in his hand, a little waft of fear touched him. Usually the moon was icy cold, but now it was warm. What was in it? Was it what he thought it was? He bent closely to sniff. Was it blood?

How was this going to help him?

But his mother had always known best, in spite of her oddity. So God did as he was told. Taking care not to spill it, he put the new moon into his kiln. He sealed the door, and began to stoke the fire beneath. The flames roared up.

As he went on sliding logs into the blaze, God began to feel very happy. It was just like old times, when his mother was teaching him how to do things. 'The hotter the brighter the brighter the better,' he sang to himself. He almost forgot about the cold clay shape of Woman away there in the forest, and Man stretched out in a trance, under a tree, among the Monkeys. And all the time the kiln glowed brighter. Soon it seemed to be throbbing, and almost transparent, the colour of apricot, with pulsing spots of dazzling whiteness. 'Can I get it white hot?' he whispered. 'Hotter hotter brighter brighter better better – ' But at that very moment the air seemed to explode in his face:

WHOOOOF–

The whole kiln had exploded and God fell over backwards with his eyebrows blown off.

And as he fell, something flashed above him, out of the explosion, like a long flame streaked with black.

He sat for a while, looking at the reeking crater where the kiln had been. Then as he got up, knocking the fiery, smouldering splinters from his hair and beard and muttering, 'Well! I'm sure that wasn't supposed to happen! What a mess!' he suddenly felt uneasy and looked round.

A strange animal stood there, watching him. A lanky, long, orange-red beast, painted from one end to the other with black stripes. Its belly and throat were frosty white. Its pelt shone. It lashed its long tail and stared into God as if it saw something moving in there. It was like no creature he had ever seen.

But the strangest thing of all was what it held in its mouth. 'It's caught a Monkey!' was God's first thought. 'It's already started killing my Monkeys!'

But then he saw it wasn't a Monkey at all. It was a tiny Human Being! A baby Human Being!

Had this leapt out of the kiln? Was this his mother's magic? How was this going to bring Woman to life? The tiny Human Being was quite nice, but that beast was more likely to frighten her to death. No, God could see his mother's magic had got all mixed up. And now he remembered why he'd left her in the corner, and heaped the rubbish on top of her, and hired the beetles to feed her.

But the beast had turned its head. Holding the Baby high, clear of the brambles and poison ivy, it went off through the

forest straight towards Woman. God began to run. He wanted to get to Woman first. But the beast began to bound. In three leaps it disappeared away ahead, in the thick jungle. Then God heard the cry of the Monkeys, and a strange, hoarse bark – not like Man at all, but God knew it was Man. And when he reached the clearing, everything had happened.

Man and the Monkeys were all together, on a high bough in the Monkeys' tree, staring down with eyes of fright. And the great beast stood over Woman's body.

As God watched, it laid the midget Human Being on Woman's stomach, stretched its own great striped length beside her, and began to lick her ear.

At once, the Baby began to stir its arms and legs. Its mouth opened like the door of a little kiln, and out of it came a thin cry.

The moment the Baby cried, the beast lifted its head and looked into Woman's face. And God, fascinated, looked at Woman's face. And the Monkeys in the tree, and Man beside them, all looked down at Woman's face. But the face remained quite still, quite lifeless.

After a while, the beast again began to lick Woman's ear gently, closing its eyes as it licked. And the wrinkled, podgy baby seemed to grow stronger, as if its cries were some kind of food. It shook its fists at the sky. It seemed to be shaking the bars of a cage.

All at once the beast leapt up and bounded away, so lightly it seemed to be weightless. And God saw it had the Baby back in its mouth. The beast stopped, sat down, and watched Woman. And the Baby hung in its mouth, silent.

God, too, watched Woman. Then he felt the hair prickle on the back of his legs. And a shiver crawled up his spine and into his hair. Woman's hand was moving. It came slowly to her head, till her fingers touched the bridge of her nose, where the Nightingale had perched with its sharp claws. She drew a deep breath and sighed.

Watching her very closely, the beast came back and laid the Baby on her thighs, and nudged it with its paw. At once the Baby opened its mouth and wailed. The air filled with its cry. And Man, too, in the Monkeys' tree, let out a cry, 'Aaaagh!' and slid down the trunk to the ground. Then he scampered across to God, and peered out from behind him. And what he saw made him cry out again: 'Aaaagh!'

Woman was sitting upright, nursing the Baby. She bent over it, her hair hanging forward like a curtain. It had happened! And the beast lay at her feet, gazing at God and Man.

God was astounded. His mother's magic had worked! But how? And what about that Frog? And what about the Baby? The Baby was a brilliant idea! Why had he never thought of it?

Wildly excited, God started forward, with Man clinging to the fringe of his apron. But the great beast rose to meet them. The hair on its shoulders lifted and spread like the tail of a peacock, its jaws opened, and a solid blast of sound hit them – a blast like the exploding of the kiln.

Man blew away like a straw, and God reeled stumbling after him, with his brain spinning. What was this beast? Was it a walking kiln exploding whenever it pleased? What was it?

'Do you know what you've done?' God cried, as he came gasping to his mother. 'Do you know what you've let loose?' She was still squatting there on the floor, above the cellar hatch. She grinned, showing him all her gums, then put back her head and cackled. Her hands, dangling over her knees, and dancing and dithering there, reminded God of the black tongue of the Puff-Adder.

'That,' she crowed, 'is the Tiger. He's an Angel. He is the Protector of the Human Child.'

God was mystified. This was the first he'd ever heard of Angels.

'Look, Mother,' he said. 'Your Tiger or Angel as you call it – it's too much. He knocked me over with one shout. He shows no respect. He's too frightful. The Baby's all right. In fact, I don't mind the Baby at all. The Baby's good. But the Tiger's overdoing it. Please take him back.'

'Take him back?' she croaked. 'How?'

'Just take him back. If he scares me, what's he going to do to the rest of my Creation? He's too much.'

His mother looked at God solemnly. 'The Human Child', she said, 'needs an Angel Protector. And the Tiger's it.'

God flew into a tantrum. 'You need a Protector,' he yelled. 'Let him protect you. My world can't handle him. He doesn't fit. If the Human Child needs a Protector, let's have something I can cope with. Something that fits.'

His mother flailed her hands loosely together – exactly, thought God, like an old Chimpanzee. 'OK!' she laughed. 'OK. I'll have him back. It's done.'

Then she clapped her palms together over her head, and held them there, fingers pointing upwards, elbows on her knees, while her face suddenly lowered and her eyes closed.

Fleeing from the Tiger's roar, Man had dived into a garbage pit. Hearing the laughter of God's mother, he'd stayed there. But now he came creeping out, and saw God returning. They went together towards Woman.

She sat as they'd left her, suckling her Baby. Man ran to her, and squatting beside her reached out to touch her hair, and gazed at her with shining eyes. The Tiger had gone.

God stood stroking his beard. He looked first at Woman,

then at the Baby, then at the small, gingery, striped animal that sat beside Woman's crossed ankles, gazing at Woman and the Baby with sleepy, half-closed eyes.

This creature looked quite like a Tiger, but it was only the size of the Baby. And after one sleepy glance and one sleepy blink, it ignored God and Man.

'So what's this?' asked God abruptly, pointing to the new creature.

Woman leaned her foot over, and the little animal rubbed its ear on her big toe. She wriggled her toes, and it pressed its chin on to them, laying back its ears and closing its eyes.

'This', she said, 'is our Pusscat. We call him Tiger.'

God nodded thoughtfully. So this was how his mother had solved the problem. But at that moment the Pusscat pricked its ears. An unfamiliar sound made God look up. It seemed to come from the clouds. No, it came from the mountains.

Steep-faced mountains surrounded the forest. A horizon of mountains. They looked like giant grey or brown or blackish faces, propped up in bed with the forests pulled up under their chins, like coverlets. Out of those mountains came a strange, echoing sound. A strange, clangorous cry, rising and falling. It was like a terrible singing. A dreadful sound really.

As he listened, God felt that same shiver creeping up from his heels into his hair. Just as when Woman's hand had moved. And he knew that this was the Tiger. He frowned. And his frown became almost a grimace. The voice of the Tiger seemed to take hold of his brain and twist it.

'Tiger!' he whispered. 'Yes, Tiger!'

As he said the word, he shivered again, and felt the hair actually stir on his head.

'Tiger!' he whispered. And the same weird electrical thrill came again. He gave a little laugh.

'Tiger!' he growled. Then again, more fiercely: 'Tiger!' His

104

eyes opened wide. He felt his hair standing up on end. And before he knew it he was roaring out: 'Tiiiigerrrr! TIIIIIgerrrrrrr! TIIIIIIGERRRRRRRRR!'

The echo of his roar came bounding and rumbling back off the mountains mingled with the appalling song of the animal. God stood there as the sounds rolled through him and over him. He had never felt anything like it. It was terrifying and yet, he had to admit it, it was wonderful. It was like nothing in his own Creation. It was wonderful in a whole new way. What was this strange new thing in his Creation?

The Tiger seemed not to have heard him. It flowed along, sometimes deep in the jungle gorges, sometimes high on the rough sides where forests hung over cliffs. Its body resounded like a giant harp, as the tree shadows and the sun's rays stroked over it. A tremendous, invisible song, it moved slowly around the mountain circle, full of its dark ideas.

God half turned and stared at the Pusscat. It occurred to him that the Pusscat too, whether it liked it or not, was breathing that sound. And Man too. And Woman, and the Baby. Everything in his Creation was having to listen. Every creature in the thickets, every tiniest insect under the leaves, they were all breathing air that was trembling with the voice of the Tiger. Nothing could escape it. And his old mother, she was breathing it too – probably still sitting where he'd left her, with her knobbly, shrivelled hands closed over her head, and her head bowed, smiling into her closed eyelids.

The Trunk

God sometimes gets tired. But he was never so tired as the day he finished making Elephant.

'It's the last time,' he was thinking, 'the last time I make anything so big.'

In fact, he was so tired that towards the end he rushed the job a little bit. Normally he would have given Elephant a thick pelt of fur. But it dawned on him that he didn't really need this. If he slapped the clay on, and made a good, really thick skin, that would do fine. And so he whacked the special Elephant clay on in great handfuls.

At last, about four in the afternoon, the job was finished. And there stood Elephant, swinging his head from side to side, lifting first one great forefoot, then the other, and looking sideways out of his wicked little brown eye.

God was pleased. He walked all round his new creation, gazing at it from every angle. Yes, it looked pretty good. He scraped the clay from his fingers, rolled it into a tiny ball, tossed it on to his workbench, and was just about to take his apron off when Elephant screamed:

'Finish me!'

God looked round in surprise. 'You are finished,' he said. 'Away with you. Out on to the plains with you. Seize the day.'

Elephant curled his trunk high over his head and let out another scream: 'Finish me!' He twisted his tail into a tight, angry knot. 'I'm unfinished. I want a coat.'

God's heart sank. All he longed to do was sink into a hot bath. But he made his face smile.

'Dear Elephant,' he said, 'you have a coat. It's a very superior coat of real Elephant leather. It's – '

His voice was drowned by Elephant's scream: 'I want a coat of fur! You've made me wrong. Show me another bald beast.'

God could feel himself getting angry. But then he saw a tear spill from Elephant's eye, and make a black streak down to his mouth corner. He made his voice gentle: 'Elephant, I'm afraid there's none of your clay left – '

'What's that you just threw away?' shrieked Elephant. 'I saw it. You had it in your hand. That clay belonged to me. It was more me.' And his little brown eye glittered with its next tear, and swivelled and fixed on the tiny ball of clay lying on the workbench.

'But that's not enough for anything,' cried God, picking it up.

'Oh yes it is,' screamed Elephant. 'Give me some hairs. Even a few would be better than nothing. I don't want to be bald from the start.'

God sighed and patted Elephant's brow. Then very carefully he began to make bristly hairs out of that tiny bit of clay. He stuck them here and there on Elephant's head and along his back. But the clay soon ran out.

'How does it look?' asked Elephant.

'It looks', said God, 'as if you're just starting to sprout a terrific crop of bushy hair. Yes, I must say it looks pretty good. You were right to insist.'

Elephant was suddenly full of happiness. Curling up his trunk, and whisking it over his bristles, he ambled off towards the plains, where the Lions glowed like heaps of crown jewels and the Gazelles drifted like shadows of clouds.

God collapsed in his chair with a gasp of relief, and gazed out into his garden. His old mother brought him a cup of tea and a bun shaped like a whelk. 'Your hands are dirty,' she muttered. 'Aren't you going to have a bath?'

But for the moment God just went on sitting there, gazing at his garden, and scraping the last Elephant clay from between his fingers and from the deep lines in his palm and from under his fingernails. He rolled it into a ball between his finger and thumb, and watched one of his Thrushes cracking open one of his Snails on the garden path. He squeezed the ball of clay flat. Then he squeezed it square. He was thinking: 'Well now, I could have made Elephant a few more hairs with this.' Then he thought about Elephant's amazing ears. And then he thought about Elephant's trunk.

God had never made a trunk before. Now that trunk was the most fascinating thing. It was a brand-new invention. He felt he'd quite like to make another, maybe smaller.

His fingers rolled the tiny piece of clay. Cleverly he shaped a trunk, with all its creases. So there it lay on his palm, a tiny trunk.

He took a sip of his tea. How if he made a really tiny Elephant? He put the trunk to his lips, to blow the nostrils through it.

Then he got a shock. The Trunk curled up, twisted and dropped from his fingers. It lay on his lap, squirming.

'Idiot!' he whispered to himself. Without thinking, he'd blown life into a tiny Elephant's trunk – a tiny trunk, all on its own, without its Elephant.

'Finish me!' squealed the Trunk, writhing as if it were in pain.

God picked it up and it flailed about between his finger and thumb.

'Finish me! Where's the rest of me? Finish me!' squealed the Trunk.

It sounded like a very tiny Elephant.

God scratched his beard. The truth was, he had no more Elephant clay. At that moment, he had no more clay of any kind. Tomorrow he'd have to go out to his clay-pits and dig some fresh. But the Elephant clay was all gone. He'd used the whole lot. That's why Elephant had turned out so big.

'Just be calm,' said God. 'I'll get you some more clay tomorrow. But it won't be Elephant clay. I'm right out of Elephant clay.'

'What?' squealed the Trunk in disbelief. 'No more Elephant clay?'

'Well,' said God, 'there might be some somewhere. But it will have to be found. It's rare and precious stuff.'

'Oh no!' wailed the Trunk. 'Oh no!' It was full of Elephant thoughts, Elephant hopes, Elephant dreams, Elephant plans. Every moment, with every breath it took, it felt more and more Elephant. And the idea of creeping about without an Elephant head or body or legs was horrible.

Then God had a brainwave.

'You could help me to find some,' he said. 'You could start right away.'

'How?' sobbed the Trunk. The Trunk was actually weeping. It glistened with tears.

'Well,' said God, 'just go and dig anywhere. Simply dig, that's all there is to it. Start down there in the garden. As soon as you come up with the right sort of clay, I'll finish you. It won't take much.'

The Trunk lifted its end.

'There you are, start where it's soft.' And God tossed the Trunk out into his garden. Then he dropped back into his chair, sighed once, and put the whole whelk into his mouth.

The Trunk began to dig. Being Elephant flesh, it was strong. It filled itself up with whatever it found down there under the grass-roots, brought it up, disgorged it all in a pile, and called: 'How's this?'

Then away down for more.

At the end of the first day God walked in his garden in the cool of the evening, and examined the tiny spirals of earth and clay that the Trunk had brought up. The Trunk peered up at him out of its best end.

'Well,' said God thoughtfully, 'some of this we might use for insects. But none of it is Elephant clay.'

The Trunk, that had been holding itself up very straight, slumped down and lay flat.

'If you like,' said God, 'you could go on a Rat tomorrow. You'd make a very fair tail. I have a good supply of Rat clay in. I've moved on to Rats.'

'No, no!' cried the Trunk, and began to dig furiously into the earth. 'I'll find it,' it cried, 'I'll find it.'

So the days passed. And the weeks. The months, the years, the centuries. Trunk toiled away, bringing up its piles of dirt. Sometimes God looked at it, but always he shook his head sadly. And more often the rain washed it away before God saw it. Or a hoof stamped it back into the soil.

But the Trunk refused to lose heart. Even though it didn't have a proper heart. 'Some day,' it cried as it burrowed among the deep stones, 'some day I shall be an Elephant. Some day I shall be whole. Some day the lands will tremble under the feet of my tribes.' And it curled itself up for joy at the very idea, and let out its trumpeting battle-cry, so fiercely that crumbs of earth fell from the ceiling of its burrow.

The Making of Parrot

In the beginning, there were even more song contests than there are now. All the creatures were just finding their voices for the first time. They were quite amazed at the sounds that came out of their mouths.

'Listen, listen to me! Listen, listen, listen to me!' they were crying. Each one wanted all the others to listen. Wolves yelled, Toads quacked, Nightingales gurgled, Alligators honked, and the Leopard made a noise like somebody sawing a table in half.

'Listen to me,' roared the Leopard. 'Oh, Oh, listen to my song! Oh, Oh, it makes me giddy with joy! Just listen!' And he went on, sawing away. It sounded wonderful to him.

But nobody was listening. Every other creature was too busy singing – head back, mouth wide, tonsils dancing. The din was terrific.

At least, it was so till the Parrot began. But at Parrot's first note, all the creatures fell silent. The Demons under the earth fell silent. The Angels in the air fell silent. And the Parrot sang on alone. Even the trees listened, breathless, to the glorious voice of the Parrot.

What a voice! Where had he come from? Who was this astounding person?

Man had just been persuading Woman to marry him. He was rubbing her whole body with coconut oil, so she glistened like a great eel. 'Marry me,' he said, 'and I'll do this to you every day.'

'Well,' she said, 'maybe.'

She loved being rubbed with oil, but what did Man mean

by marriage? That was a new word. 'Marry?' What did it mean? She wasn't so sure she liked the sound of it. But she didn't want him to stop rubbing her with oil. So she said: 'Well, maybe.'

And that was the moment the Parrot began to sing.

Man stood up. Like somebody in a trance, he walked straight out through the door. He simply left Woman lying there, as if he had forgotten she existed.

'Hey!' cried Woman. 'Come back. You haven't finished.'

But Man was already outside, gazing amazed at the Parrot.

And the surrounding trees of the forest were loaded with birds of every kind, all gazing amazed at the Parrot. And in the lower branches of the trees, and between the trunks of the trees, all the kinds of animals were jammed together, in a great circle, gazing amazed at the Parrot.

Parrot surely was something to gaze at. He was actually a Dinosaur – but a truly beautiful specimen. He didn't look like a modern parrot. He was much bigger. He was quite a lot bigger than a Peacock. Nearly as big as Woman. And he was thickly covered with every-coloured feathers. These feathers didn't lie down smooth, like the feathers on the neck of a Hen. They ruffled out, like the feathers on the neck of a Fighting Cock. He looked like a gigantic Red-Indian head-dress. His face was a huge flower of rainbow feathers. His legs and feet were thick with glossy feathers, that changed colour as he stamped about. All his body was fluorescent, and as he sang, taking deep breaths, and flinging out the great flame-feathers of his wings, he seemed to be lit from inside by pulsing strobe lights – red, then orange, then yellow, then green, then blue, then indigo, then purple – then a blinding white flash and back to red. Really magnificent! And all the time, his incredible song poured out.

What a song! The crowding creatures couldn't believe it. It

seemed to pick them up bodily. Their eyes boggled, their jaws dropped, and they felt like puppets being jerked by strings.

Man stared in delight. This was something new. What singing! What a marvel!

'Can you believe it? Just listen to it!' he shouted, turning to Woman, who was now leaning in the doorway, looking out sulkily. 'Can you believe it?' Man almost screeched with excitement.

Woman frowned. She just went on leaning there, feeling dull. What was the matter with her? All the creatures of the earth were there, swooning at the singing of the Parrot. And there was Man, who was so clever at everything, standing overpowered by the voice of that bird. 'What's so wonderful about it?' she kept thinking. 'Why don't I like it? What's wrong with me? Maybe my ears are funny.'

She did try quite hard to like the Parrot's song. She didn't want to be left out. She closed her eyes, and listened so fiercely her head began to ache. But it was no good. She simply couldn't like it.

But now Man was dancing around the Parrot, flinging up his arms and legs. 'I can't believe it!' he screeched. 'I can't believe it! This is ecstasy! Where have you been? Oh! Oh!'

That first evening, Man took Parrot into his house. And until late in the night, the creatures all stayed where they were, crowded around Man's house, hearing Parrot's great song coming from inside. The house seemed to tremble and jerk with the power of it. And every now and again they would hear Man cry:

'Fantastic! Another! Another!'

Man was so delighted by his new friend that he invited Parrot to live with him for ever. 'I'll supply all you need,' he promised. 'Whatever food you like. Shelter from the bad weather. And you can sleep in that bed.'

'Which bed?' cried Woman. She was already fed up with this gigantic bird. Her head was splitting with his pounding songs. Man hadn't even looked at her for the last eight hours. And now –

'That bed there,' said Man.

'My bed?' she gasped.

'Why not?' asked Man. He had already drunk a lot of beer. Woman choked. She was so furious she couldn't speak.

'And give our new friend another glass of beer,' said Man.

Parrot stared at her. He could see very clearly that this Woman didn't like him one bit. But that didn't worry him. He ruffled his feathers. The crest on his head stood up straight, and his eyes, big and round and cold and deadly, like a Dinosaur's, stared at her.

'Don't think you can hypnotize me, you horrible Turkey,' shouted Woman.

'Do as you're told,' snapped the Parrot.

Man laughed and drained his glass. 'More beer for his Lordship,' he said. 'And for me too.'

Woman went to fill the beer-jug, but she was thinking what Parrot would look like with all his feathers plucked off. Behind her, once again, Parrot burst into song and the jug in her hand began to vibrate.

Next morning, all the contestants for the great song contest were ready very early, outside Man's house, and the crowd was even bigger than usual. The Fox and the Turtle were bustling about, taking bets. Some of the creatures were terrible gamblers.

Today, most people thought Lion would win. He had never entered before. He had been out there on the resounding plains, perfecting his mighty song, for years, and rumours had been coming in. 'It's simply stunning,' said the Zebra. 'Knocks your head off,' said the Gnu. Everybody could see, by the way he lay there, eyes nearly closed, one forepaw laid over the other, that he was confident of winning.

Beside him the Wart-hog sat looking very nervous, twitching his ears and tail, occasionally shaking his head. Nobody had the slightest idea what to expect from him.

But next in line was the Giraffe. The general opinion was that Giraffe had no voice at all – she was simply dumb. Even so, the Burrow Owls put their bets on her. 'She's not dumb,' they said. 'You people are the dumb ones, thinking she's dumb.'

There were three others: a Cormorant, a Woodpecker and a Loon. Loon was thought to be pretty good.

At last, Man came out, scratching his head and yawning. Parrot emerged, and stood beside him. He looked as fresh as a giant firework in full blaze.

Usually, Man judged the singing at these contests. But now he spoke to the crowd. 'You all heard Parrot singing last night,' he said. 'Never have I heard singing like it. We must all admit, he's in a class of his own. And so, today, I've asked him to be our Judge.'

A Monkey clapped.

'Let's begin,' said Parrot. 'Cormorant first.'

The Cormorant had been persuaded to enter by the Seagulls. He opened his beak, flapped his scraggy wings, and began.

'Aaaaaaaaaaark!' he croaked, and stopped.

'Is that all?' asked Parrot, blinking his pebble eyes.

'No, that's only the beginning,' said the Cormorant.

'OK,' said Parrot. 'Sing it to the end.'

Cormorant stretched up his neck, shifted his feet, and croaked: 'Aaaaaaaaaaark!' and stopped. 'That's the end,' he said.

Parrot stared at him.

'Next,' he said. 'Woodpecker.'

Woodpecker set back his head and laughed. After three or four laughs he stopped, and peered at Parrot. 'That's mine,' he said.

Parrot blinked. 'Loon,' he said.

The Loon writhed. His long neck performed like a snake with the itch, then shot up straight, as his beak opened.

A howling mad laugh twisted out. A Wren fainted and Man felt a shiver go up his back. Woman poked her head out through the doorway, round-eyed.

Parrot nodded and smiled. 'Giraffe,' he said.

Giraffe swayed. What looked like a bubble travelled slowly up her neck. Giraffe opened her mouth, and after about six seconds burped.

A baby Chimpanzee turned a somersault and screeched, till its mother hit it.

'Is that your song?' asked Man. Giraffe nodded gracefully, and lowered her thick, long eyelashes.

'Wart-hog,' said Parrot.

The Wart-hog's performance was quite good. He whirled on the spot, fell on his back, threshed his legs, churned with his tusks, writhed and contorted in a cloud of dust, and all the time let out noises like a cement-mixer. At last he stood up panting. He was sure he'd won.

'Lion,' said Parrot sharply.

Lion stretched, yawned, took a deep breath, then suddenly gripped the earth with his claws and roared. The blast knocked off several rows of birds, and Man grabbed the rail of his veranda. Parrot's feathers flattened for a moment, and

all the baby animals began to cry till their mothers hushed them. Then everybody waited.

Parrot seemed to be thinking. Then he said: 'The result of this contest is – Winner: ME!'

The Lion frowned. All the animals began to chatter. 'How is that?' roared a voice. It was Lioness. 'How can that be? How can you be winner?'

'Because – ' said Parrot. And suddenly he burst into song. He leaped out into the middle of the beasts. His feathers flamed and shook, his colours throbbed. His voice was not only utterly astounding, it was amazingly loud. Man shouted with delight:

'He's right. He's the winner!'

And Man began to clap. All the animals began to clap. And when Man began to dance, they all began to dance. Clapping they danced, and dancing they clapped, while the Parrot whirled and sang.

But Lion, Giraffe, Wart-hog and Loon stood apart in a group. 'He's not a bird,' said the Loon. 'He's a lunatic!'

'I might have won!' snorted Wart-hog. 'I was in there with a fighting chance!'

And Lion said: 'Something will have to be done about this fellow.'

But Giraffe stuck her head in through a side-window in Man's house, and saw Woman lying on the floor, weeping.

'Your husband has gone crackers,' said the Giraffe. 'It's that Parrot.'

Woman looked up. 'I'm leaving,' she sobbed. 'I've had enough. That Parrot is a monster. Have you seen its eyes? And is that supposed to be singing? It's made me deaf.'

She began to push things into a suitcase. 'Man was going to marry me,' she cried. 'Since that Parrot came he never even looks at me. The Parrot orders me about and I sleep on the floor. I'm off.'

'Wait,' said the Giraffe. 'We have a plan.'

It was true. The Giraffe may have been a dumb singer, but she was a clever planner.

'Wait till we come back,' said the Giraffe. 'Give us two days.'

Woman sat on the bed weeping. She nodded wearily: 'OK. OK. But two days is the limit.'

The Giraffe, the Loon, the Lion and the Wart-hog went to God. They told him that Man was getting married to Woman and that he wanted God to be there. But he daren't ask. He was too modest. In fact, Man was a little bit afraid of God. So the animals had come to ask what Man didn't dare to ask.

'I'd like very much to come to that wedding,' said God. 'Woman is my favourite invention.'

'But what he really wants,' said Giraffe, 'is for you to sing a song.'

'What,' asked God, 'at the wedding?'

And Loon said: 'Woman thinks that if you sing at her wedding, they will be happy ever after. She believes that. She's praying you'll come.'

God laughed. 'Simple!' he said. 'No problem. When?'

'Tomorrow,' growled the Lion.

The animals came to Woman, and explained their plan. 'The wedding must be tomorrow,' they told her. 'And you must get that Parrot to sing.' So the same night, when Parrot was fast asleep in Woman's bed, a great heap of glowing feathers, Woman got up from the dirt floor where she slept with the cat, and whispered to Man:

'You begged me to marry you, do you remember?'

He woke up and lay staring into the dark.

'What's that?' he said. He thought he was dreaming Woman's voice. So she said it again: 'You begged me to marry you, do you remember? Did you mean it?'

'Yes!' he said. 'Oh yes. If you will, I'll rub you every day with warm oil. Oh yes! Will you? Will you?'

'Tomorrow,' she whispered.

He would have jumped out of bed for joy, but remembered the Parrot and lay silent. Then he said: 'I'm sorry about the Parrot. But you know how I need music. I get carried away.'

'If he'll sing at our wedding,' she said, 'I will try to like him.'

By dawn, the news of the wedding had spread. The animals assembled from every corner of the forest and plains.

'What's this about a wedding?' cried Parrot, rushing back into the house. Man was already draped with honeysuckle, and he was rubbing Woman's body with warm oil. 'It's our wedding day,' said Woman. 'Will you sing for us? Can you sing a Marriage Song?'

'Haha!' laughed Parrot. His eyes seemed to whirl, but they were actually darting to and fro. His feathers were a-tremble. 'Sing a Marriage Song?' he cried. 'Only give me the chance!'

'Oh, I knew you would, Parroty,' she cried, and flinging her arms round him she covered his feathers with oil.

As he stood at the river's edge, trying to wash the oil off, Giraffe came strolling up.

'Hello, Parrot,' she said. 'I expect you're looking forward to hearing the new singer.'

Parrot blinked. 'New singer?' he asked. 'What new singer?'

'At the wedding,' said Giraffe. 'He's supposed to be simply the best ever. They say he's already here. Some animals persuaded him to come. I think Man was hoping you'd sing. It's going to be a mix-up. I expect it will end up with both of you singing.'

Giraffe sauntered off, and Parrot glared after her. He was beginning to feel angrier and angrier. First, he was furious about the oil on his feathers. And twice as furious about this new singer butting in on his show. A new singer? The best ever?

Parrot knew what he'd do. He'd challenge this new singer to a Marriage Song contest, on the spot. And he'd flatten him. He'd just crush him with his Parrot Songpower. The poor fellow wouldn't even be able to croak.

So Parrot shook himself like a great, gaudy dog, and came up from the river raging with eagerness to challenge the new singer.

God arrived looking like a beggar. He told nobody he was God and nobody recognized him. He merely said he'd heard there was going to be a wedding, so he'd brought a present. It was a hive full of bees. Man had never seen such a thing.

Already the creatures were crushing tightly around Man's house. And Parrot stood there on the veranda, staring hard at the Beggar. Could this be the new singer? He didn't look like much competition, if he was.

Man was impatient to start. But this was the first wedding ever, and nobody knew how to do it. Then the Beggar had a bright idea. He smeared Man's and Woman's faces with honey, from the hive. Then Man licked Woman's face and Woman licked Man's face, and when all the sticky sweetness was gone – that was it, they were Man and Wife. So simple!

'And now sing a song,' roared the Lion.

The Beggar nodded and smiled. But before he could open his mouth, a bellowing shout came from the veranda: 'Wait!'

All creatures looked at the Parrot. And as they looked at him, Parrot began to sing.

But from the first moment something was wrong. Something was stuck in Parrot's throat. He stretched his beak wide open, his feathers rippled and flared, his colours throbbed – but he choked. Finally he coughed and spat out – a Fly. A big Bluefly.

It buzzed on to the veranda rail, and sat there, cleaning the back of its neck. The Beggar nodded and smiled.

Parrot began again, but he'd hardly got into full voice before the same thing happened again – another Fly, which joined the first.

Parrot braced himself in rage, and began again. His voice choked, grated, strangled, as he forced out his song – and Fly after Fly shot out, till the veranda rail was crawling with them, and Parrot's eyes were blood-red.

He gagged finally, and bent over, coughing drily – while Fly after Fly came whizzing out of his mouth.

'Perhaps while we're waiting,' said the Beggar, 'I could sing a little song.'

And the Beggar began to sing. As he sang, the animals seemed to grow in size. Woman began to pant and cry. And Man too, he suddenly collapsed to his knees, and crouched there, his elbows on the ground, clutching the top of his head. And out of the ground all round flowers began to push up and open. Huge blossoms and tiny florets. And out of every twig in the forest clusters of blossoms burst and hung down. And out of the core of every flower unfolded a different Butterfly. And Butterfly after Butterfly came out of the flowers, just as Fly after Fly had come out of Parrot's mouth, till the air was full of Butterflies, that settled everywhere on the birds and animals and covered Man and Woman like a rich, quivering cloak.

Then the Beggar began to sing more strongly. And now Parrot seemed to clear his throat and let out a screech. He was trying to sing. Everybody could see he was trying to sing, but all that came out were not Flies now but more and more horrible screeches. And as he screeched he writhed. It was truly awful to watch him. His feathers now seemed to be real flames, devouring themselves. And the Beggar stepped towards him with his eyes shining and sang a great torrent of song straight at Parrot. The poor bird whirled and blazed and screeched, while his feathers scattered like burning embers from a kicked bonfire, and his body shrank. He was like a whirling Parrot being tossed, or maybe a Parrot being bounced on the end of an elastic.

Suddenly Woman ran forward. She ran fearlessly into the blast of the Beggar's song, and caught up the Parrot, and ran into the house with it, and silence fell.

When Man uncovered his eyes and looked up, he saw the incredible garden of blossoms and Butterflies. The Beggar had disappeared. Man went into the house looking for his new wife, and found her nursing the Parrot.

He could only just recognize the bird. It was no bigger than a small Monkey. Its feet were scorched, scaly twigs. Its face was a bent lump, like glass that had melted and hardened again. Its eyes were little marbles in ashen sockets. Only a few colours. Only a few feathers. And its voice – its voice was just the burned-out wreck of its song.

'Poor Parrot,' said Woman. 'Poor little Parrot!'

But gazing at the Parrot all Man could think about was the tremendous song of the Beggar.

The Invaders

In the deep darkness, God suddenly raised his head, and listened.

What was that? Was it a voice?

He strained his ears, listening into the silence.

Whatever it was, it had wakened him up. The silence was thick, as if made of dense leaves.

All through the world, just like God, the creatures listened. Some that had been sleeping had jerked awake. Their eyes bulged, wide and moist in the pitch black, as they listened. Some that had been creeping froze – with one paw lifted. Their ears craned.

All were listening. All were astonished. It had been a new noise, like nothing before.

And though it hadn't been very loud, every ear had heard it, all over the earth, at the same moment.

As if it had come from the inside.

And now, as they listened, and just as those creeping creatures were thinking of putting their lifted paw silently down, the sound came again.

It was a voice. It was words. It said:

'I am taking over.'

It didn't come from inside. It came from far out in space. But from everywhere in space at the same time. A peculiar, hoarse, quiet, howling voice. How can a howl be quiet? But it was. It was a sort of howling whisper. Or a whisper, a harsh, thin whisper, with a howl far away down inside it. Very eerie!

All creatures on earth looked straight up into space to see

what it might be. That night was starless. Their gaze disappeared into complete black.

God at his window stared up into the perfect black. And again the voice came, louder, and as if angrier:

'I am taking over the earth. All creatures shall be my slaves and food. God shall be my slave. I am coming to enslave the earth. I am coming to enslave and devour you all.'

A terrific silence followed. God's skin had tightened with goose-pimples, and his hair was trying to stand on end, struggling in its matted curls.

Who was this? What was this? A voice from beyond? And what else?

Had he made the earth too beautiful? Had he made all its creatures too beautiful? Had he attracted the greed of some space-being – some horror, perhaps? It sounded as if he had, and it was coming.

And as he stood there at the open window he heard the little cries of fear beginning, whimperings, caterwaulings, whinings, screeches, moanings, chitterings, snufflings, roarings, wailings, mooings, bleatings – all the voices together, a sea of sounds that grew louder and wilder. Till the whole earth was crying out. He listened in dismay. What could he do? That voice from space had terrified the whole earth. Panic was beginning. A sounder of Wild Pigs went plunging through his gooseberry bushes, barking and squealing. A great Horse was churning to and fro on his lawn. He could hear it in the dark, whinnying and grunting and whining and shaking its nostrils. He could imagine its staring, frenzied eyes, its mane on end, its tail-stump stuck straight up and the long tail flaring from it, as it whirled about in terror. Foolish Horse!

He cupped his hands to his mouth and bellowed with all his strength:

'Quiet out there! Quiet! There's no reason for alarm. Have no fear. God is here! It's a false alarm!'

That sound too was heard all over the earth. But it travelled slowly. Like waves widening from a rock dropped in a pond, it swept around the globe.

Hearing it, the creatures became quiet. Was God going to make a speech? Was he going to explain? Was he going to make it all right?

Soon the whole earth was silent once more, listening now for God. And God was thinking: 'I'll just give them a few comforting words,' when that other voice came again.

So all the creatures, listening in silence for God's words, heard instead that horrible, howling, screeching whisper from space, from the very stars, it seemed to be, but from all the stars together, from every hidden star at the same time. And it said:

'I am coming. Listen, O slaves. I am your new Master and I am coming. I need blood. I need food. And you, God! Hahahaha! You poor little God! You shall be my backscratcher! Hahaha!'

The voice was no longer a whisper. It sounded a whole lot nearer. And bigger. It was a bigger, fiercer voice. Just the voice, quite apart from what it said, the voice alone was terrifying. And the wild laugh made the ground shiver a little.

At once, every creature closed its eyes, opened its mouth to the limit, and emptied its lungs. From the whole earth, one great cry went out.

The din was deafening. God slammed his window shut, and went groping for a candle. His fingers were trembling.

How long before sunrise? How fast was this voice approaching? It was obviously coming pretty fast. But space is big. He found his candle and lit it with a snap of his fingers.

He sat on his bed and clutched his hair, and tried to think, while outside his window the earth wailed and sobbed, and up in the darkness – what? What? God's eyes rolled upwards, and he listened.

It was a terrible dawn for the creatures. God walked out in the dew, doing what he could to calm them. All the smaller creatures tried to get into his clothes, to hide near him. Up his trousers, inside his shirt and his sleeves. And as he walked he looked like a walking bee swarm with all the birds trying to land on him for safety. The bigger animals had gathered around God's house. Even Elephant and Lion and Leopard were in a shocking state, especially their wives.

God called a meeting.

'This voice in space', he began, 'is very odd.'

All the creatures fell silent. Even the Flies landed and listened.

'Yes, it is very, very odd,' said God. 'Most peculiarly odd.'

They all gazed at him, full of trust. Surely God would know what to do. Surely he would protect them. But he simply stood there, scratching his beard and frowning and saying:

'Very, very, very odd,' and again he frowned, sternly.

Buffalo suddenly saw that God didn't know what to say. He didn't know what to do either. God was as baffled as they were. And Buffalo was just about to shout: 'We ought to get ready to fight,' when the sky seemed to split.

All the creatures flattened, as if a giant hand had slapped down on them. Their eyes were squeezed tight shut, their ears flattened, their jaws clenched, as the voice came from directly overhead.

The same voice, but now very loud, like a great clangour inside a huge iron ship.

'Surrender! I call on you all to surrender. You are in my power. It's already too late to fight.'

Only God still stood upright. He lifted his fists and shook

them at the morning sky, which was bright blue, a beautiful morning, with a few fluffy clouds in the west.

'Do your worst, whoever you are!' he roared. 'We're ready for you! Do your worst! We're ready!'

The answer from the skies was a long, howling laugh, and then:

'Prepare! I shall be on top of you before you know! Prepare! Countdown has begun!'

God waited. After a few minutes, when nothing happened, he roused the animals. And now, working in a fury, he began to arm all his creatures.

'Have no fear!' he called, as he fitted tusks to the Elephants. 'Go and practise with these.'

The Elephants surged off, and began to practise on big trees, levering their roots out of the ground, ripping their bark off. 'What weapons!' they cried, and blew their trumpets.

Every creature pressed towards God, crying for weapons.

The Wild Pigs stormed off, like a charge of cavalry. Their jaws had been fitted with short, hooked tusks, as sharp as razors. They slashed through a field of turnips, making the slices fly.

The Wild Bulls trotted off, knotting their tails, looking deadly under their new horns. 'We're the land rockets,' they boasted. 'When his tanks appear, watch us,' and they shook their heads, so their horns seemed to spin like propellers.

His fingers flying faster than a typist's, God fitted weapons to every creature. The Rhinoceros bounded off, in his armour-plating, tossing his long horn upwards. 'Where's the enemy?' he shouted. 'Let me topple his towers!'

'That's better!' snarled the Leopard. And he made such terrific swipes with his new bunches of claws, like clubs full of steel hooks, that some nearby tall flowers fainted and became creepers ever after.

Even the rats and mice scampered about, clashing their fangs, dying to come to grips with the enemy.

Everybody felt safer. Pretty soon they were all equipped. And all longing for the fight.

'Let me at 'em!' boomed the Bear, and he took a swing at a tree stump, which actually exploded, just as if he'd tossed a bomb into its roots.

God called his army of new warriors.

'It's no good being well armed,' he shouted, 'if we've no discipline.'

Then he showed them how to form round him in a square. The biggest and most dangerously armed creatures on the outside, the smaller and quicker creatures inside. God stood in the middle of the square. His main weapons were blinding lightning and thunderbolts. He kept in reserve earthquakes and volcanoes. He also had mists, hail the size of oranges, and tornadoes which could lift up weights bigger than Elephants and whirl them far out to sea. He had incredibly freezing winds that could refrigerate most enemies solid in about five seconds. His last resource was meteorites. He was slightly afraid of those. The damage they could do, he knew, was out of this world. But he'd practised a lot, on the moon, and knew he was pretty accurate. It was a last resort.

The creatures stood in their places, gazing upwards. God gazed upwards. The Elephants stood fast, swaying like boxers and making little lunging movements with their tusks. The Lions lifted their upper lips. The Leopards made sure their jaw muscles were loose.

But God was worried. He'd put heart into all his creatures, giving them weapons. But he still had no idea just what this enemy might be. Its voice had made him feel quite sick with anxiety. He had a feeling this was going to be some battle!

He was already thinking: 'The moment it appears, up there in the sky, I'll have a go with the old meteorite, and risk it.'

Silence descended on the strange army. All gazed upwards into the blue. It actually was a gorgeous morning, fresh and light, a little wind just nodding the flowers. A Lark suddenly burst into twitterings of joy, till a Baboon slapped it and a Mongoose gave it a fierce look. They waited.

Finally, God couldn't bear to wait any longer. He cupped his hands and roared upwards into space.

'Whoever you are, you'd better go back. I advise you to turn round and go back. We're very heavily armed and perfectly prepared. Please don't be foolish. Go and try your luck with some other Creation. You haven't a hope here.'

There followed a moment's pause, then the air shook. Even the air inside their mouths and inside their lungs seemed to shake. The noise was stunning. It came from everywhere. It was no longer above in space. It was in the earth, in the trees, in the air, and even, yes, inside each other. A most tremendous shout:

'ATTAAAAAAAAAAAAAAAAAAAAAAAACK!'

Every creature had the impression that a meteor had come rushing from nowhere and had hit them smack in the ear. On both ears. A truly shocking noise, a horrendous moment of noise!

Then came dead silence.

With clenched teeth, with wild, popping eyes, all claws out, horn-tips trembling, lips lifted from fangs, ears flattened, bodies tensed and quivering, the beasts stared at each other, waiting for IT.

God crouched, his eyes stretched very wide, to miss nothing, a meteorite at the ready, another one slowly circling his head on standby.

But still nothing happened.

A Rabbit broke down with the tension and gave a few sobs.

Gradually the creatures relaxed. They blinked, they licked their dry lips, they readjusted the positions of their tails. The Wolf glanced at God.

God's arm lowered slowly, and he straightened. A slight frown came over his brow.

Gazing round uneasily, he passed the meteorite to his left hand, pushed his right hand under his left armpit, and scratched himself.

The Wolf, as if imitating him, pointed its nose, flattened its ears, closed its eyes, and with one hind foot fiercely scratched the back of its ear.

A Cheetah, without taking its eyes off the topmost leaf of a distant tree, which had just moved the wrong way in the wind, thoughtfully lifted a hind leg and tried to scratch its belly. Then, forgetting the leaf, it sat and began to nuzzle and chew at its belly-fur savagely.

God was also scratching his belly. Then the back of his knee.

A pack of Wild Dogs began to scratch, all together, like dancers without music.

Was it catching? Was it itching powder? The densely packed square of creatures was shuddering and shaking. The Vultures fluffed their wings and burrowed in their feathers with their beaks. The Monkeys rolled on the ground, scratching fiercely, with grimacing faces. A Badger sat, teeth bared, with a blur for a hind leg. Pigs squirmed on their backs, trying to find sharp stones or twigs to scratch them.

The whole army was shuddering in a disorderly heap. Every animal and bird was scratching itself, or scratching its neighbour, or trying to do both.

And then God, scratching his belly, found what felt like a

speck of grit. It twitched between his finger and thumb as he squeezed it. It was alive.

He peered at it. A tiny bushy face peered out at him, with two ferocious red eyes. The mouth opened, and that same tremendous voice came out:

'Surrender! You are overpowered!'

And the tiny thing leaped into his beard.

God began to laugh.

'It's a Flea,' he cried. 'We've been invaded by Fleas!'

He scratched and laughed wildly. He seemed to be tickling himself. And all the creatures began to laugh and rake at their itches. And itching they scratched. And scratching they laughed. And laughing they itched and scratched and laughed and scratched and itched and laughed and scratched and scratched –

They scattered through the woods, rubbing themselves against trees and rocks, scratching and laughing, and itching and laughing, and scratching and scratching –

God went into his house for a bath.

The Snag

Right from the beginning Eel was grey. And his wife was grey. And his children were grey.

They lived in the bed of the river under a stone. There they lay, loosely folded together, Eel and his wife, and two of his children. They breathed, and they waited, under a big stone.

Eel could peer out. He saw the water insects skittering about over the gravel, and sometimes swimming up through the water, to disappear through a ring of ripples. Where did they go?

He saw the bellies of the Trout, the Dace, the Minnows, and one Salmon, hovering in the current, or resting on the points of the stones on the river-bed, their fins astir endlessly.

All day he lay under the dark stone.

But at night, when the sun went behind the wood, and the river grew suddenly dark, he slipped out. His wife and his two children followed him. Their noses were keener than any Dog's. They could smell every insect. They rootled in the gravel of the river-pool, nipping up the insects.

But wherever he went over the river-bed, he heard the cry: 'Here comes the grey snake! Look out for the grey snake! The grey snake is out! Watch for your babies!'

The fish could see him. Even in the dark, the fish with their luminous eyes could see him very well. They darted close, to see him better.

'Here he is!' piped a Trout, in a thin treble voice. 'He's coming upstream. Horrible eyes is coming upstream.'

And then: 'Here he is!' chattered the Minnows. 'He's turning back downstream.'

Wherever he moved, the fish kept up their cries: 'Here's the grey snake now. Here he comes! Watch your babies!'

Eel pretended not to care. He poked his nose under the pebbles, picking out the insects. But the endless pestering got on his nerves. And his two children were frightened. 'We're not snakes,' he would shout. 'We may be grey, but we're fish.'

Then all the fish began to laugh, so the river-pool shook. 'Fish are silver,' they cried. 'Or green, or gold, or speckled, with pinky fins. Fish are beautiful. Fish have scales. They are shaped like fish. But you are grey. You have no scales. And you are a snake. Snake! Snake! Snake!'

They would begin to chant it all together, opening and closing their mouths. And Eel and his wife and children would finally glide back under their stone and lie hidden.

In a few minutes the fish would forget about them.

If there had been anywhere else to go, Eel would have gone there, to escape the fish of that pool. Once he did take his wife downstream, to a much bigger, deeper pool. But that was worse. Nearly thirty big Salmon lay there, as well as many Trout and Dace and Minnows. The Salmon had shattering voices. They were used to calling to each other out on the stormy high seas. And now when Eel came slithering from under his stone, when night fell, a deafening chorus met him:

'Here comes the grey snake. Here he comes to eat your children. Here he comes. Watch out!'

And all the time he was hunting they kept it up: 'Go home, grey snake! Go home, grey snake!'

Finally Eel led his family back to the smaller pool, where there was only one Salmon.

*

136

His two children stopped going out at night. They lay curled up under the stone, crying. 'What are we?' they sobbed. 'Are we really grey snakes? If we aren't fish, what are we?'

Eel scowled and tried to comfort them. But he couldn't help worrying. 'What if I am a grey snake, after all? How can I prove I'm a fish?'

Eel had only one friend, a Lamprey. Lamprey was quite like Eel, but he was so ugly he didn't worry about anything. 'I know I'm a horror,' he would say. 'But so what? Being ugly makes you smart.'

One day this Lamprey said to Eel: 'I know a Fortune-teller. She could tell you what you are. Why don't you ask her?'

Eel reared up like a Swan. 'A Fortune-teller,' he cried. 'Why didn't you tell me?'

'I've told you,' said Lamprey.

This Fortune-teller, it turned out, was the new moon. 'How can the new moon tell fortunes?' asked Eel.

'She tells fortunes only for a few minutes each day,' explained Lamprey. 'You have to get to her just as she touches the sea's edge, going down. Then she tells fortunes until she sinks out of sight. You have to listen very carefully. You don't hear her with your ears. You hear her with your thoughts.'

'Let's go,' said Eel. And he wanted to set off that minute downstream, but Lamprey checked him.

'Take a witness,' said Lamprey.

'A witness?' asked Eel. 'What for?'

'Unless you have a witness to what the new moon says, the fish will never believe you. Take the Salmon.'

The Salmon was so sure the new moon would tell Eel he was really a snake, and not a fish at all, that he was eager to come. 'I want to hear that,' he cried. 'I'll bring the truth back. Then you can stay out there in the sea, you needn't come back at all. It's the truth we want, not you.'

So they set off. It was quite a journey, getting to the new moon. But finally Eel got there, with Lamprey beside him, to keep his spirits up, and, skulking behind, the Salmon.

The new moon was actually a smile without a face. It lay on the sea's rim like a face on a pillow. And the Smile smiled as Eel told his problem. It smiled as it sank slowly.

'You are a fish,' said the Smile. 'Not only are you a fish. You are a fish that God made for himself. God made you for himself.'

'Me?' cried Eel. 'God made me for himself? Why?'

'Because,' said the Smile, 'you are the sweetest of all the fish.'

The Salmon slammed the water with his tail. He'd always thought he was the sweetest. This was bad news on top of bad news.

'Say that again,' cried the Eel.

'You are the sweetest of all the fish,' said the Smile. It spoke so loud the whole sea chimed like a gong, with the words.

Eel didn't know what to say. 'Thank you,' he stammered. 'Oh, thank you.' He was thinking how his children would jump up and down, as much as they could under their rock, when he told them this.

'But,' said the Smile, as it sank. It seemed to be sinking faster and faster. There was only a little horn of light left, a little bright thorn, sticking above the sea.

'But?' cried the Eel. 'But what?'

'There's a snag,' said the Smile, and vanished.

'What snag? What's the snag?' cried Eel.

But the Smile had gone. The sea looked darker and colder.

138

A shoal of Flying Fish burst upwards with a shivering laugh, and splashed back in again.

Still, Eel had what he wanted. And both Lamprey and Salmon were witnesses. Salmon had already gone, furious, as Eel and Lamprey set off home.

Back in the pool, Eel called all the fish together and told them exactly what had been said. 'I am a fish,' he said. 'Not only that, I am God's favourite fish. God made me for himself. Because among all the fish, I am the sweetest.'

'It is true,' said the Lamprey. 'I was there.'

'Yes,' said the Salmon. 'Perhaps she did say that. But what did she mean? That's what I'd like to know, what did she mean?'

Even so, the fish were impressed. They didn't like it, but they were impressed. And from that moment, Eel and his wife and children surged about the pool throughout the day as well as the night. 'Make way for God's own fish,' he would shout, and butt the Salmon. 'Make way for the sweetest!'

The fish didn't know what to do. The story soon got about. The Heron and the Kingfisher told it to the birds. The Otter told it to the animals. A crowd of them came to Man, and told him what had happened.

Man, who was drinking very sour cider, which he had just made out of crab-apples, pondered.

'What', he said finally, 'does the Eel mean by sweetest? How sweetest? Sweetest what? Sweetest nature?'

All the creatures became thoughtful. Then they became wildly excited.

'Man's got it!' they cried. 'What does the horrible Eel mean by sweetest? Sweetest how?'

The fish came crowding around Eel and his family. 'Sweetest what?' they shouted. 'How are you sweetest? Come and prove you're the sweetest! You and your hideous infants. You and your goblin wife.'

'It's a riddle,' said the Salmon. 'The new moon posed a riddle. What does sweetest mean?'

'We are sweeter than any Eel,' cried the flowers. And the wild roses and the honeysuckles poured their perfumes over the river.

'And we are sweeter than any dumb Eel,' cried the Thrushes, the Blackbirds, the Robins, the Wrens, and they poured out their brilliant songs over the river.

'And my children are the sweetest of all the animals,' cried the Otter, holding up its kittens. 'They are not,' cried the Sheep, and she butted forward her two Lambs. 'No, they are not,' cried the Fox, suddenly standing there with a woolly cub.

'Among the fish,' cried the Eel. 'That's what she said. I am the sweetest among the fish. Who cares about perfumes? Who wants to smell? And who cares about song? What counts is the thought. And who cares about fluffy darlings? The Otter grows up to murder Eels. The Lamb grows up to butcher the flowers. The Fox-cub grows up to murder the Mice. What sort of sweetness is that? No. My sweetness is the real sweetness, the sort that God loves best.'

'Taste?' asked Man. 'That leaves only taste.'

Eel would have blinked, if he had had eyelids. Taste? He hadn't thought of that.

'That's it!' shouted the fish, sticking their heads out of the water. 'Taste! Cook us and eat us, see who's the sweetest. Taste us all. Taste us all!'

Eel felt suddenly afraid. Who was going to taste him? Was Man going to cook him? But the fish were shouting to Man: 'You can eat one of each of us. And then eat Eel as well, and then you can judge. Here we are. Here we are.'

The fish were quite ready to let one of each kind of them be eaten so long as it meant that Eel too would be eaten.

'No,' cried Eel. 'Wait.'

But fish were jumping ashore. One Trout, one Dace, one Minnow, and even that Salmon – he too was offering himself. All to get the Eel killed and eaten!

Eel twisted round and fled. But the Otter plunged in after him. And in the swirling chase, the Otter grabbed Eel's wife. She was much bigger than Eel anyway.

Eel coiled under the stone with his two children. He couldn't believe it. The oven was glowing, the fish were frying. And his wife too! It was terrible! But all he could do was stare and feel helpless.

And Man and Woman were already testing, with dainty forks and thin slices of buttered brown bread.

They didn't like Dace at all. He tasted of mud. The Minnow was quite nice – but peculiar. The Trout was fairly good – but a little too watery. He needed lemon and – and – something. And the Salmon – the Salmon, now! Well, the Salmon seemed just about the most wonderful thing possible – till they tasted Eel.

Woman uttered a cry and almost dropped her fork. Tears came into her eyes and she stared at Man.

'Was there ever anything so delicious!' she gasped. 'So sweet! So sweet!'

Man rested his brow on his hand.

'How have we lived so long,' he said, 'and not realized what gorgeous goodies lay down there, under the river-stones? How could anything be sweeter than this Eel?'

'Eel!' he shouted. 'You have won. God is right again. You are the sweetest!'

Eel heard and trembled. And he shrank back under the stone, deeper into the dark, when he heard Man say: 'Bring me another!'

142

Otter came swirling down through the current. Otter was working for Man. Eel and his two children shot downstream. But one had to be hindmost. One of the children. And when Eel looked round, only one of his children was following.

And as they slipped and squirmed down through the shallows, among the stones, towards the next pool below, the Heron peered down out of heaven and – Szwack! The other Eel-child was twisting in the Heron's long bill. The Heron too was working for Man.

But the Eels were so sweet, neither Otter nor Heron could resist eating them on the spot. From that moment, the Otter hid from Man and spent all his time hunting more Eels – for himself. And from that moment Heron was afraid of Man – flapping up and reeling away with a panicky 'Aaaark' – only to land somewhere else where he could go on hunting Eels – for himself. Neither Otter nor Heron wanted to hand over what they caught – Eels were much too sweet!

But Eel himself hid from all of them. He oiled his body, to make it hard to grip. And whenever he sees the slightest glow of light he hides deeper under the stones, or deeper into the mud. He thinks it is Man searching for him. Or he thinks it is the point of the moon sinking and he suddenly remembers THE SNAG.

Yes, the snag.

The Playmate

'I want a playmate,' said Woman.

Man stopped, turned and stared at her. Here he was, his food-gathering bag on a stick over his shoulder, and his club, to defend himself from the hoodlums among the animals, stuck in his belt, ready to tramp all day searching for tasty mushrooms, and honey, and edible snails, and all she wanted to do was play.

'A playmate?' he echoed. 'Can't you weave another carpet? They're very pretty.'

'I've woven twenty-eight. They're seven deep on the floor. I'm sick of carpets.'

'Then – make a pot,' suggested Man. 'You're a very good potter. I love your pots.'

'I'm sick of pots,' she cried.

'Then weave a basket.'

'I've woven baskets till – look! My finger-ends are raw. If you mention baskets again I'll scream.'

She sat on the bed, looking miserable. Man's heart sank.

'What happened to the pet rat?' he asked. 'He was good fun.'

'He bit me, didn't he,' she shouted.

'Be calm, be calm!' said Man. He knew he'd have to do something. But what?

'Ask God,' she said. 'Tell him if I don't get a playmate, I'm off.'

'Off?' cried Man. 'Where to?'

'Just off,' she shrieked. 'Off! Off! Off! Flap! Flap! Flap! Like a bird! Go and get myself eaten by Lions. Find some excitement. Anything. I'm withering inside!'

She was growing more and more agitated.

Man tried to calm her. 'I'll ask him,' he said. 'Today. A play-mate, you say.'

He was just about to go when he turned back. 'What kind?' he asked.

'How am I to know?' she yelled. 'It's God's job – thinking things up. All I've got is a snake. It sleeps the whole time. I'm perishing of boredom and snake-sleep!'

Man set off. His day was ruined. It wasn't always so easy, getting a word with God. First of all, it wasn't so easy to find him.

But today he was lucky. Man found God kneeling in a forest clearing. He seemed to be pressing his ear to the ground. But then Man saw he had his right arm buried to the shoulder in some sort of hole. He strolled up.

'Lost something?' he asked casually.

God frowned, rolled his eyes and twisted his mouth. He was obviously groping for something down there, deep in the earth. Then he gasped and straightened up. His hand came up out of the hole and God laughed. Between his fingers something struggled.

'There we are,' he said, and laid the creature on his palm. It took a few wriggly steps, then peered at Man over the edge of God's forefinger, a tiny froggy face, with brilliant jewel eyes.

'A Newt!' said God. 'Funny. I simply had a feeling about it. I knew there was something down there. But I'd no idea – ! Well, well, well!'

'Is he your latest?' asked Man.

'Hard to say,' God replied, peering into the Newt's eyes. 'He might have been here a while. Some things take an awful lot of work. But others – they just seem to turn up, somehow. All ready-made. Very odd!'

'Maybe somebody else is making them too,' suggested Man, getting interested. But God turned angry eyes on him, and stared at him, and so Man said quickly: 'Actually, I have a request. For a special kind of creature.'

Now it was God's turn to be interested. 'Really? A special creature, eh? How special?'

'My wife needs a playmate,' said Man. 'She says she wants some excitement.'

God's eyes became grave. He lowered the Newt on to a lily leaf in a swampy pond. He pushed the lily leaf under the surface, with one finger, and the Newt floated off. Then, laying its arms and legs close to its sides, it wriggled away downwards into the gloom, like a dart with ribbons.

God sat back on his heels, and gazed at Man. 'An exciting playmate for Woman!' He nodded thoughtfully. 'Well,' he said, 'I already have one or two ideas. How soon?'

'Tonight, maybe?' said Man. 'Suppertime, about?'

'OK,' said God. 'Tonight.' And he stood up and strode away, his head bowed in thought.

Man licked his lips nervously. He would have liked to say a little bit more. He would have liked to say: 'Something not too big, not too noisy, not too wild.' But God had gone. Man began to gather frilly orange mushrooms, pausing now and again. What he didn't want God to do, was make another Man.

That evening Man and Woman ate their supper in silence. As the sun set, the glow of the fire seemed to grow brighter. Man could feel himself becoming more and more anxious. His wife wasn't angry, and she wasn't exactly sulking. If anything, she was just sad.

'Well,' he said at last, 'your playmate's coming this evening.'

She looked up, with round eyes, but said nothing.

'God didn't exactly say what sort,' Man went on. 'Only we can be sure it will – do the trick.'

Woman blinked and gazed into the fire. Man thought she looked a little bit less unhappy, so he felt happier. He told her about the Newt. All she said was:

'I hope it isn't going to be a Newt.'

They sat on, waiting. Wolf began to howl. Bats began to snatch Moths from the edges of the fire's little flames. But still no playmate. Finally they went to bed. Man couldn't sleep. Was God going to fail him? Or maybe the playmate had already arrived, and they hadn't noticed. Maybe it was a Moth. Or a Bat. These didn't seem like very good playmates. But then, thought Man, God had some funny ideas. Not all were what you might call perfect.

The moon rose full and shone into the room. Man closed his eyes and tried to force the morning to come. Maybe in the morning –

But suddenly, he knew his wife beside him had lifted her head off the pillow. He opened his eyes and listened.

Something was coming through the forest, towards the house. And not very quietly either. Branches cracked and broke.

'Ooooh!' his wife whimpered.

Man got out of bed. Some of the animals did not like him too much. His hand found his club in the dark. He waited, standing in the middle of the room, as the crashing came closer.

And now he heard celery stalks snapping in the garden, and a crunching and a munching.

Was it an Elephant? The chomping noises came still closer. Now the thing was standing just outside the door, slurping and chewing and breathing hard.

147

Very gently, Man pulled the door tightly closed and slid the big wooden bar-bolt into its sockets.

At the same moment something pounded on the door. The whole house shook slightly, and a mouse screamed.

'Who's there?' shouted Man.

Dead silence answered him. Then the breathing started again, with gasps and grunts as the door creaked. Something was trying to force a lever or maybe tusks into the edge of the door. Man swung his club and slammed that spot with all his strength. A screech of pain went up, and a heavy creature thudded away. More screeches followed, then whinings, and finally silence. Man and Woman waited, hardly daring to breathe, straining their ears.

Suddenly a dark shape appeared at the window and Woman screamed. A huge bulk blocked the moonlight. It was coming in.

Again, with all his strength Man whirled his club, and after a few thuds and more screeches the dark thing fell away from the window, and the moon looked in as before.

Man stood panting, waiting for the next attack. His wife crouched behind his knees, sobbing.

Suddenly, to his amazement, the whole house began to rock. He had built it on low pillars, and now something seemed to have got under it, and to be hoisting up one corner.

A groaning series of gasps came from under the floor, as the house reared higher. Man and Woman crashed to the back wall and the whole house toppled over. They struggled under a heap of pots and carpets and baskets.

They were hardly clear when the house began to heave up again and with another groaning gasp toppled right over on to its roof. Now Man and Woman were lying on the ceiling, which had become the floor, and on top of them were all the pots, baskets, carpets, and the bed too.

'Don't worry,' shouted Man, 'I built this house to last.'

But already it was toppling again. And again. And again. And the dreadful groaning gasps outside had become a sort of laugh. And the house was trundling over like a giant, creaky crate. And Man and Woman and all their possessions were tumbling inside it like clothes inside a washing machine. And the terrible creature, whatever it was, kept on heaving it over, like some sort of toy, with horrible grunty laughs.

Inside, Man and Woman dived and rolled, bruised and dizzy, in a hail of broken crockery, in a great writhing tangle of carpets. There was nothing to cling on to. Man kept trying to push his wife out through the window, but she screamed and clung to him. 'Don't throw me to that monster,' she cried. So then he tried to climb out while he carried her. But each time, before he could get more than his leg over the sill, the house heaved up and crashed over, and there came another gibbering laugh from somewhere out in the dark, and they were both in a heap under their furniture.

At the end of the garden, the ground sloped steeply to the river. And finally it happened. After toppling the house to and fro, and round and round and about, the powerful mystery beast rolled the house to the top of the sloping bank and down it went. Kerrash! Kerrrrack! Kerrrash! Kerrrackity! Splooooonge!

Water poured in through the window and the loosened joints, and Man and Woman heard the wild laugh rise to crazy shrieks. Their dark prison rocked gently and the water deepened.

Man pulled his wife out through the window. They sat on the roof with a Snake and a Mouse. Their half-sunk house was floating in mid-river, revolving slowly. The sky over the forest was pink with dawn. And they could just make out, in the pinky-grey light, a black massive creature leaping up and down on their garden, at the top of the slope, turning somersaults and shrieking, waving immense, long arms.

God rescued them, and their house, and brought them back home. He just couldn't understand it. 'But I made him specially as an exciting playmate!' he said. 'He only wanted to play.'

'With our house?' cried Man. 'He thought we were a squarish sort of ball. He bounced us about all night.'

'Still,' said God, 'he was only playing. He just wanted you to play.'

They found a gigantic black hairy ape, asleep among the remains of the melon patch, worn out with his fierce all-night game. Woman gazed down at the creature in horror.

'It's only a Gorilla,' said God mildly. 'He's really very sweet.'

'That thing a playmate for me?' she gasped, and she cringed close to Man. He put his arm round her as she began to sob again.

'You'll have to take it back, God,' he said. 'It won't do. You can see it won't.'

So God sent Gorilla off into the forest, and thought again. He asked Woman: 'What sort of playmate do you want? I thought you wanted excitement?'

She gazed dreamily down the river. They were sitting at the end of the garden, at the top of the slope. Man was away finding food.

'Like the sea,' she said at last. 'The beautiful sea!'

The sea was a blue haze, beyond the headlands at the mouth of the river. God gnawed his thumbnail.

'Like the sea!' he pondered. 'How like the sea?'

'Beautiful – like the sea,' she said.

'So,' said God. 'A beautiful friend. I thought you wanted an exciting one.'

'Beautiful,' she said. 'And exciting.'

God gazed at her. She smiled at him, hazily.

'Right,' he said. 'I'll have another go. But this time, you help.'

He sat Woman on the dunes, at the top of the beach, and walked down towards the sea's edge.

'Now,' he called, 'give me some sort of hint.'

They both stared at the sea. And suddenly:

'There!' she shouted. 'Look! Like that. Oh, lovely!'

A great green comber was heaving up, a long hollow wall of glassy green. Full of lights and weedy rags, it reared and reared, higher and steeper, as it raced towards them. Its top burst into flower, the foam began to topple towards them, spilling down its face.

'Lovely!' shouted Woman, and her voice was lost as the whole colossal cliff of water collapsed, exploding in foam, and the beach shook. Long arms of boiling milk froth shot up the sands and piled around God's ankles.

He nodded. 'I think I've got it.' And with those words, he ran at the sea, dived into the face of the next great comber, and disappeared.

For a long time Woman waited, watching the breakers. The tide was coming in. The wind blew off the land, so the white bursting crests of the breakers flamed over their backs.

Then she noticed a white commotion out at sea. She thought it must be a great fish fighting at the surface. Then she saw God, sitting astride something silver and glistery. He vanished, in an eruption of foam. But he re-emerged, much closer. He was racing towards the land. He was astride something, a racing bulge under the surface of the sea. And as he rode up into the breakers a huge shaggy head reared out of the water ahead of him. She saw its deep-sea staring eyes. It reared a long neck, draped with seaweed. She watched in horror. It was bigger than Elephant. Then its shoulders heaved up, and as the great comber burst around it, it turned. She saw its long side, like a giant white-silver shark. For a moment, it seemed to writhe and melt, as if it were itself exploding into foam, and the next thing God was rolling up the beach, battered by foam.

He got up and looked towards her, waved, then ran again into the sea, diving like a seal under the next comber.

Soon she saw it again, that struggling out at sea. And once more, God was riding towards the beach. He seemed to be riding in the crest of one of the towering combers of surf. But she saw he was having a problem.

And again she saw the shaggy head lifted, and an arching body with God astride it. In a smother and welter of foam, uptossing spray, and amid the earthshaking thunder of the breaking surf, this time God rode up the beach on the back of some animal. She saw it now, nothing like so big as a whale, or a whale-shark. It tried to turn and go back into the combers, as the foam sucked back into the undertow. But God forced it to go on up the beach. It wheeled to left and to right but he forced it ahead.

And so it came, tossing its head and lifting its knees high as if it only wanted to go backward or maybe straight up into the air. Its whole body seemed to be tossing and quivering.

God rode it up on to dry sand and right to the dunes. There he dismounted. And the beast stood, glistening, shivering and snorting. A dazzling smoke seemed to rise off it. God had tied a thick sinew of kelp weed-stem round its nose, and that seemed to hold it. At any moment Woman expected to see it

melt and spill foaming away down the sand into the sea. Instead, it reared and surged and stamped. It was bursting with fierceness, as if a whole sea were somehow packed inside it. Glaring pulses of dazzle seemed to come out of it, like flashes off the sea. Its skin quivered and rippled like the skin of a blown wave. Woman stared, dumbfounded, thrilled and frightened.

'What is it?' she shouted, over the sea's hoarse, constant roar. 'It's gorgeous!'

'It's a She,' said God. 'Not an It.' And then he reached out, and before she knew what he was doing he took hold of her long hair, and sheared through it with his thumbnail, as if he were plucking a flower. Woman clasped her cropped head. Then she watched as God laid one hank of her hair over the creature's neck, and one great bunch of it he coiled round the creature's stumpy tail, and let it trail and flow.

At once the beast became quieter. It seemed to change. It looked at Woman, its ears pricked up, its nostrils opened wide. It stepped towards her and gently sniffed her face. She could feel the power-waves coming off it, so that her skin prickled.

And suddenly Woman had the strangest feeling. Part of her was there, lifting in the wind, on the creature's neck and tail, like its own banner. And she felt the beast was part of her.

'She's me!' she shouted excitedly. 'I can feel she's me!'

It was a completely new feeling. It twisted in her, making her want to leap and run.

'Up you get,' said God, and he set her astride the strange animal. He slapped its rump.

'Away home, Horse,' he shouted.

It surged forward, it bounded over the dunes. She hung on to its neck. It knew the way. It ran as if it floated. Some of the sea's sound came with it.

And so, as Man set down his bag of mushrooms and nuts and sweet roots and snails and whelks and loganberries, he heard a drumming. And as he looked up, a great glare of light seemed to burst over him, and this strange, silvery beast swirled to a stop in front of him, as if a flame had blazed up out of the earth, and now stood there, flaming and trembling, waiting for a command. To his amazement, his wife jumped down, out of the dazzle.

'What's this?' was all he could gasp.

'Just what I wanted,' she said. 'My new playmate. God calls it Horse.'

So it was, the playmate God had created for her. And so it still is. And Man has learned, whenever Woman grows sad, she is missing her Horse.

The Shawl of the Beauty of the World

God rubbed his eyes and yawned. His candle blinked. Out through the open doorway, in the dark blue sky, a star blinked.

It was late. Again he yawned. As he yawned, a thin squirt of juice from somewhere at the back of his throat sprayed over what he was making.

Straight away, the creature-shape squirmed. He held it tight.

'Now then!' he said sternly. 'You're not finished. Don't start living yet.'

But the thing squirmed again. The juice from the back of God's yawn had somehow brought it to life.

It was a funny-looking object. Just like a Turkey all plucked and ready for the oven. Even its head was pink and bare. And it had no legs.

God felt cross. If this thing had come to life, he really would have to finish it. He'd wanted to go to bed and finish it in the morning. Was it really alive? It had become still again. God shook it carefully. It lay still.

He wondered if he dare leave it. He stood up, walked to the door of his bedroom, taking the candle. He stood there awhile, watching the dark lump on the workbench. It lay still.

So God went to bed, and left the strange creature as it was, unfinished.

Early next morning, God was awakened by a wild banging at his door. It was Elephant's wife. Elephant had fallen into a crevasse. God called his old mother up, and set her in a rocking-chair, to keep watch over his unfinished creature, still there on his bench. Then he took his ropes and started off, to rescue Elephant.

As the sun rose, Man's two children, Boy and Girl, came peeping in through the door of God's workshop. They saw God's grizzle-haired old mother asleep in the chair. They saw the plucked Turkey shape on the bench. They tiptoed in.

Boy took the creature cautiously by the sharp beak. He lifted its head, on its long limp neck.

'Wake up, baldy!' he said, and gave it a little shake.

The creature opened its eye and blinked. Boy let go of the beak and stepped back. But the head didn't just drop on a limp neck on to the bench. Instead, it craned up. And now the head was looking at its own bare body and the stumps of its no legs. It certainly was wide awake.

'Oh!' cried Girl. 'Poor thing! Oh you poor thing!'

The creature burst into sobs. At least, it would have burst into sobs if it had had a voice. It gaped its beak and gasped, but nothing came out. Only tears bulged from its eyes and dropped on to its own goose-pimpled chest. It felt terrible. And suddenly it wanted to shout terrible things. It wanted to shout: 'Where are my legs?' And: 'Where are my feathers?' And: 'Why am I only half made?' And: 'Why me?'

But no matter how much it stretched its mouth, and strained its lungs, not a sound would come out.

And now it wanted to yell: 'And no voice either! Where is my voice?'

It writhed and heaved and squirmed on the bench, and rowed at the air with its stumps.

'Oh!' cried Girl, and began to cry, watching the Poor Thing's efforts. Then she looked round and saw two clawed feet, bundled together, lying on the end of the bench.

'These must be meant for you,' she cried, and began to loosen the chain that was wound and knotted tightly round the ankles of the two scaly, clawed feet. They did look like a bird's feet, but they were actually the feet of a Demon. That was another story. And God had bound the feet in this fine but very strong chain because though they no longer grew on the Demon, they were still full of devilish tricks. And he'd laid them there in full view, on the end of the bench, so he could keep an eye on them.

Now Girl stuck each foot in place on the Poor Thing's stumps, and with lightning devilish power they took root. They clenched and unclenched. And suddenly, with a heave, the creature rolled off the bench and flailing its naked wing-stumps landed on its new feet, on the floor, with a thud.

It took three steps, then put back its head, opened its beak and – nothing came out.

'Find a voice for it,' cried Girl. But Boy had already found a small bottle. He peered at the label, and spelled out: 'Voice of Voices.'

'Is this creature called Voices?' he asked.

Girl snatched the bottle, opened it, opened the Poor Thing's beak and upended the bottle. A brilliant, heavy, green vapour poured down the Poor Thing's throat.

It blinked. It felt, all at once, that it no longer existed. It closed its eyes, and saw all the stars. But all the stars, in a funny way, were inside itself. All space was inside itself!

Then it opened its eyes and saw Girl again gazing with her large brown eyes, and Boy behind her, and the old woman crumpled in the rocking-chair. And out through the door it saw the red rising sun.

Then the Poor Thing's beak opened and out came the most tremendous yell: 'WOOOWWW!'

God's mother jumped straight out of the chair on to the bench. Boy's hair stood on end. Girl fainted.

158

And where Poor Thing had stood was nothing. Poor Thing had vanished. And at that moment the room went dark.

God's figure blocked the doorway. He was panting. 'What did I hear?' he bellowed. 'What's happened?'

What had happened was this – at that dreadful yell from the Poor Thing's new voice, the Demon Feet had been frightened out of their wits. And they had simply fled! And they had taken the Poor Thing with them – new voice and all.

And as the Feet scampered through the woods, and through the swamps, whenever the Poor Thing tried to cry, 'Oh, please stop,' out came that dreadful yell again:

'WOOOWWW!'

And away the Feet went, more terrified than ever.

And as they went, out came that yell, again and again: 'WOOOOWWW! WWOOOOW!' And 'WHAA-AAAAAAAAOW!'

'It's nearly got me!' thought the Feet. 'Oh! Oh! I'm done for! Oh! Oh!'

And they leaped into a thorn-bush, and the yell came again:

'WAAAAAAOW!'

And the Feet leaped over a cliff, thinking: 'It will never dare follow me.'

But straight away, right on top of them, the yell came again, out of the beak that was fastened to the neck that was fastened to the body that was fastened to the legs and the Demon Feet:

'WAAAAAAAAOW!'

Then the Feet ran into a black burrow and straight away the yell came deafening in the blackness of the hole:

'WOW!'

And the Feet thought: 'Help! It's in here with me!' And they shot out of that hole and ran and ran till the Poor Thing collapsed exhausted on a sandy plain.

All the creatures gathered around it and began to laugh. Poor Thing didn't dare utter a sound for fear his Demon Feet should start running again.

But all on their own, the Feet began to caper about. They began to dance. They leaped and twirled. And of course, since they were growing on the end of the Poor Thing's legs the Poor Thing leaped and twirled, whether it liked it or not. Stark naked, flapping its foolish naked wing-stumps, it leaped and twirled.

The animals laughed harder than ever. And the Demon Feet were just thinking 'Why are those creatures laughing? Don't they appreciate a Demon Dance? I'll kick sand in their eyes if they don't stop laughing.' But at that moment the Poor Thing couldn't stand any more, and it shouted: 'I can't help it!'

But all that came out was a dreadful:

'WAAAOW!'

In a cloud of dust, a scatter of pebbles, the animals fled.

But the Feet stood. This time they didn't flee. It had suddenly dawned on them where the voice came from. And now they wanted to laugh. Yes, the Feet laughed. And:

'WOW! WOW! WOW!' yelled the Poor Thing – though actually that was the Demon Feet laughing.

'WAAAAAOW! WOW! WOW!'

Then the Feet set off after the fleeing animals. In no time, they overtook the Wart-hogs:

'WOW!' they yelled, and the poor Wart-hogs almost died with fright. They scattered, they jammed their heads down holes and under the roots of trees.

Now the Demon Feet raced on, and overtook the Gnus:

'WAAAOW!' yelled the Feet. And the Poor Thing just could not do a thing about it. When the Feet ran, and the Feet yelled, the Poor Thing had to run and yell. And now the Gnus tried to scatter. But they fell in heaps, their gangly long legs tied in knots, and the Demon Feet laughed madly, at the top of their voice:

'WOW! WOW! WOW!'

The Feet were enjoying themselves all right. And so they raced on. And wherever they found an animal, that animal saw this stark naked Turkey creature hurtling towards it out of the distance, right up close, and then heard that ear-splitting:

'WAAAAAOW!'

Some animals went white with shock, instantly. Some simply fell stunned. Some plunged into lakes.

And what did the Poor Thing think about it? The Poor Thing was helpless, in the power of the Demon Feet. The Poor Thing didn't know what to do. The Poor Thing simply rolled its eyes, as the Feet rushed it towards yet another poor animal, and as it felt its beak being forced open from the inside, and the terrible voice getting ready to blast out, it thought: 'Oh no! Not again! Not again!'

But it couldn't stop it. And out it would come:

'WAAAAAAAAAAOW!'

And the poor animal had to hear it. And it might be only a tiny shrew that actually died on the spot.

Suddenly – a flurry of darkness in the air, and Crow landed just in front of the Poor Thing.

'God', said Crow, 'is looking for you. He wants to give you your feathers. You do realize, I hope, that you are featherless, stark naked, and an embarrassment to the birds.'

162

The Demon Feet became still. They listened, through the Poor Thing's ears. And the Poor Thing too, of course, listened.

'Well, feathers would be very nice,' it was thinking. And suddenly it felt excited. Perhaps they were pretty feathers. Some of the birds were gorgeous, though not Crow. And so the Poor Thing cried: 'Oh please! Oh yes! Oh please!' But all that came out was a terrific:

'WAAAAAAAAAAAAAAAAAOW!'

Crow closed his eyes, as a cat does when you blow in its face, and gripped the earth with his feet.

'OK,' he said. 'Come to God at once.'

The Demon Feet needed no urging. In no time, the Poor Thing arrived at God's workshop. But God was out in the hills, the coat of feathers draped over one arm, looking for it.

God's mother saw it, peering about. 'There you are,' she cried. 'Oh, I am sorry. It was all my fault. Oh, I'll never forgive myself!'

The Poor Thing stared at this old lady who stood wringing her hands and screwing up her face in the strangest way. It kept its beak tightly shut.

'If only I'd stayed awake,' she went on, 'Man's little brats would never have given you the wrong feet and the wrong voice.'

The Poor Thing blinked. And the Demon Feet listened. What was this about wrong feet? They suddenly remembered the chain that had bound them so tightly.

'And now it's too late,' wailed God's mother. 'I saw these spare funny-looking feet, and I thought they were mistakes or leftovers. I threw them to the Fox. He ate them. And they were your feet. Oh! Oh!'

She was actually weeping. The Demon Feet crimped slightly, as they tried to smile.

'And your voice,' sobbed the old lady. 'Your charming voice! Oh, it was so pretty! My Magpie stole it. He fed it to his baby Magpies. Oh! Oh! God was so furious!'

She mopped her eyes with the edge of her shawl.

'But I want to make amends,' she said finally. 'I want to give you something.'

And now she laid in front of the Poor Thing the most astounding robe. It was blue, but inside the blue every other colour raced and glimmered. It was green, but inside the green every fiery colour flared and throbbed.

'God made it for me,' said the old lady. 'He called it the Peacock, which means: the shawl of the beauty of the world. He said: "Mother, my most beautiful creation is for you." But now I want you to have it. And wear it. Oh please. Please, please accept it!'

The Poor Thing couldn't believe its eyes or its ears. The Demon Feet were aghast with amazement and joy.

Trembling, like somebody stepping carefully under a freezing waterfall, the Poor Thing put on the robe.

Behind it, the long train swept, full of eyes like coloured moons racing through their changes. It lifted the train and spread it, and it was like a whole heaven full of big, darkly blazing planets spinning in their rings.

God's mother clapped her hands with delight.

'WAAAAAAAOW!' yelled the Poor Thing and the Demon Feet together.

Then the Demon Feet leaped, and danced a few steps. Then they and the Poor Thing together stamped and danced in a circle, shuddering the great lifted spread of feather heaven and all the suns and moons and planets. A tall, fine crown shuddered on the Poor Thing's head.

'WAAAOW!' it cried. 'WAAAAAAOW! WAAAAAA-AAAAAAAAAAAAAAAAAAOW!'

And God's old mother stamped and danced with him, and clapped her wrinkled old hands, and yelled:

'WOW! WOW! WOW!'

And God appeared. A short, rather dowdy brown, tasselled drape of feathers dropped from his hand. He stood amazed at what he saw. Then he began to laugh. He too clapped his hands.

'The Peacock!' he cried, and he laughed till his tears ran down. And he breathed to himself:

'Wow!'

Leftovers

At the end of his working day, God usually had a few bits and pieces left over. Sometimes, just to clear up his worktable, he would stick these together and make a funny-looking mixture of a creature. Then he would breathe life into it.

The creatures he made in this way felt very mixed up. They had a hard time knowing how to carry on. 'What am I?' asked the Okapi. 'Am I a Giraffe? Or a Bushbuck? Or a Zebra? Or what?' He hid in dark forest, trying to work out what he was. But he would never work it out. He had been mixed up by God.

One day God felt he ought to give his workshop a spring-clean. He set to. It was amazing what ragged bits and pieces came out from under his workbench, as he swept. Beginnings of creatures, bits that looked useful but had seemed wrong, ideas that he'd mislaid and forgotten. He stared at the pile of odds and ends. There were off-cuts and waste scraps of bad weather, which was his very latest invention, only just completed. And bits of the flowers from long, long ago. There was even a tiny lump of sun.

He scratched his head. What could be done with all this rubbish? At that moment he smelt sausages. His mother was cooking his dinner. Suddenly he felt ravenous. It had been a hard day. So now, in a great hurry, he mixed the whole heap of sweepings together, squeezed it into shape, breathed life into it, and set it down on the edge of the plains. 'There we are,' he said. 'Run off and play.'

As God let go of it, the creature lifted its head, and opened its mouth. What it wanted to say was: 'Give me a sausage!' Because it too felt ravenous. A little bit of God's hunger for

the sausages had got in there, along with all the other scraps.
But what came out of it was a long roll of thunder. God stared
at his new animal in alarm. But then he laughed. He'd noticed
a bushy clump of blue-black cloud among the sweepings. It
must have been a piece of thunder cloud. He hoped there
were no lightnings or thunderbolts in it. Still, it couldn't be
helped. So he laughed and called: 'Not bad for leftovers!' and
went off to chomp his sausages.

The creature shook himself. He felt very uncomfortable. He
blinked. There was something terribly bright behind his eyes.
He did not know it, but that was a chunk of the sun – just a
leftover scrap. He wrinkled his face and shook his head. Then
he lowered his nose and again a long roll of thunder came out
of him. All the creatures of the plains lifted their heads with
question marks in their eyes.

But he was thinking: 'So I am Leftovers, am I? Made out of
the scraps. Made out of the bits that couldn't be fitted into
anything else.'

And as he thought this he became more and more angry.
And that little bit of God's hunger in him made it worse.
Again he shook his dazzled head and let out another roll of
thunder. 'God made all his other creatures with great care and
with great love,' he said to himself. 'But me – he just screwed
me into shape like a ball of waste paper, and dropped me on
to the earth as if he were throwing me away! Aaaaaah!' And
he thundered again. 'I am rubbish!' he thundered. 'I am
Leftovers.' Thunder after thunder rolled out of him. And at
every roll of thunder he grew more and more bitter. He was
working himself up.

'If I had God here now,' he rumbled, 'I'd swat him like a
Fly! I'd splat him to a splodge! I'd swallow him alive and
howling! Yes! Yes! Revenge!' he thundered. 'Revenge!'

A Wild Cow standing nearby stared at him. 'Shame on you,' she cried. 'You scruffy-looking ruffian. Go and get yourself washed. Go and get yourself combed.'

Leftovers glared. Then, before he knew what he was doing, he rolled out a great crash of thunder, soared through the air and landed on top of the Wild Cow. 'Help!' she cried, as her legs crumpled. She thought heaven had fallen.

All the animals watched horrified as Leftovers killed her and ate her. This was new!

They came trotting closer, twitching their tails and flicking their ears. The Gazelles stamped. The Wild Bull pawed up clods of dirt. He couldn't believe what had happened, but it was beginning to sink in. The Elephants lifted their trunks.

'You can't do that,' squealed the Elephants. 'You should eat leaves and twigs.'

'That's not done,' brayed the Zebra. 'You should eat grass.

'Eat flowers,' bleated the Gazelles.

'I shall tell God,' bellowed the Wild Bull. 'You shall be punished. God will not like this. I shall have justice!'

But Leftovers seemed not to understand them. He thought he'd just eaten a wonderful pile of sausages. He watched them through his eye-pupils that looked like tiny keyholes. He licked his lips. Then he yawned.

The animals became more and more excited. 'Eat flowers! Eat grass! Eat leaves! Not the Wild Cow! Not the Wild Cow! We shall tell God. Now you'll be punished.'

But they all kept their distance. There was something in his yellow dazzled eyes they did not like. And none of them wanted to end up like the Wild Cow.

Then, to their amazement, he laid his head on his paw and fell asleep, right there among the bloody bones of the Wild Cow. The animals were enraged. In a great mob, they turned and rushed off over the plains, to tell God.

'He's a cannibal!' squealed the Elephants.

'He's a gluttonous, ghastly, ghoulish ogre!' bleated the Bonteboks.

'He's a big, bad, bloodthirsty bandit!' bleated the Blesbok.

'He's a scruffianly, ruffianly, rag-bag hooligan!' bleated the Springboks.

'God will punish him!' bellowed the Wild Bull.

And they milled around on the hilltop, raising a red cloud of dust, stretching their necks up, or their trunks, and crying:

'Oh God, you've made a mistake! Do you know what you've done? Leftovers is killing our wives! Help! Help! Take him back! Take him back! Leftovers is killing our wives!'

And the Wild Bull humped his shoulders and bellowed: 'Justice! I demand justice from God!'

God could not hear the animals, but he could see them, leaping and churning about in the dust-cloud. He thought they were dancing to celebrate their happiness and the beauty of the earth. He nodded in Heaven. And to show them that he understood, he stirred the top of a thundercloud with his right hand and let a roll of thunder rumble out across the horizons.

When they heard that, they scattered in terror. They did not know it was God's new toy, which pleased him almost more than anything he had created so far.

'A giant Leftovers in Heaven!' they cried. 'He'll fall out of the sky on top of us, just as Leftovers dropped on the Wild Cow. It must be his unborn brother!'

God frowned and stopped chewing for a moment. 'Funny!' he muttered. 'What's got into them?'

But from that moment all the animals were afraid of Leftovers and his titanic brother in Heaven. And from that moment too the Wild Bull began to follow him, peering out from the deep thickets of thorn and watching him, waiting for the moment of revenge.

Leftovers was uncontrollable. Every third day, the craving for sausages, that hunger of God, came over him and would not let him rest. It drove him over the rocky ridges, slouching from thorn-bush to thorn-bush. He truly was a scruffy-looking object, like an old tatty blanket draped over a broken-down sofa. His face looked like a giant, battered, dried sunflower. The animals would have laughed at him if it hadn't been for the rolls of thunder that came pouring out of his mouth, and the way he would suddenly stop, and stare through his deadly keyholes. Then they knew what to expect. Next thing, some fat happy animal would suddenly let out a honk, and collapse, as if struck by lightning. And that would be Leftovers, lying on top of it.

And when his skin was stretched as tight as a huge sausage, he'd roll on to his back and sleep, frowning over the lump of sun behind his eyebrows. Then he looked exactly like a bursting sackful of rags, till his skin began to slacken a little, and once again the hunger of God woke him up.

Meanwhile, every day, the Wild Bull's rage grew worse. He slammed his horns into an Ant-hill, and tossed the lumps about, to strengthen his neck. 'God cannot feel my grief,' he bellowed. 'God cannot hear us.'

The animals tried to calm him down. 'You mustn't take justice into your own hands,' cried the Tree-Shrew. 'That's bad. Be patient. Leave Leftovers to God. God will punish him.'

But the Wild Bull crashed his horns into the trunk of a baobab tree, to toughen his brains. 'I can't wait for God,' he bellowed. 'I shall deal with Leftovers alone.'

The animals were horrified. If Wild Bull started fighting, where would it end? 'God must be told,' squeaked the Meerkat. 'And soon.'

At last a Weasel managed to get to God, and gave him the whole story. God slapped his brow. He remembered Leftovers. But where had those eating habits come from? God had forgotten how his mother had been frying sausages, and how he had breathed life into Leftovers with breath full of craving for sizzling sausages, out of a mouth watering at the very idea of sausages. But he felt it must be his fault somehow. He came hurrying down to earth, very upset. Was he really to blame for Leftovers' horrible behaviour?

All the animals gathered around God, to tell him how Leftovers was killing their grandmothers and grandfathers, and their wives and their children.

'Leave it to me,' said God at last. 'Just leave it to me.'

He found Leftovers licking his paws. 'Do you realize,' he said very sternly, 'what you're doing?'

Leftovers gazed at God. He'd just eaten so much he could not get up. He blinked.

'You can't carry on like this,' said God. 'This – well, it's murder, isn't it?'

Leftovers yawned.

'Do you hear me?' roared God, and he slapped a couple of thunderclouds. Lightning plunged into lakes and forests.

'It's no good shouting at me,' said Leftovers mildly. 'You made me. I am what I am. And that's all there is to it.'

'I am what I am!' screeched God. He sounded like an Almighty Elephant, and he shook his thunderclouds like separate fists. Lightnings spattered the sky.

The animals crouched on the plains. 'They're at it now,' cried the Hare. 'Leftovers must have sent for his brother. Somebody'll be hurt now! Oh boy!'

'I'm your fault,' said Leftovers quietly.

'My fault?' gasped God. He was nearly speechless at Leftovers' insolence.

'You shouldn't have made me of rubbish. I'm rubbish, aren't I? What do you expect from rubbish? I can't help it. Now go away.'

And while God stood there, Leftovers laid his head on his paw and fell asleep.

God sat on a stone, thinking. What could he do? Leftovers was right. God shouldn't have made him so carelessly. He should never have let that little bit of thundercloud get into him, for one thing. But where had that hunger come from? Because that was the dreadful part, the hunger.

As he sat there thinking, Man came strolling up.

'There's a very easy answer to your problem,' said Man.

'There's a reward,' said God, 'for the right answer.'

'Listen to this,' said Man. 'Leftovers is bitter because you made him of rubbish. Isn't that true? He's taking his revenge on your Creation. Killing the animals.'

'So it seems,' said God.

'So all you need to do', said Man, 'is make him King of the animals.'

God gave a little laugh, and raised one eyebrow.

'A King has to protect his subjects, doesn't he?' said Man. 'Instead of being rubbish, an outcast on the earth, he'll be King. He'll be your representative over the animals. He'll become good. He'll stop being bitter. He'll feel so good, he won't need to take any more revenge. It will change him.'

'What about that hunger of his?' asked God. 'Will that change too?'

'Oh, that!' said Man. 'Well, you could always feed him on your sausages.'

God liked this idea. He called all the animals together and explained his plan. But all they did was stare at him, saying nothing. None of them trusted Leftovers.

'We'll put a crown on him now, while he's asleep,' explained God. 'And when he wakes up, you all kneel and say: "Greetings, O King!" And you, Hyena, will say: "And here, O Your Mighty Majesty, are God's own sausages for your royal breakfast." I'll supply some. Then while he's eating I'll come by and talk to him.'

The animals looked fearful.

'What if he doesn't believe us?' bleated a Sheep.

'If the crown's on his head. And the sausages are there sizzling. And you all act your parts. He'll believe it,' said God.

They all thought hard how they would act. But they still weren't sure.

Then the Fox cried:

'King Leftovers doesn't sound right. That name Leftovers will remind him. That will set his thunder rolling. That will bring the lightning out of the ends of his great paws. He needs a new name.'

God thought. He didn't like wasting anything. 'If we knock a few letters out of his name, we could call him Love.'

'No,' bellowed the Wild Bull. 'He's a convicted murderer, remember. I do not forget the past. You're letting him get away with it. I'm having nothing to do with this.' And he plunged away into the dense thorns.

'Very well,' said God. 'How about Leo?'

So they agreed. And God produced a crown from his

174

treasury in Heaven. It was actually a small-scale model of the Zodiac. The sausages were prepared. And when Leftovers awoke, he was greeted by all the animals kneeling and touching the ground with their foreheads.

'Greetings, O Mighty King,' they cried. 'Greetings, O Mighty King Leo!'

And Hyena crawled forward, pushing a huge plate of hot sausages in front of him. 'O Mighty King Leo,' he chanted. 'O representative of God among the animals, here is your royal breakfast, hot from Heaven.'

Leftovers looked around. He was puzzled. But there was no denying the sausages. And now he saw them, he knew they were exactly what he had always wanted. And as he tasted the first, he closed his eyes in bliss. This was the taste he was always searching for. Heavenly sausages!

Hyena spoke: 'Your Majesty, you have forgotten to hand your crown to me.'

'Crown?' asked Leftovers.

'While you eat your royal breakfast, I always polish your royal crown, given to you by God,' said Hyena.

Then Leftovers noticed the weight on his head. He took off the crown and gazed at the shining gold and at the jewels in seven different colours. He pretended not to be surprised, as he handed it to Hyena, who began to polish it with his little tail.

'Of course,' said Leftovers. 'It slipped my mind.'

'Blessings on his Mighty Majesty King Leo!' yelled a Baboon.

And all the animals, in one great voice, shouted: 'Blessings on his Mighty Majesty King Leo!' And the Elephants stood in a row and blew a majestic fanfare, as Leftovers ate his sausages.

As he ate he thought: 'Am I me or am I Leftovers?' But he

couldn't answer. He really couldn't tell. 'It seems,' he thought, 'that I dreamed I was a ragged, nasty creature roaming about in the thorns, murdering my subjects and eating them!' He shuddered with horror, and picked up another sausage.

And as he munched he thought: 'This is the life!'

At that moment God came strolling by.

'Good morning, King Leo,' God greeted him. 'How is the kingdom of the animals? Is everybody happy?'

'Indeed,' said King Leo, speaking in a slow, dignified way, 'my subjects are all happy.'

'It must be thanks to your care,' said God. 'Everything depends on you. You are my representative here on earth, among the animals. I have complete faith in you.' Then he added: 'I am just on my way to the kingdom of the insects, where Stag-Beetle is King. Like you, he is a perfect King: brave, wise, generous, tireless and kind.'

God raised his hand in salute, and was just about to disappear into the roots of a clump of grass when King Leo said: 'By the way, God, I had a strange dream.'

'What was it?' asked God. 'Perhaps I can tell you what it means.'

'I dreamed I was an outlaw, very dirty and ragged. I was murdering the animals and eating them. With a truly horrible hunger. I was called Leftovers. What does it mean?'

God laughed. 'That is easy. Dreams are memories of a former life. That was the life in which you got everything wrong. Now, as you see, you are getting everything right. Isn't it so?'

'It is,' said King Leo, puzzled. 'Yes, it is. I do seem to be getting everything right.'

God raised his hand again, smiled, and vanished into the grassroots.

Hyena handed King Leo his crown.

'It is time now,' said Hyena, 'for your Majesty to choose. Will you be carried through your kingdom on Elephant's back, or will you sleep?'

'Of course,' said King Leo. He felt sleepy, after the sausages. So there and then he closed his eyes and slept.

At that moment, all the animals breathed a sigh of relief. They got up off their knees and started doing what they usually did, playing and feeding.

All except the Wild Bull.

Now the Wild Bull stepped from the thorns. He stepped from the thorns, and the sun glistened on his blue-black body. There, at the edge of the thorns, he levelled his nose like a black stumpy cannon, and sniffed with his great black nostrils. His tail rose in the air and twirled its tassel. He was remembering his wife. He groaned softly and his dewlap trembled.

It seemed to him the murderer had been rewarded too well. He dragged his right hoof backward through the stony earth, and flung gravel up over his flank and back. Was King Leo going to be King for ever? Feasting on sausages, bowed to by all the animals, wearing a crown that looked like the starry heavens? He groaned louder, with a weird, hollow, booming sound, and flung more earth over his back. He glared at his enemy and the empty plate. This was not justice. To make a murderer King, this was not justice.

The Wild Bull stepped forward, slowly, till he stood right over the shaggy, sleeping King. His moment had come. With a flick of his horns, he tossed the crown into a swamp, where a watersnake grabbed it and sank out of sight with it, leaving a bubble.

Then he put his horns under the King and with one jerk

tossed him into the top of a thorn tree – a big, strong-trunked thorn tree of ten million thorns.

'Leftovers!' he thundered. 'Leftovers! You have not paid for my wife. But now you shall pay.'

Leftovers woke up falling through the thorns, which raked his body and clawed his face. But he did not hit the ground. He fell smack on to the Wild Bull's horns, who hurled him up again – back into the top of the thorn tree.

'Leftovers!' bellowed the Wild Bull. 'I am God's Judge. And Judgement Day has come!'

And again the torn and bleeding King fell through the dreadful tree, and again he fell on to the waiting horns, and it was as if he had fallen on to a trampoline. Up he went again, higher than ever, turning in the air, his legs outflung, as if he were no bigger than a rabbit, and the Wild Bull gazed up, his eyes flaming with joyful fury.

But as he came down through the whipping and slashing thorns for the third time, Leftovers grabbed the trunk and hung there. Was he awake or asleep? He shook his dazzled head. Where was his crown? Where was his kingdom? And his subjects? And his sausages? Where was God?

And there, clinging for dear life halfway up a thorn tree, above a demented Wild Bull, he knew he was Leftovers. And the rest was a dream. The crown, the sausages, the Hyena, the fanfare of Elephants, God – all were a dream.

But this was real. This real Wild Bull was the real husband of the real Wild Cow he really had killed and eaten. And these were real thorns.

He roared an enraged clap of thunder. And down below him the Wild Bull tore up the earth with his hooves, and he too bellowed thunder. God crouched in the grass clump, peering out between the fibres of the roots. 'All my fault!' he was muttering. 'All my fault!' as he tried to think what to do.

But then the Wild Bull charged the tree. There came a crack, the earth jumped, and the whole tree blurred. In a shower of thorns, Leftovers dropped on to the Wild Bull's back, biting and clawing. The Wild Bull rolled over, but Leftovers sprang away, and with one bound he was gone – into the high grass where the Elephants too were hiding from the uproar, with their trunks curled into their mouths. The Wild Bull stormed and trampled in circles, hunting for Leftovers, tearing up small trees and bushes, till finally he stood panting, letting his red eyes slowly darken to a bright, burning black.

That was the end of King Leo's reign.

And now Leftovers roams the land as before, hungry as before, terrible as before. But he keeps out of the way of the Wild Bull, because the Wild Bull is ready for him, always sniffing for him, always alert.

And just as before, all the animals go in fear of Leftovers' unrolling carpet of thunder and his thunderbolt leap.

What can God do? He knows his trick would not work a second time. But it nearly had worked. If the Wild Bull had not burst out of the thorns, it might have worked. And so when Leftovers walks along the skyline at evening, when the sky flames red, God listens sadly. And all the animals listen too, as Leftovers' thunder rolls away across the plains and crumbles against the surrounding wall of sky.

'King Leo!' shouts Hyena, and laughs.

And Man, too, listens in his house. It seems to him that Leftovers' thunder is a sad sound. Peal after peal of thunder, shorter and shorter, ending in a few grunty coughs. Man can tell that Leftovers is remembering his dream of being King, his dream of being wise, generous, kind and beloved by all. 'Was it a dream?' says the first roll of thunder. 'Or was it real?' says the second. 'Or is this a dream now?' says the third. 'Or is this real?' says the fourth. And then, very fierce, as if he could hardly bear it, 'Was that a dream and is this real?' And after a pause: 'Or was that real and is this a dream?' Then shorter and shorter: 'Which is it? Which is it?' And shorter and shorter and shorter: 'Which? Which? Which?'

Then, in the silence, Leftovers frowns over the lump of sun behind his eyebrows. And he lowers his head, and half opens his mouth to cool the hunger of God that urges him forward.

The Dancers

A great, flaming star was falling. Owls looked up and the ball
of fire, with its long tail, was reflected in their bulging eyes.

Most falling stars burn out to nothing, before they get
near the earth. But this one did not. And the wide eyes of the
Owls widened wider as the flaming ball grew and grew
and – plunged silently into the dark mountains.

God was asleep. When dawn rose, he woke and started
work, knowing nothing about the great star that had crashed
into the Mountains.

Later that day God sighed and leaned back in his chair. His
work just wasn't going right. He'd been trying for three days,
and somehow it still wasn't right.

He'd been trying to make a Dancer. He wanted an animal
that would dance for him. And what had he ended up with?
A Cat!

There it sat, on his workbench, gazing at him sleepily out
of slit eyes.

God lifted Cat down to the floor.

'Go on,' he said. 'Dance.'

Cat looked at him, lifted her tail straight, and gently curled
and uncurled the tip of it.

'Is that all you can do?' asked God. 'You're my dancer.
Dance.'

Cat yawned.

'I'm sleepy just now,' she said. 'It's quite hard work, you
know, being created.'

And she settled down there and then, and closed her eyes.

God scratched his beard. He liked the look of Cat. And

maybe she could dance as well as he'd hoped. But if she wouldn't, if she was just too lazy, what could he do about it?

He looked out through his window and rested his eyes on the mountains.

And now, as he gazed at those mountains, he noticed something different about them. They looked sick.

He went out on to the balcony to get a better view. Yes, they looked sick.

Then, in front of his eyes, they moved. It was like a hiccup. And again, they seemed to shrug.

What was going on? The Crow flew down on to his balcony rail.

Now the mountains were definitely up to something. They seemed to swell, then abruptly collapsed. They jigged. They shivered. They stretched up.

'The mountains are having some sort of fit,' said God. 'I wonder what's got into them?'

The Crow stared.

'I think,' said the Crow, 'I think they're trying to dance.'

God couldn't believe that. They both went on watching. And the mountains went on stretching and swaying and jigging. God could feel the vibration under his feet. Other creatures came out of the forest.

'It's an earthquake,' said Giraffe, bracing her legs wide.

And the birds flew up from the shuddering trees, till the whole sky was full of their circling, fluttering or gliding specks, all crying:

'What's got into the mountains?'

God set out to get a closer look. He arrived under the shadow of the mountains, and all the creatures were with him, and above him the birds. Even new-made Cat was there, peering from behind God's ankle.

182

Surely the Crow was right. Surely the mountains were dancing. At least they looked to be dancing.

Or they looked rather as if something inside them were dancing. As if creatures the size of the mountains were dancing under the gigantic fallen tent of the mountains, like people dancing under a great sheet.

But as they all watched, the mountains began to split. With a booming roar, a jagged crack ran up the rock face. The mountains were tearing themselves apart.

God watched that huge crack as it widened. Was something coming out? Were the mountains coming out from under the mountains?

It was an amazing sight, the eyes of God, and of all the creatures, all the birds, all the reptiles, so shining and round and still.

And there, out of the vast, gaping crevasse, came a tiny animal.

A dancing creature.

A Mouse!

It was a Mouse! A dancing Mouse!

The mountains became still. But the Mouse danced. He twirled, and leaped, and cavorted. He frisked, and jumped and twirled. God watched him, speechless with delight.

Mouse danced up to God and danced on to his hand. God held him up, on his palm. Cat saw the wide smile on God's face, and dug her claws into a root. She tore fibres from the root. Her teeth chattered together. She was sick with jealousy! God had made her as his very special dancer, and suddenly here was this Mouse!

'Mouse!' she hissed. 'A Mouse! A paltry, piddling, pitter-patter, pin-claw string-tail!'

And she buried her fangs in the root. Otherwise, she just might have leapt and swept the Mouse off God's hand with a single swipe of her thorny fist.

Back in God's workshop, Mouse became his favourite new creature. As God worked, Mouse danced at the end of the bench. He would leap and twirl, skip and frolic, with his long-fingered pink hands, and his elegant pink tail, and his black eyes so full of feeling.

Cat refused to come back to the workshop. She slunk through the forest. Passing a tree, she would suddenly lash out and rip a lump of bark clean off. 'The Mouse will pay. My day will come and Mouse will have to pay!' she yowled, and knocked the head off an orchid.

One day God was making Thrush. The voice-box of Thrush was in place. Perfect. Now the tongue. But as he eased the tongue into position – Barrummmmph!

The earth shook, just slightly.

Crow hammered on God's window.

'The mountains are at it again!' he cawed.

God frowned. He waited, without taking his eyes off the Thrush's tongue. He knew how vital it was to keep his eyes fixed on the job. And he didn't want to bungle this.

Nothing more happened. He gave the tongue its final touch. There!

And straight away - Barrrummmph! And the workbench jolted so hard, Mouse, who had been cleaning his belly-fur, fell over and clutched the grain of the wood.

Crow hammered on the window. 'Come and see! It looks like another Mouse!'

God looked up then and saw the peaks shudder. He passed his hand over his brow and sighed. He really wanted to finish Thrush. He still had the most finicky job of all – fitting the song into the voice-box.

Then he saw Mouse gazing at him with excited eyes.

'Might it be another Mouse?' cried Mouse.

God smiled and nodded. 'Maybe a partner for you,' he said.

Mouse's nose began to tremble.

'A friend?' he squeaked.

'Who knows?' said God. 'Maybe a wife.'

'A wife!' cried Mouse. 'Oh, let me see her. Oh, are you sure?'

And Mouse leapt down on to the floor, and scampered towards the doorway. He stopped, waiting for God.

'You go on,' said God. 'I'll sit here and finish what I'm doing. Bring your wife back here.'

Mouse was already running.

'But mind,' shouted God after him, laughing, 'don't bring anybody else. If it isn't another Mouse, tell it to go back where it came from. We don't want it.'

Mouse raced through the forest, with wildly beating heart. No, he wouldn't bring anybody else back. He was already imagining the fantastic dances he would soon be having with his partner – with his wife!

From every corner of the forest, the creatures came hurrying towards the mountains. Last time it had been so comical! After all that tremendous commotion of mountains, to see nothing come out but a tiny midget Mouse – even if it was a dancing Mouse.

This time, all the creatures agreed, the mountains were dancing even more wildly. If it was dancing. They seemed to swell, and flop down. Then great bulges raced from one end to the other. Sometimes it looked as if the whole range was going to lift off and jig in the air.

Mouse too, standing there, out in front of all the other creatures, jigged and hopped with impatience.

186

'It's my wife!' he called. 'She's on her way! She's dancing through the darkness towards us. Yes, yes! I remember what it's like in there. Pretty frightening, I can tell you. You have to dance, or you just might get too frightened.'

And cupping his tiny, pink hands to his mouth he squealed: 'Hurry up, my darling wife!'

But no crack appeared in the rock face. The mountains went on shivering, squirming and teetering. They tossed their tops, like horns. They surged, like trees in a storm. They almost swirled like water. But still no crack.

Mouse had become still and silent. Was something wrong? Why was it taking so long?

Suddenly a Mongoose barked and pointed. A tiny crack had appeared in a great slab of cliff. Had it been there before?

'It's beginning! The hills are going to hatch!' screamed the Cockatoo.

At last Mouse couldn't stand it any longer. He snatched up a stalk of dry grass, ran forward, pushed one end of the stalk into the fine crack, and heaved on the other with all his strength, as if it were a crowbar.

The boom was so stunning, so immense, that all the animals cowered. It really sounded as if the mountains had exploded. And sure enough, the cliffs were tearing apart.

And out of the gaping rent in the cliffs came –

Elephants!

Dancing Elephants!

Great flapping and cracking ears, great coiling and swinging trunks, great swooshing and sweeping tusks, great looming and frowning foreheads, great baggy and bouncing bodies, great stamping and trampling feet!

They danced out over the creatures. How many? It seemed

187

to the poor creatures, flattened in the dust, rolling in the dust, whirling in the dust, that the mountains were turning into Elephants, as if there'd be nothing left after this but the skin of the empty mountains lying flat on the earth. Howls and shrieks went up, and trees fell splintering down, showering monkeys, marmosets, martens and squirrels, not to speak of Owls' eggs. Wildly, not caring at all where their huge flatteners came down, the Elephants danced.

'Help!' came the cry of the creatures of the world. 'Oh God, help us!'

But far away in his workshop God was bowed over the open throat of the Thrush. He wasn't even aware of the tremor of the chair he sat in.

While the creatures whirled about, this way and that, under the whirling dance of the Elephants.

But Mouse was coming to his senses.

Where was his wife? After all his hopes, where was his wife?

He leaped up among the Elephants. And in his tiny voice, with terrific fury, he squeaked:

'Where is my wife?'

The effect was unbelievable. The whole churning mass of Elephants came to a dead stop.

'Who are you all?' squeaked Mouse. 'We don't want you. God doesn't want you, he wants my wife. God has ordered you to get back under the mountains, get back where you came from. Get straight back there and SEND ME MY WIFE.'

The effect of this astonished even the furious Mouse. With trumpetings of fear, with ears flung back over their shoulders,

188

with trunks curled up tight above their heads or stretched out forwards, the Elephants scattered. Anywhere but back under the mountains! At top speed, in every direction, they bolted.

They didn't want to go back under the black mountains. Anywhere but that. So they simply fled, out across the bright world. They smashed broad roads through the forest, and where the jungle was too dense they surfed over the top, like great power-boats, and now, hearing their screams of panic, God looked up from the throat of the Thrush.

He frowned. What a hideous uproar in the world! And surely that was the voice of the Mouse! Yes, it was the shouting of Mouse, as he hurtled through the trees, chasing the Elephants with 'Where's my wife?' and 'God doesn't want you. Get back where you came from and send my wife,' and then again, louder than ever, the fleeing screams of the poor Elephants.

The Elephants faded away into the edges of the world. The rest of the creatures couldn't stop talking about it. What a fantastic thing, the fury of the Mouse. With a single shout, he had scattered a whole mountain range of Elephants!

But Mouse himself was heartbroken. He dragged his tail along. He didn't want to dance for God any more. He went back to look at the ruined and shattered mountains. Was his wife somewhere under all that? It didn't look as if the mountains would ever dance again. It didn't look as if they had anything left.

He crept into Man's house. He made his home in a crack in the wall, under Man's bed. And at night he crept out quietly, to eat Man's crumbs. He danced no more.

God missed his Mouse. Cat had begun to dance for him

now. Just now and again, especially in the evening. But it wasn't the same. Once you've seen a dancing Mouse a Cat seems just clumsy.

One day, as he was kneading a bit of clay, God was thinking about his Mouse. He wondered what had happened to him. Nobody seemed to know. All the animals agreed he must have been flattened into the clay by the foot of an Elephant. But suddenly, as he sat there thinking, God realized what his fingers had done. They had made a Mouse.

Carefully, he breathed life into the tiny, perfect creature.

She stood up on his hand. She lifted her little arms. And to God's absolute delight, she began to dance.

Cat could not believe it. She clamped her jaws tight shut, so that the boiling steam of her rage shouldn't flash hissing across the room. Then she made one leap. Cat cleared God's hand, like a horse going over a fence, but Mouse was already out through the doorway.

Cat leaped again, but Mouse was already in the forest. Cat leaped through the leaves, but Mouse was already among Man's carrots. And as Cat leaped again, Mouse shot in through Man's doorway.

Cat came in so fast her claws tore splinters from the floorboards, but Mouse was already down the hole, under Man's bed.

And at that moment, Man's wife appeared with a broom, and saw the strange animal with its hair all on end, its eyes like raging lamps, its white fangs bared, and she thought: 'That looks nasty.' And with one whack of her broom she swept Cat back out among the carrots.

Down the hole, the Mouse from God's hands dashed straight into the arms of the Mouse from the Mountains.

Think of their happiness!

Each evening, after supper, while they lay in their bed together, Man would play his flute to Woman. He played softly. And under the bed, the two Mice held each other tightly and listened. After the flute had fallen silent, the two Mice came out from under the bed, out on to the middle of the floor, and there in the firelight they began to dance.

The first evening, Woman, lying half asleep, saw them, and shook Man gently. 'Look!' she whispered. 'What are those?'

Then Man and Woman lay there, watching the two Mice dancing in the firelight.

And so it happened each evening. Man would play his flute softly to Woman, and afterwards they would lie quietly and watch, till the two tiny creatures came out from under the bed and began to dance together, in the middle of the room, in the firelight. And their happiness was so great, as they danced, that even God became aware of it. He lay awake, unable to sleep, tossing and turning, and muttering: 'Something is keeping me awake! What can it be? Something strange is going on somewhere. I can feel it. But where is it? And what is it?' And he had the feeling that somewhere in his Creation, somehow, there was a huge happiness hidden from him.

And strangely enough, the Elephants could feel it too. They didn't know what it was, but out in the forest, as the stars rose, they became more and more restless, and shifting from great foot to great foot they began to dance. And under the flickering stars the jumbled range of mountains began to dance softly. The whole night was filling up with the happiness of the Mice, as they danced in the firelight. While Man and Woman, gazing out from under their bedclothes with the flames of the fire reflecting in their eyes, watched them. Till

God had to get out of bed, muttering: 'What is keeping me awake? What is it?' And he paced to and fro in his bedroom, and stood at his window and stared out over the forests at the hills, and at the shaking stars above the hills, and again he walked to and fro, his arms clasped tightly across his chest and his eyes glittering.

BOOK THREE

The Dreamfighter and Other Creation Tales

*The stories in 'Dreamfighter' are particularly
suitable for children 10+.*

for Carol

Contents

Goku

Right in the beginning, when everything was being made, God worked night and day, and his helpers were the Angels and the Demons. His Angels made the insides of things. His Demons made the outsides. God told them how it should be done and they did it. They were tireless workers.

But one of the Demons was different. His name was Goku. Goku would not work. Or rather, he would work only in his own way. He worked in such a clownish way, all the other Demons laughed, sometimes so hard that they had to stop work, which made God angry.

Here is the sort of thing Goku did. When they were making the river Amazon, God had given his instructions. And the Angels had made a gigantic River Spirit. This was the inside part of the river Amazon. God was pleased. It was one of his masterpieces. From one angle it looked like an enormous Indian woman lying across the landscape, naked and draped only with flower garlands, beside a full-length mirror, admiring herself as she combed her hair. From another angle, it looked like a colossal snake, looped and coiled across the map, with a huge great-lipped mouth resting on the edge of the sea, into which it sang gloomy songs. Every one of its scales was like a lens, and when you looked into one of those lenses you saw a fish, or a crab, or an insect, or a bird, or a reptile peering out, as if it were hiding inside the lens.

From another angle the River Spirit looked like a horde of ragged goblins, pouring towards the sea. Every one of them was monstrous, and every one different. Imagine for yourself. Some were luminous, and were half frog, half monkey. Some bounded along on a single leg, with the bone sharpened to a

197

point. Some were simply heads, happily or unhappily rolling. And so on. The hubbub was deafening. Their wagons, loaded with magic drums, flutes, fishing tackle, looms and cooking pots, trundled along with them, pulled by alligators, tapirs, jaguars and wild pigs.

From another angle, it was nothing but an old man, trudging along. Just one lonely old man. Yet wherever you looked, along the whole length of the river, there he was, trudging along, the same old man.

From every angle it appeared to be something different.

This was the inside of the river, the River Spirit, made by the Angels.

When the Demons started making the outside of the river, they had a problem. They had to invent an endless supply of water. Plain, ordinary water. They all thought hard how to do it.

The Goku cried: 'I've got it!'

He grabbed the River Spirit, tied a mountain range round its neck, and threw this huge weight out into the middle of the Atlantic Ocean. The whole River Spirit flew through the air like a long streamer tied to a cannonball. As it disappeared under the Atlantic, Goku let out his laugh. He really had thought it was a good idea. He had plunged the River Spirit into endless water, just as God had wanted. But now he saw how alarming his solution was. And how wrong. And how funny.

The Demons lay laughing helplessly all around him. The Angels rushed to rescue the River Spirit before it perished in the salt water, and God was furious. But Goku only said: 'You told us it needed water. Now it's got it.'

When God invented Man, it was just the same. This was quite a tricky job, especially when it came to making the head. The Angels had made the inside of Man's head – the Head

Spirit, thinking brilliant thoughts, planning a happy future, solving every problem, and dreaming of songs.

But then the Demons had to make the outside. They sat in thought, wrinkling their demon brows. Suddenly Goku cried: 'I've got it!'

He pulled up a turnip, which God had invented a few days before, and stuck it on Man's shoulders. 'There,' he said. 'Two birds with one stone.'

But then when he saw what he'd done he laughed so hard all the Demons laughed with him, rolling up and down Heaven, the Earth and the Underworld. They thought it was very funny. But the Angels frowned. The part of God that was black went white with rage. And the part that was white went black.

Man did look very odd with a leafy turnip for a head. But God's rage frightened Goku. 'I'll fix it,' cried the Demon. And with quick scoops and gougings of his demon claws, he carved the turnip into a face.

'What's wrong with that?' he asked. But then when he saw what his claws had done, he let out his wild earsplitting laugh.

God threw down his book of ideas and went storming off into a far corner of Heaven. He thought he might explode and annihilate his own Creation. He really did feel dangerous. Even the Angels were frightened.

Quickly, before God came back, the Angels made the inside of Woman. And this time, before Goku could spoil things with one of his crazy ideas, the Demons gave Woman's head and face a beautiful outside, just like the most beautiful of the Demons. And before God came back, Man and Woman had two children, Boy and Girl – but their heads were half turnip, just as they are to this day. It was too late for God to correct. After that, whenever Goku saw Man or one of his children he let out his awful laugh. God began to dread the sound of it.

And so God planned how to get rid of Goku.

But just at that moment Goku found another Demon exactly like himself. A female Demon named Goka. He recognized her on sight as one of his own kind and she recognized him. They stared at each other with joyful faces and let out a fierce wild laugh that ripped the paint off God's toy motor car, which he was saving up to give to Man when the right moment came.

Goka was almost crazier than Goku. 'Where have you been all these billions of years?' cried Goku, gazing at her in rapture.

'I've been up my mother's nostril, plugged in with a poggle,' she explained, and let out her loopy wild laugh.

Whatever they said to each other, they followed it with a laugh. The Demons grinned, waiting for what amusing thing they would do next. But the Angels watched sternly.

'One day,' said Goka, 'I'll make those Angels laugh so hard their jaws will break off. They'll laugh so hard they'll be treading on their tongues. They'll laugh so hard their eyes will come bouncing off the wall. They'll laugh so hard their hearts will be jumping about on their plates – '

Goku silenced her with a kiss.

'Let's do it together, my love,' he said.

So she and Goku set out to make the Angels laugh.

They almost brought Creation to a standstill. God was inventing new things all the time, and the Angels, as ever, were making angelic insides for them. But when it came to the turn of the Demons to make the outsides – Goku and Goka were there, making trouble.

That is how so many things came to be made wrong.

Suddenly God had a brainwave. If Goka has a baby, he

thought, she will calm down. She'll become sensible. And Goku too, he will become serious. Fathers become serious.

God gave a quiet little laugh – and there was Goka, about to have a baby. She burst into tears. Goku licked his lips, scratched his head, then got up and walked to and fro, uttering a wild laugh. Then he sat down again and frowned.

Suddenly Goka jumped up. 'I've got it!' she cried. 'I know what!'

She flew down to Woman and whispered in her ear: 'You are going to have God's child.'

Woman, who was dozing on her veranda, woke with a start. She told Man. 'An Angel just came,' she said. 'It told me I'm going to have God's child.'

'Are you sure it was an Angel?' Man asked. He knew something about the Demons.

'It was made of light,' Woman said. 'It had fierce eyes.'

Man also knew something about the Angels. He knew they were made of light. The Demons were made of darkness.

His eyes grew round, gazing at his wife. 'An Angel!' he whispered.

'It looked exactly like me,' she added.

Man's eyes narrowed. How angelic was his wife?

Next day, there was the Babe in its cradle.

'My little darling!' cried Woman.

'Can this be God's child?' whispered Man.

The Babe looked at them with bright eyes like a bird, and let out a wild, unearthly laugh.

When God saw what Goka had done with her baby, he shook his head. 'Just like a Demon!' he exclaimed. The time had come to do something drastic about her and her mad husband. He called to the Demons to heat his furnace white-hot, and he rolled up his sleeves. Then he bound Goku and Goka together, face to face, with heavenly wire, and heated them white-hot in the furnace. Then, laying them on his anvil, he pounded them with his mighty hammer till the sparks flew.

Again he heated them white-hot, and again he pounded them on the anvil, gripping them with his pincers as his almighty arm rose and fell, and the hammer blows shook Heaven and Earth.

Goku and Goka no longer laughed. Their faces were squeezed into one face, their bodies into one body, as God hammered them into a single lump.

Again he heated them white-hot, and again he hammered them. And as he hammered, the lump grew smaller. And smaller. Till it was only the size of a thrush's egg.

Then he plunged it into icy water, with a bang of steam.

He took it out, and rolled it between his palms. In spite of the icy dip, it was warm and dry. He gave it to an Angel. 'Take this,' he said, 'and give it to any bird who will take it.'

So the Angel came down to Earth, where the birds were singing. He called them together and explained that God had invented a new egg. He showed them the ball. 'So which of you will take it and hatch it and nurse what comes out?'

The birds were silent. But finally the Hedge Sparrow piped up: 'If it's God's,' she said, 'then I'll take it.' And she put it with her own five eggs.

Out of that egg two chicks hatched. They screamed to be fed. And screamed. And screamed. They took all the food their parents brought. And they grew.

They tossed the Hedge Sparrow's own children out of the nest. And screamed to be fed.

'Are these truly God's?' asked the male Hedge Sparrow. His head was worn bare with pushing food down the throats of these two gaping mouths.

One day, the two strange creatures flew up and away.

They began to fly to and fro over the Earth. One was male, one female. She called 'Goku!' and he called 'Goka!'

When she lays an egg, she does what she did before, and what the Angel did. She gives it to somebody else. She finds Hedge Sparrow's nest, and pops it in, and flies off with a weird laugh.

They ignore the other birds. They try to attract the attention of the Angels, and of the Demons, that stream to and fro in the air invisibly, going about God's business.

'Goku!' they cry, and 'Goka!' at the tops of their voices, all day long. And as the days pass, they grow more and more desperate. They turn somersaults. They shout their names and follow that with a mad demonic laugh, hoping they will be recognized.

But the Angels and the Demons are still too busy. And God refuses to take any notice. Only Man listens. He pauses, and listens. And as he listens to that endless 'Goku!' and 'Goka!', and now and then that laugh echoing between the woods, a strange feeling comes over him. He feels he wants to laugh madly. He feels something is missing – something very important. And he feels the Angels watching him sternly.

The Dreamfighter

God was in a bad way. The trouble was – things from outer space. These alien beings would land at night, dress themselves in nightmare, and creep into his ear.

His sleep was gone. The only way he could escape the attacks of these ferocious beings was to stay awake. So night after night he paced to and fro in his workshop. Sometimes, for sheer weariness, he would sit. But then if he closed his eyes, even for a moment, his head would loll forward and he would be asleep.

And a nightmare would creep into his ear.

He'd stopped doing any real work, creating real creatures. He made a few plants. Doodling with clay, he made a few kinds of fly. But his heart wasn't in it. The truth was, he felt too sleepy.

One afternoon sleep was weighing heavy on him. Struggling to keep awake, he began to doodle with clay. And this time, yawning, rubbing his eyelids that kept trying to stick together, and almost dreaming with his eyes open, he made an odd thing.

It was red, with red eyes. About the size of an Alsatian dog. Six skinny legs. It waved two feelers. And it stared at him. And it cried: 'What am I?'

God stared back. He had simply no idea what it was, or what to call it. Usually when he made a creature he had a pretty strong picture of what he wanted and why he wanted it. But this time his mind was blank.

'What am I?' it cried again, shivering.

God scratched his head and yawned. He supposed he ought to give it a name.

'Tell me what I am,' cried the creature. 'Tell me what I have to do.'

But God's head had already fallen forward, and a snore came out of his beard.

The creature blinked its red eyes and strayed into the forest.

For a long time it simply stood under a tree. Other creatures going busily past looked sideways at it and said: 'A new one! What are you?'

But the creature didn't know what to say.

A Baboon marched past. 'Haha!' it barked. 'A newcomer! Name please.'

When the creature didn't answer, Baboon gave it a shove, and it collapsed like an ironing board. It got up slowly.

'Can't you speak?' asked the Baboon. 'Then you must be a Mutant. Get it? Mute Ant. Hahaha!' And the Baboon rolled over backwards, beating its head with mirth. It ran off to tell some Gazelles.

'Mutant?' thought the creature. 'Well, maybe I am. Maybe the Monkey's right.'

But that didn't help. He still didn't know what to do. And the trouble was, he didn't feel like doing anything either.

The Cheetah hurtled past, along the trail of dust left by a Gerenuk, and he heard its claws hissing: 'Faster! Faster!' What was the hurry?

A long line of Gnu, heads bowed with effort, climbed away north, grunting: 'North! North!' Where were they all going?

And just above him, two Wrens came and went, came and went, came and went, every half-minute, holding a feather, or a string of moss, or a stalk of grass. Why were they so busy?

He watched some Flamingoes holding their heads upside down, half under water. What were they trying to do?

'If I'm a Mutant,' he thought, 'what does a Mutant do? Why

did God make me? I'm not properly made. I don't seem to fit. He must have left something out of my works.'

He walked around, watching the animals and the birds all so busy. 'How do they know what to be busy with?' he thought. He did feel completely left out.

That same day, God advertised for a bodyguard, to defend him from his nightmares. *Must be a good nightworker and dreamfighter*, said his ad. Three creatures had applied: Leopard, Wolf and Owl. God was giving each one a try. Leopard first, then Wolf, then Owl.

But none of them could stand up to the Space Beings.

The first night, Leopard saw two eyes coming closer. They were very like his own, but much bigger. 'They look like eyes,' thought Leopard, 'but they are probably flying saucers.' He decided to attack. But when he leapt, the moment his feet left the ground he felt suddenly dizzy. When he landed he was spinning like a top. Not only was he spinning like a top, somebody was lashing him with a whip, to keep him spinning. With an extra crack, the whip lifted him out over the forest, and he crashed into a thorn bush. Scrambling out of the thorns, he shot off to his cave.

That night God had a shocking nightmare. He was a Leopard spinning down a plughole. The plughole was too small. So he was having to become very thin, till he was no thicker than his own tail. So he spun down the plughole and came out as an immensely long, twisting Leopard's tail writhing among the stars, which were all quaking with laughter. He woke up shouting, and no wonder.

The Wolf did no better. The Wolf didn't know what had happened to Leopard. He saw two eyes coming closer. He thought it was another Wolf. He went forward warily. It seemed to be another Wolf, very like himself. They touched noses.

As they touched noses, the other breathed in fiercely, with a sudden, whistling, sucking breath. And Wolf felt himself being sucked in and actually turned inside out inside the other Wolf. 'How can this be?' he howled, and his howl, too, was inside out.

Then the other Wolf sneezed, and Wolf shot away into the darkness, once again outside out and inside in, but so terrified that when he landed he went on running till next morning. From this moment he became three times as wary.

But while Wolf was still running, God had a shocking nightmare. He dreamed he was first turned inside out, then blown up like a very big, very tight balloon. And that's how he spent the night, inside out, blown up as a big balloon, bobbing among the freezing, prickling stars.

Owl had the worst time. Owl saw two eyes coming closer. He'd heard what had happened to Leopard and to Wolf, so he wasn't very happy. He was wishing he hadn't taken this work on. But he was brave, and he was thinking: 'I'll attack, and just grab at those eyes. If I can get my hands on his eyes, he'll be helpless.'

So he attacked. But instead of landing with outstretched, grasping feet on a solid creature's head, as poor Owl expected, he was hit by something springy, light, flat and very tough. It sent him spinning. And then the same thing, with a whiffling whop, hit him again, from the other direction and sent him spinning back. And hit him again from the other direction. And so it went on. And Owl had no idea what was hitting him, or what was going on, except he was being slapped helplessly through the air, first one way then the other, with whacking, whiffling blows.

Making a terrific effort, he flung out his wings and flew straight upwards. He was free. He hurtled home, all his feathers broken and bent. He squeezed himself into the back of his tree hole. He closed his eyes tight. No more bodyguard jobs for him!

Meanwhile God was having an awful nightmare. Two gigantic tennis rackets were batting him to and fro across a net in which the knots were stars. Every sort of shot, lob and whack, slice and volley slam. God spun in the air, or he flashed like a bullet. Sometimes he hit the net and stars showered. Then the racket flipped him up and – Bop! – away he went again. He woke next morning hardly able to move.

After this, animals stopped applying. So God advertised again, and this time, as well as asking for a good nightworker and dreamfighter, the ad said: *Pay in advance: one wish fulfilled.*

When Mutant heard of this, he thought: 'What if I ask him to make me busy. That's my only wish.' So he applied.

When God saw him, he was astonished. He couldn't remember making him. And when he heard the wish that Mutant wanted fulfilled, as advance pay, he laughed. Sleepy as he was, he actually laughed.

'Oh well,' he sighed. 'Granted. You'll certainly need to be busy to keep the nightmares off me. Yes, I grant you ten times the natural dose of busyness. That should be about right!' And he laughed again.

Mutant's eyes blinked furiously. Without waiting for God to say any more, he dashed outside. It was already dusk. What time did the Space Beings start their attack?

He raced over God's roof, through the forest and up a mountain. On the peak, he stood on his hind legs, waving his feelers.

Then he raced along the hills, from peak to peak. He raced the whole way round the circle of hills and back to God's house. He felt very strange. 'So this,' he thought, 'is what it is to be busy!'

He felt as if all his limbs were about to burst into flames. He had to move, and move very fast, and keep moving, to escape the feeling, which was actually rather awful.

But what now? Where were the attackers? It was dark. Where were the eyes he'd heard so much about?

He raced in a circle round God's house, up over the roof and back again.

And there they were – the eyes.

Mutant didn't wait for a second. He dashed straight in.

He felt the dizziness bounce off his hard skin. It knocked him off balance, but only for one of his lightning strides. Then he felt the dreadful suction pump clamped over his face. But he clashed his pincers and shredded it, before it could suck him inside out. Then the springy, hard, light bat hit him, but he clung to it, ran over the mesh, and down the handle, and over the fingers gripping the handle, and seized the wrist in his pincers.

A most horrible screech went up. God peered out through his window and saw an immense shape floundering in the darkness, and he heard trees crashing. Then a tearing cry of pain, and then more cries, and groans, going off, through the forest, with splintering tree boughs. The cries seemed to climb the mountainside, then go off up into space.

Mutant appeared in God's doorway. He was dragging something. At first God thought it was a Rhinoceros without a head. Then he saw it was a colossal hand. Mutant had brought him the nightmare's hand.

From that night, Mutant's life changed. He became God's bodyguard and all the creatures heard about him with awe.

And he certainly did some amazing things. The Space

Beings didn't stop trying to get at God. Every night Mutant raced through the forests and over the mountains, to and fro, to and fro, and here and there, over God's roof and around his house, all at top speed, and the Space Beings simply couldn't outwit him.

No matter what shape they took, he was ready, he was there, with his terrific activity.

One came as a fog, but Mutant grabbed a blazing log from God's kiln and raced through and through the fog till he found the heart of it – a kind of big soft spider dangling on a thread from space. When he plunged the torch deep in the spider, the whole fog fell as a two-minute rain of honey blobs.

Mutant licked his feet and tasted the honey blobs. He had seen the other creatures eating. In fact, they did little else but eat. This was the first time Mutant had tasted anything. He whistled with delight. He spent the rest of that night licking the leaves, the grass, even the bare ground.

'At last,' he thought, 'I've found something to live for.'

Next night, as he raced in his protective circles, he noticed a slender bamboo shoot growing beside God's door. 'Strange!' he thought, and raced on. By midnight, no Space Being had appeared, but the bamboo was as thick as an Elephant's leg, and its leaves leaned in through God's doorway. And then, as Mutant dashed over God's roof for the fiftieth time that night, he heard God groan on his bed.

Had the nightmare got through?

Mutant hurled himself at the bamboo, and crushed its thickness with his pincers. The splintering was also a screech, and all the leaves flew like knives. Mutant shook his head, like a Dog, and the bamboo toppled. Honey welled out of the mangled stump, and Mutant was still feeding there when God got up next morning. Looking at the stump and the fallen bamboo, God said: 'That reminds me. I dreamed. My spine was a bamboo tree. I was growing in a swamp. It was horrible. Then Man came in a canoe, cut me down, and made me into an organ pipe, a giant flute, and that was beautiful.'

Mutant, his pincers deep in the oozing honey, tried to smile.

Every night Mutant overpowered a different Space Being. But now he was not only defending God from Space Beings and the nightmares they came in, he was keeping up the honey supply for himself, since every Space Being, somehow or other, shed honey.

Feeding on the honey, his busy energy became fiercer than ever. But something else was happening too. Mutant was growing.

At the end of the first month, after about thirty nights of victorious dreamfighting, Mutant was the size of a Camel. At the end of the second month, he was the size of an Elephant. 'God's bodyguard,' he cried, 'needs the weight.'

Now as he raced through the forest and over the mountains, he travelled along the deep lanes he had worn. His passing sounded like a motorboat, as his six feet pounded the earth.

God was sleeping well. He was so pleased with Mutant, he built him a special tower beside his own house. Mutant would race to the top of it, and survey space. During the day, to use up his busyness, he dug cellars under it, and deepened tunnels down to deeper cellars. He called the tower the Palace. And God, seeing him grow, changed his name from Mutant to Giant.

The other creatures began to be alarmed. For one thing, when was Giant going to stop growing? That worried them. He was already bigger than any of them.

For another thing, it was becoming quite difficult to sleep. All night long Giant was charging along his trails, through the forest, up the mountain, over the peaks, back through the forest, on his maze of different paths. And the din was terrific. It was like living in the middle of a permanent speedtrack. And not only was the noise impossible, the earthquaking was worse. He was getting to be so tremendously heavy. And every three minutes or so he let out a shattering roar: 'Make way for God's bodyguard!'

At last the creatures came to God and complained.

'As he gets heavier and bigger,' cried Sloth, 'he gets faster. He's forever shaking me off my branch, just by pounding past.'

'And the accident rate,' cried a Shrew, 'it's going up and up. Why can't he fly?'

Giant listened as he paused deep in the earth, working at one of his cellars. He dashed up and sprang out in front of the creatures.

'Complaints?' he bellowed. 'What do you want? Me or no me and God going crazy with nightmares? Which of you serves God as I do? Which of you will take my place to defend God?'

The creatures all sidled away. Giant certainly scared them. His eyes were really quite terrible, and he was obviously trembling with eagerness to attack somebody.

God frowned and scratched his chin through his beard. If it weren't for those Space Beings and the nightmares, he was thinking, the world might be a nicer place without Giant. He was getting to be a bit too much of a good thing. But so long as the Space Beings kept coming . . .

*

The night after that they stopped. Had Giant finished them off? He raced along his trails. On into the dawn, he was rushing from peak to peak, gazing into space, waving his feelers. Where were the Space Beings?

That was his first night without honey. But the second night was the same. And the third.

On the fourth day he lay still on his tower. He was thinking: 'What if Space Beings are over?' Then he whispered: 'What if the honey's finished?'

His legs jumped into action. He raced into the forest. At one point he stopped and roared: 'All creatures great and small will bring honey to Giant. Failure will be punished.'

He then seized Linnet by the scruff of the neck: 'Where is the honey? You pay your taxes in honey. And you pay them to me.'

Linnet squirmed. What could he say? So Giant flung him into one of the cellars under the Palace.

When Bullfinch, Newt and Giraffe had joined Linnet in Giant's cellars, the other creatures learned. They began to squeeze nectar out of the flowers, and brought it to Giant. Even Leopard brought him some on a leaf.

'Not enough,' roared Giant, and pushed Leopard down into one of the cellars.

Few of the animals brought much. Pretty soon the cellars of the Palace hummed like a great beehive with the sobbing and wailing of the imprisoned animals.

God realized something had to be done. 'Giant,' he thought, 'has gone crazy.'

When he asked Giant to let the animals go, Giant stared at him, incredulous.

'But,' he gasped, 'they didn't bring me any honey.'

God nodded, and keeping his voice very gentle and calm he asked: 'But does that really matter?'

Giant almost squeaked. 'Matter?' he cried. 'But if I don't have honey, how can I guard you? I need the strength.'

God nodded again. 'Very true,' he said. 'But,' he added, 'maybe I don't need guarding any more. The Space Beings have stopped.'

Giant let out a blasting screech, like a steam whistle, and stared at God thunderstruck.

'I serve you,' he bellowed finally. 'I am your bodyguard. That is my life. Don't you understand what it means, to be the bodyguard of God?'

God gazed at Giant. 'This peculiar creature,' he was thinking, 'really has gone crazy!'

'Who else but I can fight the Space Beings?' Giant continued at the top of his voice. 'Without me you'd be a sleepless wreck, your Creation would fall to bits. So I need energy. I NEED HONEY!'

Giant stood there. He looked exactly like a house-size statue made of girders and ship's boilers, all glowing red-hot. His eyes looked like welder's flames. Even God felt quite alarmed. But then he had a brainwave.

'What about the Bees?' he asked.

Giant frowned and sparks crackled. 'Bees?'

'The Honeybees,' said God. 'Let all the animals go free, and Honeybee, henceforth, will work only for you.'

So Giant let all the animals go free, and waited. Now that his limbs were still his mind was going faster and faster. He was trying to calculate how many Bees he would need.

But God was also thinking hard, and at last he knew what to do.

First of all he hung a wet sack over the Sun. Next the Wild

Goose and the Swan brought him snow. He modelled this snow into a figure exactly like Woman, but as big as himself. There she stood, in front of his workshop.

Now he sent Magpie to advertise a new job: a bodyguard for God's bride.

A bodyguard for God's bride!

All the creatures came running. Even Wild Goose and Swan gazed in wonder at the beautiful Snow Maiden. Was God getting married? The creatures were wild with excitement.

But Giant, too, had emerged. He stared at the dazzling white figure.

He was very angry. And when he spoke, he had difficulty forming the words, because all he wanted to do was roar with rage.

'All creatures,' he cried, 'will go home. The bodyguard of God is also the bodyguard of the bride of God.'

God came out of his workshop. 'But, Giant,' he said, 'I thought you couldn't work without honey. The Bees will take some time, you know, getting you a good enough supply to start you off again. I'm afraid my bride needs a bodyguard now.'

'I don't need honey,' choked Giant. 'I am her bodyguard. I am your bodyguard. I am the only bodyguard.'

'But she is so beautiful,' said God. 'Something will surely steal her. While you're racing about over the mountains, she'll be snatched by the Bridesnatcher from inside the Earth.'

'By who?' Giant had never heard of the Bridesnatcher inside the Earth.

God sighed. 'A terrible being. Worse than any Space Being. He comes light as a breath. Invisible as a breath. Soundless as a breath.'

'Test me,' cried Giant.

215

But God only shook his head.

'If she were to be stolen – ' he began. Then he stopped and sighed again.

'I'd find her,' Giant cried, 'I would never stop till I found her and rescued her.'

God seemed to think deeply. 'All right,' he said at last. 'But promise. If she is stolen, you will never stop till you have found her and brought her back.'

Giant nodded. He felt if he spoke he would burst into tears of rage. How could God doubt him?

'Swear,' said God sternly.

'I swear!' cried Giant, through his clenched teeth.

'Very good then,' said God. 'You are her bodyguard.' And as he went back into his workshop he casually drew the sack, now almost dry, off the sun.

The next hour was the most terrible time of Giant's life. The sun's great beams blazed down on the Snow Bride. And as Giant stood, staring at her, she began to sink slowly into the ground.

He raced round her in tight circles, trying to see where she was going. But it was no use. And the moment came when the last glint of snow melted into the sodden ground.

He could not believe it. He stared at the place till the ground was dry.

Then he began to race to and fro over it, looking for a way in, and whimpering like a little puppy dog.

God came out. He stood there, simply nodding. He seemed to be beyond anger. And when Giant saw the grim look on his face he cried: 'I'll find her, I'll find her.'

'How?' asked God, and stood silent.

'Somehow, somehow,' cried Giant.

'However are you going to get into the crannies of the

Earth, where the Bridesnatcher's carried her off? I knew this would happen.'

'Make me small, make me tiny,' wept Giant. 'I'll find her.'

'Well,' said God. 'If I did that, at least you'd have no problem finding enough honey. Very well, I'm relying on you.'

And God snapped his fingers.

Giant saw everything grow suddenly enormous. The grass blades towered far above him. The forest loomed like a green, stirring thunderstorm.

God looked down. Giant, no bigger than a fly, was scrambling over the crumbs of soil.

'Try every hole,' boomed God, high up in the sky. 'Try every cranny. And when you've found her, let me know.'

He went back into his workshop, whistling a little tune under his breath.

Then the Baboon danced up. 'Gee-up, Giant,' he laughed. 'She's getting further away all the time. Now you'll need your famous speed. Gee-up!'

And Parrot cried: 'Gee-up, Giant!'

And the Elephants, blinking sleepily, rumbled: 'Gee-up, Giant!'

Pretty soon, Geeup Giant was simply called Geeupant.

'Gee-up, Geeupant,' laughed the Jackass.

Giant, now so tiny, began racing in and out of the wormholes. And he has never since been able to rest. Where can he ever find the maiden of melted snow? Where did she go? But still he races along, deep in forests, under all the roots, and far out over deserts, down every crack in the baking crust. He races over the world, unresting. Where could she be? Where is she?

'Poor old Ant!' sighs the Sloth.

Gozzie

To amuse his mother, God invented the little fluffy yellow Gosling, and gave it to her. She was very pleased. Its comical little eyes at the corners of its beak made her smile. And she loved its soft, broad, purplish webbed feet that waddled along with their toes turned in.

It followed her everywhere. At night it jumped on to her bed and slept as close to her as it could get. It was very proud to be the pet of God's mother. While the other birds watched from bushes and trees, or from high in the air, Gosling waddled along at her heels.

'Well,' he would say to himself, 'aren't I the lucky one!'

And the birds would mutter to each other: 'How did he do it? What's so special about him?'

Even as he grew bigger, and his yellow fluff became grey feathers, he still followed God's mother everywhere. And she still called to him constantly: 'Come on, Gozzie, have a nibble.' And she would feed him some delicious little bit of something from her fingers.

'He's lucky,' rattled Magpie. 'But wow! Isn't he ugly! And what a voice!'

It was true, Gozzie was ponderous-looking. He looked too fat, for one thing. And as he grew bigger, his fat belly sagged deeper between his legs.

But he didn't care. 'Jealous!' he'd quack. 'Absolutely everybody is jealous of me. Sometimes even I'm a little bit jealous of me!' And he laughed: 'Wak! Wak! Wak! Wak! Wak!'

'Ugh!' cried the Owls, covering their ears.

'You could be good for one thing,' chattered the Starlings.

'God's alarm clock. With a bit of practice at getting the time right.'

'Jealous!' quacked Gozzie.

But it was true. His voice was not pretty. His voice, in fact, was ugly. It worried him a lot. Sometimes, when he was sitting in the grass close to God's mother, perhaps when she was peeling mushrooms or shelling peas, he would think: 'How is it I'm so lucky in everything, yet have such a horrible voice?'

And sometimes he would listen to Thrush in the evening, or Robin, and he would feel so miserable he would actually weep. Then he would think: 'If only I could sing like that! I think I would exchange everything just to be able to sing. Yes, if I could sing, I don't think I'd mind living in the rough old forest. Or out on the windy river.'

Then he would go down to the river and swim a bit, dipping his head under the water so the other birds wouldn't see that he'd been weeping.

If only God had given him a proper voice!

Soon he was thinking about his voice all the time. Worrying about his voice. 'I can't sing. I can only honk and yodel in a cranky way, and quack. I'd sooner be a fish.'

God's mother had no idea, of course, that her darling pet was so wretched. He never told her. He never breathed a word about it to anybody. He was too proud.

One day it was announced: the creatures were having another song contest. Everybody was wildly excited, as usual. All except Gozzie.

'Oh no!' cried Gozzie. 'I can't bear it. Oh! I think I'll go and stick my head in the mud of the river bed till it's over.'

The birds were sure the winner would be a bird. The animals, the reptiles and the insects had their champions.

But they all secretly suspected the winner would be a bird.

Which bird? A favourite was Nightingale. A close runner-up favourite was Skylark. Another was Missel Thrush.

But suddenly – a sensation! Everybody was talking about Water Snake.

Water Snake was a new creature. God had never meant to give Water Snake an unusual voice. But something went wrong in her making. A lucky accident! Anyway, the result was, Water Snake had an absolutely stunning voice.

A delicious, liquid, heart-stopping voice! When she lifted her head up between lily pads, and sang a melody, even Alligator's tail curled slowly upwards, in an agony of pleasure. Yes, the beauty of Water Snake's voice was so keen it was painful.

When she draped herself on a floating log in some back-water, and sang a full song, practising for the competition, even God found himself rooted to the spot. Wild Bull set his brow to the ground and leaned on it, groaning softly. Flying Beetle lost control of his wings in his effort to listen. He fell into the grass and lay there, legs in the air, just letting the song happen to him. Other kinds of snakes, that were coiled in trees, became limp and simply slithered loosely to the ground, lying there maybe on their backs, motionless as long as the song lasted.

And Nightingale, Skylark and Missel Thrush, and the other favourites, fell silent.

It surely was an incredible song.

But nobody was listening so hard, or so painfully, as Gozzie. Yes, for Gozzie that song was pure cruelty.

'Oh!' he sobbed in the reeds. 'Oh! Oh! Oh! If only! If only! Why Water Snake? When God made me for his mother, couldn't he do me a favour? A voice isn't much of an extra. And I could have sung for her, his own mother.'

And he plunged his head into the mud beneath the water. But straightaway he lifted it out again, not to miss a note of the song.

Magpie decided to take action against the new rival of the birds. He flew out over Water Snake.

'Hey, knot-neck!' he bawled. 'When you stop singing do you know what? You vanish into ugliness. Your ugliness is so impossible – you're invisible. We can't help hearing you, but do we have to look at you?'

Woodpecker joined in with a laugh: 'Hey, creepy, you've won a prize – for the wettest worm and the droopiest drape. Give us another spaghetti solo.'

Then Kookaburra came, with an even worse laugh. 'Nice of you to sing for my supper!' he cried and dived down, great beak wide open, to catch and gobble Water Snake. She dived under water in a flash, but only just made it.

After that, these three birds made Water Snake's life a misery. Whenever she lifted her head out of the water, to practise her singing, these three came flying, and Kookaburra made a grab at her.

'Seems like Water Snake's not in the running any more,' the birds said.

Meanwhile, Gozzie's heart was breaking. At last, he couldn't bear it any longer, and he told God's mother. She listened in surprise. She had never guessed.

'You poor darling!' she cried at last. 'Why didn't you say something before? Of course my son will make you into a singer. You just leave it to me.'

And gathering him up, big as he now was, she took him in to God. And she told God what was making her pet so unhappy. Gozzie simply laid his head over her shoulder and sobbed openly.

'Well, who'd have thought!' said God, and he dropped into his chair. Gozzie's grief was so plain to see, God was quite upset.

'But what can I do now?' God asked helplessly. 'Once he's got his voice, he's got it for good.'

'You're God, aren't you?' cried his mother. 'Simply give him another voice. A standby. Any kind of decent singing voice. You're the Creator – think something up.'

'Well, I'll try, I'll try,' said God. And he leaned his brow on his hands. 'You'll have to give me time, though. It's not going to be easy.'

What on earth could he do? But then, as his mother went into the kitchen, crooning over Gozzie, God noticed a movement down in the corner of his doorway.

It was Water Snake. She had managed to reach God without being seen by the birds. And now she told him her tale. Her tears splashed on to the floor. God sat listening, deep in thought. What a day! First Gozzie, now Water Snake! It was all getting too much. At last he burst out:

'But what can I do? So the birds scream insults at you whenever you sing. And Kookaburra tries to grab you and gobble you up. Can't you stay silent under water? You're a water snake, remember.'

'And waste my beautiful voice?' cried Water Snake. 'Can't you get rid of those birds.'

'Certainly not!' said God sharply. 'Not once they're made.'

'Why don't you make me a bird?' wailed Water Snake. 'Then they'd be on my side. It's all because I'm not a bird.'

When Water Snake said that, God slapped his brow. He had a sudden brainwave.

'Wait,' he cried. And he called his mother and asked her to

bring in Gozzie. Gozzie, who was now a big, heavy goose, came waddling in, and stopped, craning his beak towards Water Snake. Water Snake curled up into a tight ball and peered out from between her coils. This looked like another bird to her.

'Now,' said God to Gozzie. 'Here is Water Snake.'

'I know, I know,' moaned Gozzie. 'The heavenly singer!'

'Well, how would you like to have her voice?' asked God.

'Me?' gasped Gozzie. And he jerked up his wings as if he might fall over.

He couldn't believe his ears. After all, this was God speaking. God did not make jokes.

'Wait, wait,' cried Water Snake. 'What's going on?' And she uncoiled and writhed herself into a tangle of question marks. Her brows came down and her black eyes scowled from under them. Her tongue flashed like a little whip.

'Will you be patient and listen,' said God. 'Both of you.'

Then he explained. He would remake them into a single creature. So Water Snake, inside Gozzie, would be a bird. And Gozzie, with Water Snake inside him, would be the singer of singers.

Gozzie blinked. The idea of having Water Snake's voice drove every other thought out of his head. That voice coming out of his mouth!

'Oh please!' he sobbed. 'Oh, that sounds wonderful! Oh, could it really happen?'

But Water Snake let out a screech and went lashing all over God's workshop like a firecracker.

'Never!' she screamed. 'Never! Live inside that stupid, ugly-looking goose? The birds say I'm ugly only because they're jealous of my voice and my beauty. I'm a beautiful black whip of water lightning. Oh I am, I am. And I love being me!'

'Listen!' cried God. 'Why don't you listen? Let me finish.'

Water Snake lay in a tangle, as God went on:

'I will make Gozzie the most beautiful of the birds. He will be perfectly beautiful. More beautiful than any other beauty. Beautiful without a flaw. And you will be gazing out through his eyes, seeing the whole world gazing amazed at you.'

'And singing through my mouth,' whispered Gozzie, 'seeing the whole world listening. Oh please, please.'

'The other birds,' said God, 'will no longer insult you. They will adore you. They will worship you. And with your voice, you will be – well – you know what you'll be. You will be the absolute star.'

Water Snake's tongue flickered.

'Maybe I'll – just try it,' she hissed. 'But if it doesn't work – '

'Try it!' said God loudly. 'Good. Close your eyes, both of you.'

Then he tossed Gozzie and Water Snake into his furnace of creative fire, brought them out magically white-hot, and with his magical hammer on his magical anvil pounded and beat the two shapes into one. The sparks flew. It all seemed to happen in a flash.

His mother brought a bucket of water up from the holy well and poured it over the finished creature with a crash and a great explosion of steam.

And there it stood, the new creature, in a puddle of water. Bigger than Gozzie, and white as fiery new snow. And there, peering out from under its brows, were Water Snake's black eyes. And Water Snake's black skin was there too, over the great webbed feet.

It turned its head on its snaky neck. God's mother saw how snaky her Gozzie had become. And when it looked at her she knew: this was no longer her Gozzie.

God planted his big mirror in front of this new creature. The head reared up, and out of the beak came a long hiss.

'Horrible!' It was Water Snake's voice, from the great white bird's throat. 'Let me out! Let me out!'

'But you're incredibly beautiful!' cried God. 'Look at you. You really do look like an Angel. You look like a bride in her lace.'

'I don't,' cried Water Snake. 'Look at my great fat body. I look like Gozzie, only bigger. Let me out!'

'Nonsense,' said God. 'You'll get used to it. Just stroll down to the water – but sing as you go. Then you'll see what the birds do. They'll fall out of the trees with surprise. And remember, you're gorgeous.'

Gozzie's great feet waddled out into the garden and down towards the river. As he went he stretched up his neck – and hissed.

Not a word came out. Not a note.

'Sing,' cried Gozzie to his voice. But all that came out was a funny sort of grunt. It wasn't even a honk or a quack any more.

God frowned, rubbing his chin. He watched Gozzie swim out on to the river.

'Give us a song now,' he called. 'It will sound wonderful over the water.' Gozzie stretched up his neck, but again all that came out was a hiss.

'What's wrong? Where's the voice?' shouted God.

'When you let me out,' cried Water Snake. 'Then I'll sing. Till then I sulk.'

'In that case,' shouted God, getting angry, 'you stay in there till you sing! Now sing!'

'Not till you've let me out,' screeched Water Snake.

'Sing,' ordered God. 'When I say sing, you sing.'

'Never never never never,' screeched Water Snake. 'Never till you let me out.'

God clamped his jaws tight shut and glared at the white shape on the river. Gozzie dipped his neck and upended his whole body, as if his eyes and beak were trying to bury themselves in the mud at the bottom.

'You've done it again,' said God's mother, shaking her head. 'Poor little Gozzie!'

'You're right,' said God. 'If ever I made a mistake, there's one.'

'It will need a new name,' said his mother.

'Hmmm!' said God. His mind was a blank. What on earth could he call such a mixture? 'Let's leave that to Man,' he said at last. 'I don't want to make another mistake. Man might get it right.'

How God Got His Golden Head

Poltergeist lived in God's workshop. Where had it come from? It had no idea.

It lived inside an old candlestick that God had carved long ago from a piece of driftwood. God never used the candlestick. Nowadays, if he worked after sunset, he worked by the light of his own eyes.

So the candlestick sat up on the shelf, collecting dust. And Poltergeist lived inside it.

Poltergeist had no shape, no weight, and not even God could see it.

'Am I a him?' it asked itself sometimes as it watched God bent at his work.

Or sometimes, when it saw God's old mother moving about in the shadows of her bedroom, it thought: 'Maybe I'm a her.'

It could fly. It loved to swoop about the workshop. It loved to fling things from one end of the room to the other. Most of all, it loved to hear things go smash.

Sometimes, when God's mother brought him a cup of tea, the cup would rise from the saucer, empty itself over God's head, then shatter itself against the ceiling. Poltergeist would laugh silently and flit back into the candlestick.

Another time, when God went into his workshop one morning, he found the whole room upside down. There he was, walking across the ceiling, and looking up at the floor above him, with his chair, his workbench, all upside down above him, and still on the workbench was his nearly completed Centipede. Was the Centipede having to cling, or was it just somehow lying there?

With a great effort, God twisted the whole workshop round, and got it the right way up again, with the floor under his feet. But now he saw something peculiar. In his mirror, everything was still upside down. How could that be?

He gripped the mirror in both hands and with a terrific effort he twisted everything in the mirror, to get it the right way up. And with a bang, he fell on to the ceiling.

Now everything inside the mirror was the right way up, but the workshop was upside down again.

On the shelf, the upside-down candlestick tittered.

Again, with an effort, God got the workshop the right way up. But once again, everything in the mirror was upside down. He turned the mirror's face to the wall and looked at the candlestick.

He knew there was something very funny going on in his workshop. And he knew there was something funny about that candlestick. Was there a connection?

Sometimes Poltergeist tried to take a hand in God's work. As it watched him, working away, creating his wonderful creatures one after the other, it longed to do the same.

One day God made Wolf. Before he'd quite finished it, he sat back, pondering. Somehow, this animal was turning out too gloomy. It sat there on his bench, glowering at him. 'How can I brighten you up?' murmured God.

For answer, the Wolf yawned. But as it yawned, a blazing log from the fire soared across the room and disappeared down the Wolf's throat. The Wolf gave a yell and all its hair spiked on end. God managed to grab it, and hold it, while he reached inside and pulled out the log. But the Wolf was now on fire inside. Its eyes glowed and the froth boiled out of the corners of its mouth.

'What now?' cried God. 'Oh lord, this is a mess!'

'Something to drink!' cried Wolf. 'Quick, oh quick, a drink!'

228

God tried water. It was no good. He tried treacle. It was no good. He tried milk. No good. God tried all kinds of things, but he had to go to bed at last, leaving the Wolf chained to the leg of his bench, lying there in the dark with blazing eyes and lolling tongue.

When God came into the workshop next morning, Wolf was nowhere to be seen. The chain lay there, and the empty collar.

Then God noticed a few hairs sticking up out of the neck of his brandy bottle. He picked up the bottle and peered through the glass. There was his big Wolf, crammed into the brandy bottle. Its eyes seemed to squirm, pressed tight against the glass inside.

Carefully he broke the bottle. Wolf burst back to its full stretch and shot out through the open doorway with a yowl.

The candlestick chuckled.

This time God heard it. He grabbed the candlestick, strode to his doorway, and hurled the wicked object as far as he could. Instantly, with a crash, all the glass of the window behind him showered in over his bench and the candlestick rolled across the workshop floor.

'Tricks!' bellowed God. 'I'll settle your tricks!'

He snatched up the candlestick again, strode again to the doorway, and again, harder than ever, with all his strength, hurled it at the far sky. With a ringing crack it hit the back of his own head and bounced away over the workshop floor, as he fell on to his knees watching a shower of stars.

Carefully now, he put the candlestick back on its shelf.

Then he stood at his open door rubbing the back of his head and frowning, and listening to the Wolf, running through the deep forest, howling for whatever it might be that would quench the flame inside it.

Soon after this, one afternoon, God was dozing in his chair.

Often in the middle of his work, he would doze off like this. Some of his best ideas came to him in these little naps.

He yawned, and felt a tickling inside his ear. Putting his little finger-end in his ear he felt a big round lump of ear-wax, simply sitting there, in the porch of his ear.

He half woke, looked at it, yawning, and idly flicked it away across his workshop.

By sheer fluke, it hit the candlestick, bounced to the floor, and rolled. Before it had come to a stop, God was asleep again.

But Poltergeist was awake. It peered out, and its gaze fastened on the ball of ear-wax. 'Did you knock?' it whispered.

It floated out of the candlestick, and sank to the floor. Close-up it gazed at the ear-wax. It poked the ear-wax. It picked up the ear-wax and gently rolled it between its palms.

Was this a little bit of God? Out of God's own ear? It was still warm with God's warmth. It was golden, like a kernel of sweet corn. And it was quite soft.

Poltergeist suddenly had a wild idea. It would make a creature out of this ear-wax. Poltergeist almost laughed out loud. It would make a creature not out of clay, like God, but one out of a little bit of God himself.

A creature made out of God! At the very idea, Poltergeist shuddered with excitement.

It had always wanted to make a bird, a swift, swooping sort of bird like a Swallow. It started to shape the ear-wax. Wings, and a tiny streamlined body, then the face.

But as it worked, it remembered God's Wolf. What if it made a tiny Wolf? Or better still a Dog. A Dog made of God!

This time Poltergeist did laugh out loud, and stared at the thing in its fingers. But then in mid-laugh it stopped. The thought about the Wolf-Dog had got into the ear-wax. And there it was, with wings, like a bird, but with a little snarly face, and fangs, like a Wolfy Dog. And it was now very nearly black. That was all the dust from living so long in the old candlestick.

Poltergeist gazed at what it had made. Actually, it looked quite interesting. Different from anything else. But Poltergeist liked that.

The creature had no life, of course. But that didn't worry Poltergeist. Stealthily, it placed the tiny beast of ear-wax on the back of God's sleeping hand, and, with a plink! like a snapping harp-string, shot back into the candlestick.

When God woke he found himself looking at the tiny snarler on the back of his hand. At first he thought: 'I've dreamed another monster! This time a midget!' That some-times did happen. Wart Hog had arrived like that. One night God had dreamed of a Wild Pig with a face like the root-ball of a torn-up tree, and it was trying to tip him out of bed. Next day he got the shock of his life when he walked in his garden and met Wart Hog itself, rooting up his tiger lilies and crunching the bulbs.

But now he saw that this new little creature had no life. So where had it come from? And what was it made of?

He had to admit, it was beautifully formed. 'Has my mother made it?' he wondered. Surely she would have given it life, because she too had the gift of giving life.

He blew the breath of life into its face. The creature squeezed its eyes shut, then suddenly took off. It dithered about the room. It could fly all right, but it seemed to spend all its energy trying not to hit things. God smiled. 'Practise hard,' he said. 'Practice makes perfect.' Then he went back to work on Desert Rat.

The new-made creature beat its wings wildly. It had no idea what it was or where it was. It saw a wall spinning towards it, then a ceiling, then a floor. Every beat of its wings brought something rushing towards it. Or at least, that's how it seemed to the little beast, as it swerved and dodged and doubled back.

It kept seeing God, bent at his work. And suddenly, in mid-whirl, it had a brainwave: 'If only I could get into his ear! There I'd be safe!'

So it tried to attract his attention, flying to and fro in front of his face, between his nose and the Desert Rat, and crying: 'Let me live in your ear.'

But its voice was so thin God could not hear it. It was really a Poltergeist voice. The Poltergeist could hear it, and he smiled silently as he watched from his candlestick.

Then the Wolf-Swallow or whatever it was thought it might just as well fly straight into God's ear, whether he liked it or not. But at that very instant, God snatched it out of the air, and tied it to his harp by one of the broken strings.

'There,' he ordered. 'Rest a while. You're getting on my nerves.'

The harp leaned against the wall, at the back of God's workbench. For a moment the Wolf-Swallow hung head downward, peering up at the string tied round his ankle. 'What's happening now?' he thought. 'This life is all surprises.'

Then he tried to fly straight at God's ear. But the string round his ankle jerked him back, and he bounced fluttering against the other unbroken strings of the harp.

A shower of plinketty-twangling notes showered out of the harp, under the strokes of the wings.

The Wolf-Swallow couldn't believe his ears. He fluttered at the strings again, and another shower of notes sprinkled around the room.

He laughed. He suddenly felt joyful. Now he felt really

alive. He forgot how dreadful it had been, reeling about in the air, with walls and furniture spinning towards him wherever he turned. He flittered again over the harp-strings, and back again, and to and fro, making the notes tumble.

God stopped his work and listened, astonished. He knew he had never heard music like this. And yet, somehow, it was familiar. It was a haunting, eerie music. Actually, it was partly Poltergeist music, but also partly music from God's own ear-drum. Nobody had ever played God's ear-drum, so God had never heard the music hidden in it. Inside the candlestick the Poltergeist clapped his hands, and hugged himself tightly and rocked to and fro with delight.

But much as he liked this music, God had soon had enough.

'Enough!' he commanded. 'Rest now. A little peace now.'

But the Wolf-Swallow would not stop. He had not had enough. He danced over the strings, flinging his wings, whirling on the end of his leash, hurtling to and fro across the harp like a mad hand, or like a mad glove rather, in a storm of notes.

'Joy!' he cried. 'Joy! Joy! Oh! Oh! Oh!'

He wanted to go on for ever. But God could not hear his cries of happiness. He caught him again, untied his leash, and was just about to toss him out through his open doorway into the world when he got a shock. When Wolf-Swallow saw that glare of daylight in the doorway, he knew more than ever where he wanted to be. He twisted from God's hand and like a black flash flew up and straight into God's ear.

'Aaaagh!' cried God, and clapped his hand to his ear. Then tenderly he wormed his finger-end into his ear as deeply as he could. Too late. The fluttering beast had gone right in. And as God wriggled his finger-end probing deeper, the creature fled in deeper. And now it was right inside God's head,

233

skittering about among his thoughts. God clutched his head and strode about his workshop.

'Oh!' he cried, and 'Aaaagh!' and 'Eeeegh!' He turned his mirror to see himself. And there was his own bewildered face, upside down, with the upside down hands clutching his hair.

Then the creature dived down through his body into his heart. Suddenly, it felt at home. Everything here felt familiar and friendly. And here he found something even better than a harp. He started hurtling about inside God's heart, playing his heart-strings just as he had played the harp on the bench. But here the music was far deeper, stranger, richer.

'Wonderful!' he cried to himself, as he hurled himself about among the strings. And the more fiercely he played, the more excited he became.

But God felt all this as an awful sensation. It was more than he could stand. He couldn't hear any music. All he knew was the ghostly plucking and twangling, the fluttering wings of the Wolf-Swallow right inside his heart, as if his heart itself were flying about on wings inside his ribs.

He beat his chest with his fists, trying to drive the crazy creature out through his mouth. But it wouldn't come out. And it wouldn't stop. He roared, like his own Gorilla, pounding his chest. His mother came running in. She stood there helplessly, wringing her hands, watching her mighty son hurl himself about the workshop, beating his chest, and roaring as if he hoped to blow his own heart right out through his mouth.

God looked at his mother with terrible eyes. 'What shall I do?' he wailed. 'What's the cure? Don't you know the cure for this?'

She only went on wringing her hands, and all the wrinkles around her eyes began to shine with tears.

'Ask the Earth,' she said at last. 'The Earth's the wise one.'

God almost fell out of his workshop. He stumbled on to his hands and knees and crawled over his lawn. He beat on the lawn with his fist.

'What's the cure for this?' he roared. 'Tell me the cure for this!' Then he kneeled up, and grappled at his chest with his great hands. It was as if he had a fire in there, like the Wolf. Only this wasn't a flame. This was a living and fluttering shadow, with a bird's wings and a Wolfy head, whirling inside his heart.

The Earth suddenly spoke. For a second God managed to hold still and he heard:

'Ask the Moon.'

God ran to the top of the nearest hill where, as it happened, the full Moon was just rising.

'Moon!' he shouted. 'What is the cure for this! This – whatever it is?'

His mother could see him outlined against the full Moon, like a mad dancer. And she heard the Moon's whispering reply:

'Ask the Sun.'

God uttered a roar of anguish and disappointment. But he set off, bounding over the ridges of forest and the ravines. And the Wolf-Swallow played more wildly than ever. He couldn't tell what God was doing, but it seemed to him that God was dancing, leaping up and down, with now and again a somersault. So the Wolf-Swallow played louder, harder. He uttered thin howls of ecstatic joy. It seemed to him, the more wildly he hurled himself into his music, the more wonderfully he broke into huge new gulfs of music, grander and more vast. 'More!' he howled to God. 'More! More!', urging him to leap higher, to dance more madly. But God only cried: 'Oh! This is horrible!' as he stumbled across the world to where the Sun was sinking behind the sea.

'What's the cure,' he bellowed, 'the cure – for this?'

And he beat his chest as his bellowing shout ended in a roar, that seemed to shake the flat, resounding shine of the sea.

The Sun was silent awhile. Then the voice came, out of the centre of the fiery ball.

'The cure,' said the voice, 'is severe.'

'Anything!' shouted God. 'I don't care! Anything!'

And again his shout ended in a bellowing roar and he pounded his chest.

'The cure,' said the Sun, 'is to put your head into my furnace.'

'What?' squeaked God. He couldn't believe what he'd heard. Also, his voice was wearing out.

At that moment the crazy player inside his heart flung himself into new efforts. He knew God had become still. He thought he'd simply stopped dancing. So now he tried to get him going again, dancing again, with new rhythms. He strummed and slammed, he plucked and leaped.

God placed his hands in the sea and leaned forwards towards the Sun. With all his courage, closing his eyes, and wrapping his hair and beard around his face, he thrust his head deep into the white-hot furnace of the Sun.

For a few moments, he thought he'd made a shocking mistake. Surely, he thought, I am going to burst into flames. I'm going to explode, like a barrel of petrol. He could feel all his atoms glowing towards flashpoint.

But then he realized his heart was quiet.

From inside his heart, the Wolf-Swallow was gazing into the glare of God's head. He did not like this at all. And as the glare became more intense, and the Sun's great heat began to brighten through God's body, he became afraid. He felt his wings growing soft. They no longer plucked at the heart-strings.

A sudden terrible fear came over him. As the dazzling glare surged down through God's neck and shoulders, he suddenly knew he was going to melt. He had to move fast.

God felt a peculiar sensation behind his knee. It moved down into his ankle. It writhed across the sole of his foot, under the skin.

With a puff of smoke, the winged and wolfy-headed creature of ear-wax shot out from under the nail of his left big toe.

It whirled down to the Earth, a black falling star, and plunged through a crevice into a deep cave. It hung itself under the ceiling, in a dark niche, panting.

God pulled his head out of the Sun. He had been bright before, but now he glowed, as if his head itself had turned into Sun. All his hair and beard dazzled whitely, and vibrated, like the element in an electric lamp, like white-hot white gold, and his face glowed like pure, new, polished gold.

He came back to Earth and stood on the hill behind his workshop, listening. From far away, among all the evening hubbub of Earth's creatures, he could hear a new sound. A tiny thudding. He smiled. It was the heart of the mad musician, the Wolf-Swallow, hanging upside down in the damp dark of its cave, squeezing its eyes shut against the terrible memory of the Sun.

This was Bat. Now he comes out only after the sunset. He hurls himself about, plucking at invisible strings. He is remembering God's harp and the music that poured out of it under his wild flying. And he is remembering God's heart, and the fantastic music he'd played inside there, that had made God himself roar and leap.

The Moon and Loopy Downtail

The Poltergeist in God's candlestick could not rest. He'd watched and watched, as God fashioned the perfect creatures. And they really were perfect. Even the most horrifying ones, like Angler Fish, Lamprey, Giant Medusa Jellyfish – no matter how ghastly, they were still somehow wonderfully perfect. They made Poltergeist want to weep and laugh and writhe, all at the same time, they were so perfect.

If only he could make something like that! Something so perfect. Finally, he knew he would have to have another go. His efforts so far had all gone wrong, in one way or another. What he needed to do, he felt, was to let his fingers imitate God's fingers exactly. He needed to follow him exactly, in every move he made, as he created a creature. But how could Poltergeist do that, without God seeing him? And if God were ever to see him – well, there was simply no telling what he would do. Probably cram him into a blazing star and hurl him into outer space.

Also, he needed something more. It wasn't good enough just to imitate. 'Inspiration! That's what I need,' cried Poltergeist. But where could he get that? Where could a Poltergeist find inspiration?

One night he was thinking of this after God had gone to bed. As he pondered, a white light slowly filled the workshop. It was the full moon, rising and looking in through the window. Poltergeist saw the great white disc reflected in God's mirror. He stared at that reflection. How brilliant and pure it was! Somehow it looked better in the mirror than it did in the sky. But then, as he stared at that great light in the mirror, it seemed to Poltergeist that he heard something. A voice.

'Do it,' said the voice.

'Do it?' thought Poltergeist. 'Do what? And whose voice is this, anyway?'

'Do it,' said the voice again. And suddenly a dazzling idea came into Poltergeist's head. He stared at the Moon's reflection. He suddenly saw how he could make a creature that would be exactly like God's. What a brainwave! He was so excited, his candlestick wobbled on its shelf. But he forced himself to wait. Yes, he would do it. The very next chance, he would do it.

'Thank you very much, Mystery Voice,' he said to the Moon's reflection.

Seeming to smile, the Moon rose slowly past the top edge of the mirror and the workshop became dark.

That next day, Man came to God asking for a friend.

'But I've already given you Woman,' said God in surprise. 'Delightful Woman. And you've also got Baby. I thought you were happy.'

'Oh, no complaints,' said Man. 'It's just that when I'm away in the forests sometimes, I don't know how it is, I get an eerie feeling.'

'Eerie?' queried God.

'I know,' Man went on, 'the world is a wonderful place. A wonderful wonderful place. I wouldn't have it one bit different. But it's also – well – a bit spooky. At times.'

'Spooky?' murmured God, fingering his beard. 'Hm! I wonder what you mean.'

'You know,' said Man, 'I'd like somebody along with me, a happy little friend, so I could say: "Come on, let's be off!" or

"Did you hear that?" or maybe: "Why don't you go and have a look behind that bush?"'

'Hm!' said God. 'I see. A trusty companion.'

'Whatever you think would do the job,' said Man.

God thought for a moment, then said: 'I'll tell you what. You have a go. Come on, make just the friend you want, and I'll breathe life into it.'

'But I can't make things!' cried Man.

'Oh yes you can,' said God. 'You've never tried. But I'll show you. Just do as I say.' And he hoisted a big ball of fresh clay on to his workbench.

'Now first,' said God, 'do this.'

And so he began to show Man how easy it was to shape an animal. All you did was imagine it, then fill up the shape of the thought with clay.

Man suddenly had a vivid picture in his head of the friend he wanted. He laughed with excitement as God guided his hands.

Poltergeist watched closely as Man's fingers, guided by God, worked the clay. He felt intensely jealous. If God could teach Man, why couldn't he teach Poltergeist? Still, in its way this was a perfect lesson. Man was learning. And as Man learned, Poltergeist, too, tried to learn.

Poltergeist could soon see this was going to be a very pretty creature indeed. Lovely slender legs, a lovely bright face with a long, very sweet snout, and brown eyes, really startling brown eyes, almost golden eyes. And a grand tail sweeping upwards, bushy.

God showed Man how to take particular care with the teeth, the toenails, and getting the angle of the ears just right. They worked on it through the whole day. Evening came, and at last the creature seemed to be all but finished. God stroked it, making its fur glisten. Then God set it on the floor and turned it this way and that. He was thinking: 'Because of Man I've put far more care into this than into anything else for quite a while. I want it to be absolutely perfect. And I think that's it. I really think there's no more to be done, except for the life.'

Now Poltergeist knew his moment had come. He had to move fast. Once God breathed life into this creature, it would be too late. God would send it off with Man, and Poltergeist might never see it again. He might never get another chance to do what he planned to do.

So he hurled himself into action.

With a terrific scream, like a thousand Elephants, he tore a wide circle through the forest around God's home.

'Fire!' he screamed. 'Fire! Fire!'

God looked up. The leaping flames reflected in his eyes. So sudden! He hadn't even smelled the smoke. He dashed out where the Poltergeist's scream was being taken up by the real Elephants, along with the screams of the Leopards, the Monkeys, the Cockatoos. All the creatures of the forest were yelling at the top of their voices: 'Help! Help! Fire!'

God set to work, beating out the fire with the palms of his broad hands, occasionally clapping his hands in the clouds to bring out the down-pouring rains. And the rains did come down. Even so it was touch and go as he coughed and choked, reeling in the clouds of sparks and rolling smoke, while the trees exploded around him like soft bombs, and Man bounded home through the forest to warn his wife, and get their belongings together, ready to flee to safety if the fire began to blow that way.

All this time, Man's finished but still unliving companion stood in the middle of the workshop floor, like a stuffed animal, gazing at nothing with bright golden eyes, waiting for life.

Poltergeist sat up on the windowsill, peering at the shaking red mane of the great fire. Now and again, when it looked as though God might be getting the upper hand, Poltergeist shot out and with another tremendous scream blazed a new roaring and popping and cracking and crashing swathe of flames into some untouched part of the jungle.

So God laboured, fighting the conflagration till past midnight. Finally he stamped out the last spark. The rain stopped and the sky cleared. The last reddish billowings of smoke blew off the full Moon, which now hung over the scorched forest tremendously bright and round. It was so bright, it threw God's shadow blackly ahead of him as he trudged home.

Aching, he flopped into his bath. Wearily he crawled into bed. It was only then, as his head sank into the pillow, that he remembered the bright ready creature on his workshop floor, waiting for its breath of life. He smiled. 'Tomorrow's a new day,' he murmured, and was already asleep.

Just as Poltergeist had planned!

The workshop was dark, except for the shaft of brilliant moonlight that came in through the window. Poltergeist did not want to light candles. God might see the glow in the crack of space at the bottom of his bedroom door. Poltergeist had a better idea for lighting up what he wanted to do. Pausing only to listen for God's steady breathing, he lifted the big mirror off the wall, and propped it leaning, nearly upright, against the nose of the new, wonderful, but still lifeless creature, which now stared with unseeing eyes at its double in the mirror. It looked as if it were sniffing at the nose of its own image in the mirror. But the strangest thing was, Poltergeist had so positioned the mirror that the full Moon shone behind the creature's image, reflected in the glass. Its black pricking ears were silhouetted against the Moon. It looked to be wearing a bright silver halo, a dazzling halo.

With the help of the bright moonlight, Poltergeist began to work fast. He pulled out a good-sized lump of clay from beneath God's workbench, and simply filled in that reflected shape in the mirror. This had been his great brainwave, and it worked. All he had to do was pack the clay into that perfect reflection, like clay into a mould. It sounds complicated, but for a Poltergeist it was the easiest thing. Because it was so easy he could work very fast. The Moon rose swiftly from behind the creature's ears, but it still had not passed out of the top of the mirror when Poltergeist had finished. He gave his creation one last close inspection, checking every hair, then he lifted away the mirror from between the creature that Man had made with God's help and the creature he himself had made by the light of the Moon. And there the two creatures stood, facing each other, nose to nose, exactly alike, drenched in moonlight.

It was then that Poltergeist saw his only mistake.

Because he'd leaned the mirror against the nose-end of the creature made by God and Man, the two creatures were not merely nose to nose – they were actually joined at the nose.

Poltergeist examined the noses. There was no sign of a join. One nose simply grew into the other. There was no doubt about it, he'd made a funny sort of mistake here. He stared and stared at the single nose of the double creature. What could he do? Time was passing. Dawn would be here soon, and God would probably choose this day to get up early. What could be done? But he was still thinking when the bedroom door swung open and God strolled into the workshop yawning and stretching.

With a click, Poltergeist was back in his candlestick. And God gazed down, bemused at first, then puzzled, then baffled, then outraged, at the eight-legged monster, the strange double creature that stared at itself with four eyes.

'What?' he shouted, incredulous. His first thought was that he must have sleepwalked. 'Somehow,' he thought, 'I came out here and I did this in my sleep. How else could it have happened?'

He couldn't think of any other explanation. He laughed then, and scratched his head. 'Maybe,' he thought, 'maybe I did just that. What a peculiar business!'

Suddenly he was filled with curiosity. What if he gave this oddity life? How would it manage?

Still not properly awake, he kneeled down and looked under the joined noses. The chins were separate but just touching, just kissing. He pulled them gently down, and with a single breath blew life into both the open mouths at the same time.

But even as he sat back he knew he'd made an error. The four eyes of the double creature rolled wildly. They stared at each other in dismay, over the joined noses, then stared sideways at God. And the eyes seemed to be saying: 'What's this? This can't be right. What's happened?'

Their upcurling bushy tails waved uneasily and they whined softly.

At that very moment, Man appeared in the doorway.

'Just in time,' said God. 'I've just finished your new friend.'

Man stared, licked his lips, blinked, and stared again. Maybe God would explain it to him. 'Are you sure it's right?' he said at last.

'What do you mean, am I sure?' cried God. 'Did you ever see such a pretty beast. Such pretty legs. And ears. And eyes. Such a gorgeous fur. Look at its ruff. And what a tail! One of the finest ever tails.'

'Two of them,' corrected Man.

God frowned. 'Try it,' he said sternly. 'Give it a chance.'

Man looked carefully at the joined noses, and now the two beasts rolled their eyes sideways looking at him. They couldn't bend their heads because their noses had no joint. It was just as if the nose bone went from between the eyes of one to between the eyes of the other.

'Take it,' urged God. 'You might be surprised.'

But the creature could not move. If one had walked forwards, the other would have had to walk backwards. And how many creatures do you see walking backwards? So this creature stood, and swivelled its eyes towards God, then towards Man, then back to God, and whined again.

'Pick it up,' said God. 'Show it you love it.'

And so Man picked up the double beast, one in the crook of each arm, with the joined noses over his head, and carried it home.

Woman gave a short, sharp laugh when he set it down in front of her. Then she stared at it.

'Is it a piece of furniture?' she asked.

Man simply sighed, and went on gazing at the eight-legged freak.

'I know!' cried Woman suddenly, laying her finger in the middle of the long connecting nose. 'Chop it through here. Then we'll have two for one. One for you and one for me. Get the axe.'

The four eyes jerked wildly this way and that way, between Man and Woman, then stared at the finger. First the nose! Now the axe!

Man carried the creature back to God and explained Woman's idea.

'It's a risky thing,' said God, 'to interfere with creation. I'll do it. But we might be sorry. It might cause trouble.'

'Oh!' said Man. 'What's a bit more trouble?'

So, with his thumbnail, God nipped through the middle of the long nose that the two creatures shared. With a yelp, they leaped apart, shaking their heads and pawing at their snouts. God caught one of them, examined the raw nose end, then spat on it and rubbed it.

The other whined and its tail drooped.

'Come on, then,' said God. 'You too. Don't sulk.'

He did the same with that one. And the two creatures, exactly alike, stood there, quite separate, licking their noses. One of them gazed brightly at God, and wagged its upturned tail. The other gazed sidelong at its partner. Its tail still drooped. It yawned, then licked its chops, blinked and gazed out through the doorway.

'Now, my dears,' said God, 'that might have felt a bit painful. But I had to do it, because I wanted to give you both very special noses. Very very special noses. Now you both have the keenest, keenest sense of smell. You might well ask: Why do we need this special sense of smell? Well, why do you need it? Do you know?'

God looked at them as if he expected them to answer. Uptail gazed at him boldly, his big ears angled forward, his eyes gold and bright. Uptail did not know. Downtail gazed at him with lowered head. His eyes were grey, not gold like Uptail's. And his eye-pupils were tiny pinpoints of black. His ears moved, angling this way and that. He did not know either. He gazed at God, waiting for an answer. But as he waited, his ears never stopped listening to all the sounds of the world.

'Your special sense of smell,' said God, 'is to lead you to your maker. Nothing will really satisfy your nose except one thing: the smell of your maker. Once a day, you will have to lick the fingers of your maker. Now, away with you.'

Man was happy. 'Come on, boys,' he cried.

God called after him. 'Just remember. You don't have two creatures there. You have two halves of what was created as one. Halves can be very odd. Keep your eyes open.'

Man strode off, one creature leaping around him, jumping up to him, putting its forepaws on his chest, the other following a few paces behind, its nose and its tail low to the ground, occasionally lifting its head and staring at flowers, as if it heard sounds coming out of them.

From the first moment, the two were quite different. There was no doubt which one was going to be Man's companion. Uptail never left him. When he sat, it rested its chin on his knee and gazed up at him. When he walked, it walked just behind him, keeping its nose within inches of his knee. When he spoke to it, it laughed silently and dangled its tongue.

Man was delighted. 'Fido, I'll call you,' he said. 'Hey, Fido!'

And Fido yelped with excitement, seeming to bounce, then stood with its forepaws on Man's shoulders and gave his whole face a wash with two swipes of its big wet tongue.

'Come on,' cried Man. 'Let's be off!' And he strode away into the forest, with Fido bouncing beside him like a thing made of springs.

Woman looked at Fido's partner. 'I suppose this one's mine,' she was thinking. As she looked into its eyes, it lowered its head, lowered its ears, and glanced away. For some reason she suddenly felt slightly afraid. The house seemed very silent. 'I'll have to make friends,' she thought.

'Come on, Loopy,' she called in a sudden loud voice, and slapped her knee. To her horror Loopy, as she'd called him, leapt up, its legs rigid, all its hair spikily on end, its ears flattened, and snarled into her face. Such a horrible, long, deep snarl that its whole body vibrated.

'Now, now!' she chided. 'Don't you like your new name?

Isn't Loopy quite a good name?' And she reached her hand towards him. She knew she must not let him see she was afraid. She made her voice cheerful and soft. 'Come on, give me a lick, like Fido.'

But it made no difference. Loopy flattened to the floor, his whole face bunched up like a cloth being wrung out, and again he gave a crashing snarl.

Then, with one leap, he was out through the door and gone.

Woman ran to the door and bolted it. She sat down and looked at her hands, which were trembling. 'Well,' she whispered, 'he didn't give me much chance to make friends with him!'

When Man came home and heard her story he remembered God's words about the two halves. Meanwhile Fido searched all over the house, busily sniffing at everything. Man thought: 'Is he glad the other's gone? Or does he miss him?'

Fido seemed to have read his thoughts. His tail swung in great circles, he squirmed his body and reared up at Man with whining yelps. He licked his face again, then licked his hands and fingers. Then across to Woman and before she could stop him he did the same to her, whimpering with happiness. He seemed to have his forelegs almost around her neck.

'Strange!' thought Man. 'Very strange!'

Fido certainly seemed happy.

But out in the forest, Loopy was not happy at all. He wandered along, sometimes his nose to the ground, sometimes sniffing the wind. 'I'm looking for something,' he was thinking, 'but what is it?'

Tirelessly he went on. After a while he began to trot. Then he began to run. As he ran, a thousand smells came drifting past his keen nose.

'But which is my maker?' he thought. 'God said my nose would lead me to my maker.'

He ran on and on through the forest, then out on the ridges of the hills. Sometimes he stopped and sniffed and licked at a stone. Then he ran on. Night fell and he was still running.

Later that night, as Man's fire glowed red, and the potful of mushroom soup bubbled on the flames, Uptail Fido sat with his head on Man's knee, gazing up at the sparks of red fire-glow reflected in his eyes. When Man spoke, Fido laughed silently. And when Man fondled his head, Fido tried to tie his fingers in the slippery loose knot of his tongue.

But suddenly they heard a strange sound. A new sound. Man, Woman and Fido looked up. The round, full, bright Moon now sailed directly above, a great white blaze in mid-heaven. The new sound seemed to come from the Moon. Or perhaps it echoed off the Moon.

High on a rocky hill, above the forest, sat Loopy Downtail. His nose, glistening with God's spittle, pointed at the Moon. Out of his mouth came the new sound, the strange, wailing howl. The forest was motionless. No other creature made a sound. Were they all listening to this new noise among them? What was Loopy Downtail trying to say? Was he crying or singing?

He seemed to be trying to talk. Man and Woman could almost hear words and sentences in the ups and downs of that thin, faraway howl. He seemed to be winding his voice round and round the moonlight. It made Man think of the long tongue of his new companion, Fido, licking and winding round his fingers.

But Fido did not like it at all. He growled a deep angry growl. He did not like to see Man and Woman listening to that howl. He knew who was making it. He wanted to rush off into the forest and silence it. He wanted to chase Loopy Downtail away, right out of hearing.

'Shhh, Fido!' said Man. 'Quiet, boy.'

Woman had stood up. She had turned away from the fire, facing the forest.

'Eat your soup,' said Man. 'It will go cold.'

But she went on standing there. 'Listen to it,' she whispered. 'Only listen.'

And there she stood, ignoring Man and his new friend, and her soup, simply listening to the long wavering howl that seemed to be climbing and climbing towards the Moon.

The Gambler

God was making Frog. He had almost finished. There it sat, green and yellow, with its front toes turned in, and its great golden eyes gazing from two bumps on top of its head.

No fur, no feathers, no scales. Just shiny smooth skin, like wet plastic.

God stared at the creature thoughtfully. It looked very bare.

'Maybe some feathers,' he murmured. 'Or short velvety fur, like Mole. Hm! That might be nice.'

But before he could give anything else to Frog, a shadow fell across the open doorway of his workshop. Man stood there, his face glowing with excitement.

'Well, well, well!' said God. 'What a nice surprise! Any news from the great forest?'

Man held out his two clenched fists in front of him, their backs upwards. He stared at God brightly.

'Guess which holds the black pebble,' he said.

God smiled. Did Man truly think he did not know? He saw the black pebble glowing darkly through the knuckles of Man's left fist. And in his right fist, veiled with a faint pink, he could see a white pebble.

'So what's this?' asked God.

'Don't you see?' cried Man. 'It's a game. Woman invented it. She said: "If you choose which fist holds the black pebble, I'll give you a kiss. But if you choose the white pebble, I give you a slap." '

'So what did you get?' asked God.

'Three slaps. I got it wrong three times in a row.'

'A lot of fun, eh?' smiled God.

'Pretty exciting,' said Man. 'The fourth time I got a kiss.'

God laughed. 'Well,' he said. 'And what if I get it wrong? What do I get? A slap?'

Now it was Man's turn to laugh. Or at least, his mouth laughed. His eyes stayed excited, bright and wild.

'Well,' he said, 'you could give me power to create an animal. A living animal. How about that?'

God became more interested. What sort of animal would Man create, he wondered, if he had the power to do it? He would love to test him. Would he create a beautiful thing? Or a gigantic monster? Or what?

'Very well,' God said. 'Let's say the black pebble is in that hand.' And he tapped the hand that he knew held the white pebble. With a strange croaking shout of glee, Man opened the fist and showed God the white pebble in it.

'Wrong!' he yelled. 'Give me the power.'

God pretended to look surprised. 'Oh dear!' he said. 'What a good thing I'm not going to get a slap. Yes, you've won the power. Use it wisely. Only one creature, remember. What a clever game!'

Man leaped from the workshop doorway on to the lawn. He stabbed both fists into the air. 'I have the power to create,' he yelled. 'I won it!' And he bounded into the forest, eager to tell Woman that he had defeated God in her great new game, and that now he had the power to create a new creature.

God smiled and turned to the Frog. He was still thinking so hard about Woman's strange invention that he forgot all about the extra trimmings he was going to give to Frog. He simply breathed life into it as it was, all bare-skinned and cold-looking.

As Frog drew his first breath, and looked out through his golden eyes for the first time, he croaked: 'Which fist holds the black pebble?' and held his clenched fists up to God. God sat back and laughed. Somehow he had breathed the idea of Woman's game into Frog.

'But you haven't got a pebble,' he said. 'You can't play this game without pebbles.'

'Where are my pebbles?' cried Frog, staring at his empty palms. 'Give me my pebbles, so I can play.'

'You'll have to look in the river,' said God. 'That's where the pebbles are. All colours.'

'Where's the river?' cried Frog. 'Quick! Quick! I can't wait!'

God took him to the river. Frog plunged in and in no time came up with a black pebble in one hand and a glittering jewel in the other. He held out his fists.

'Guess the black,' he croaked.

'And what if I get it wrong?' asked God.

'We change places,' cried Frog. 'I become God and you become a Frog.'

'And what if I get it right?' asked God.

'I give you a kiss,' said Frog.

God laughed again and tapped the little green fist in which he could see the black pebble glowing through quite clearly, just as clearly as he could see the jewel glittering through the other one.

Frog stared at the black pebble on his open palm. God had won. He shrugged. 'Oh well!' he sighed. 'It was a try.' And he jumped back into the river.

'Hey!' called God. 'What about my kiss? Come on – pay your debt. That's the law. If you win, you collect your winnings. If you lose, you pay. That's God's law.'

Frog surfaced and blew him a kiss.

God went laughing back into his workshop. But Frog stared after him. A breeze rippled the river, and Frog felt suddenly very cold. Why did he feel so cold? He dived to the river bed, and buried himself in soft silt, trying to find warmth.

Frog soon realized that every creature had more than him. They all had either fur, or feathers, or scales. Or teeth. Or horns. Or tails. He had only his thin smooth skin. And no tail.

Or they had beautiful voices. Or loud alarming voices. Roars, bellowings, whinings. Or clear, lovely song. Frog could only croak, with a funny little gasping croak.

Also, the other creatures were nearly all wonderful movers. They could fly. Or they could run. They could hurtle about in the bushes and the treetops, or over the stony ground. They could build nests among the spines, or dash through the thorns.

Frog couldn't do any of these things. He had not a single one of these useful ways. He could only crawl very slowly. He could swim, sure enough. But not like the fish, that flashed through the water like bright thoughts, and spun on a twinkle, or vanished into pure speed. All he could do was swim from the bottom of the water up to the surface. And from the surface back down to the bottom. But that didn't seem like very much.

'God forgot to give me the extras,' he muttered to himself. 'I don't have a single thing except what I look like. The other creatures have everything. It's God's fault that I'm so cold and have nothing.'

But then he thought about his black pebble and his jewel. Yes, he had those. And they were something. And suddenly, down there in the silt, he burped a tremendous bubble. It wobbled to the surface and burst there with a booming croak. Frog had just had a most fantastic brainwave. Quickly, he started to search among the river gravels. He had no difficulty in finding another black pebble. Another jewel took a bit more finding, but pretty soon he had one, exactly like the first. Now he had two of each. He put them in the pouch under his chin.

Crocodile was lying on a sandbank, imitating sleep, when suddenly Frog popped his eyes above the surface of the water quite close to the great creature's nose.

'Wakey, wakey!' cried Frog. 'I've got a new game.'

Crocodile's first thought was: 'What a plump little snack!' But he pretended to be interested. 'Oh really?' he said. 'What sort of game?' As he spoke, he moved his feet slightly, ready for a quick rush and a clashing snap.

Frog held out his fists. 'One of my hands holds a black pebble. The other holds a jewel. Which holds the jewel?'

'And what happens if I guess correctly?' asked Crocodile, shifting his chin slightly.

'Well,' said Frog, 'you can eat me.'

'And what if I get it wrong? Obviously you can't eat me,' said Crocodile.

'In that case,' said Frog, 'let's see. Eating me is pretty serious. So it has to be something to match. I'll tell you what. If you get it wrong, you give me all your fangs.'

Crocodile smiled. 'Stupid little beast,' he was thinking. 'Right or wrong, you're my starters.' But he said: 'OK. It's a deal. The black pebble is in your right hand.'

Frog opened his right hand, and there lay a jewel. 'Your fangs are mine,' he croaked. 'And you have to pay up. It's God's law.'

To his absolute horror, Crocodile felt something like a zip fastener unzipping down either side of his jaws, top and bottom, and saw his teeth tumbling out on to the sand. Quick as lightning Frog gathered them all up and stuffed them into his mouth. Crocodile saw them bulging in the baggy pouch under Frog's chin.

Frog couldn't speak, his pouch and mouth were so crammed with Crocodile's fangs. They stuck out between his tightly closed lips at all angles. He gave Crocodile a big wave and dived out of sight. Crocodile let out a toothless roar of fury and flailed the sandbank with his immense, jagged tail – whumpetty-whack! But what could he do? He had lost the game and his teeth were gone. He was astonished. He simply lay there and wept.

Very soon after this, the great black-maned Lion was drinking at the river's edge. He had just eaten an entire Wart Hog. Very salty. But he drank warily, because he knew the river hid Crocodile, with his sudden rush and his dreadful fangs. So Lion jumped back a yard when two golden eyes popped up a yard from his nose. He stared at the green, flat-mouthed face of Frog.

'Who are you?' he growled.

'I am Frog,' croaked Frog. 'And this river is my gambling casino. Do you want to play? Have you the courage to gamble?'

'Play?' rumbled Lion. 'Gamble? For what?'

Frog held out his fists.

'One of my fists holds a black pebble,' he croaked. 'And one holds a jewel. Guess which holds the jewel?'

'Why should I guess?' growled Lion. But then Frog began juggling the black pebble and the jewel from hand to hand, very fast. Lion couldn't help staring at the flashing jewel.

'Well,' said Frog. 'If you guess right, you get the jewel. You can keep it under your tongue, so when you roar your mouth will flash with beauty and all the animals, and the Lionesses as well, will come closer to look.'

Lion blinked.

Frog held his hands behind his back and wriggled his shoulders. Then suddenly brought his fists forward.

'Which?' he cried.

'But what if I guess wrong?' purred Lion.

'Oh, in that case,' said Frog, 'let's see. How much is this jewel worth? Quite a lot. I'll tell you what. If you guess wrong, you give me your roar and your mane.'

Lion laughed with surprise. He was thinking: 'If I lose, I'll whack my great spread hooky paw down on that silly little head, and I'll simply take the jewel off him.'

'OK?' cried Frog. 'Is it a deal?'

'It's a deal,' said Lion. 'And the jewel is in your left hand.'

Frog opened his left hand and there lay the black pebble. 'You've lost,' he croaked. 'And both your roar and your mane are mine. And the loser must pay without fail. It's God's law.'

Then to his horror and bewilderment, Lion felt his mane tearing off like a great Velcro collar. He tried to roar with rage, but to his worse horror no sound came from his throat – only a dry whistle.

And there stood Frog, in the shallows of the river, packing the mane into a tight bale. 'Better luck next time,' he roared, and Lion flattened back his ears in the blast of sound from Frog's mouth – a blast of genuine Lion roar, out of that tiny mouth!

Then Frog was gone, down to the bottom of the river. Lion staggered to the top of a nearby ridge and lay down. He was stunned. How had it happened so quickly? No mane. And no roar. He covered his head with his great paws, and let the tears seep down through the furry wrinkles of his great face. His chest was heaving with rage. But what could he do? He had lost.

*

So Frog started his amazing career as a gambler. He challenged every animal. 'If you win,' he would say, 'you can eat me.' Or: 'If you win, you get this big jewel.' No animal could resist.

The forfeit for losing was always the thing they valued most: their fur, or their speed, or their strength, or their tails, or their beautiful feathers. Elephant lost his trunk and his tusks and his great ears. Giraffe lost her superb tail and her thrilling jigsaw spots. Tiger lost his stripes, his leap, and the talons of his right front paw. Humming Bird lost her brilliant cloak of feathers and had to hop about like a tiny plucked chicken the size of a beetle. Cobra lost her fangs and Rattlesnake his rattle. Rhinoceros lost his horn, his sense of smell and the toughness of his thorn-munching mouth. Weasel lost her dance and the whiteness of her belly. Porcupine lost his spines and Skunk her stink weapon and her gorgeous feathery black tail. Jaguar lost his black rosettes and the power of his green gaze. Macaw lost his fiery feathers and the beak that could crack a brazil nut.

And so on. Every animal lost their best possession to the cold-eyed smiling Frog. Frog stored all these winnings in a cave under the river bank. And never once did he lose. Oh no, he was far too smart for that. How could he lose?

What the animals did not know was that Frog was cheating. That had been his brainwave: how to cheat. That was why he had collected two black pebbles, and two jewels.

When he said: 'Which hand holds the black pebble?' both black pebbles were in his pouch, while his two fists each held a jewel. The guesser could not possibly win. Whichever hand he then chose for the black pebble always held a jewel. And when Frog said: 'Which hand holds the beautiful jewel I just showed you?' he had already hidden both jewels in the pouch under his chin and each of his fists held a black pebble. He

258

was so nimble and swift with his hands, no animal ever saw
him do the trick. And none of them ever suspected a trick. It
was the first time any of them had ever gambled. They were
all still so trusting!

But what was Frog going to do with his winnings? His plan
was simple. When he had won enough, he was going to go to
God and gamble again with God – this time using his trick.
Yes, he would cheat God. And the deal would be, when God
lost he would have to let Frog use and wear all his winnings
as his very own, whenever he wanted. So he would be able to
stroll out in his Porcupine armour. Or he would leap across
the plains like a Gazelle. Or he could shake down a tree-load
of ripe fruit with his Elephant trunk. And he would always be
warm, wrapped in his Otter's pelt with its seal-fur lining.

But what about the animals who had lost? They were
raging, weeping, wailing, whining. At first they had been
ashamed of losing their most precious possessions, and had
kept their losses secret. But soon they were telling each other.
Frog had defeated them all. Frog was worse than a tyrant. He
was taking everything from everybody with his two little
green fists and his great wide green smile and his cold golden
eyes.

The animals came to God. They told him about Frog's
game. 'You've made him too lucky,' they cried. 'He never
never never never never loses. He's taken everything we
had.'

God listened gravely and nodded. Frog had certainly been
busy. Finally he said to them: 'Go home quietly and leave it
to me.'

As God sat on his veranda, thinking what to do about Frog,
he saw a movement on his lawn. Frog was crawling slowly
towards him. God waited as Frog heaved himself slowly up

the steps and on to God's veranda, where he squatted, pulsing his chin pouch and gazing up at God through his brilliant eyes.

'What's the news today?' asked God in a friendly voice. 'How are you enjoying the river?'

Frog's answer was to hold up his two fists. 'The game!' he croaked. 'Remember? Let's have another round. I challenge you.'

God waited a moment, then said: 'I'll tell you what. First, we play your game, then we play mine. How about that?'

Frog lowered his fists. He wasn't sure he liked the sound of this.

'What's your game?' he asked.

'Oh, you'll see,' said God. 'Quite exciting, in its way. Let's play yours first, then I'll show you mine.'

Frog showed God the jewel and the black pebble. Then he held his hands behind his back and fumbled there. Finally, he brought his two fists forward.

He had a special gambling voice. 'Which hand holds the black pebble?' he cried.

'And if I win?' asked God.

'Whatever you like. I'll give you a kiss if you like,' said Frog. And he laughed a croaky laugh.

'And if I lose?' asked God.

'Then you let me wear and use all my winnings as if they were my own,' cried Frog. And his chin pouch pulsed. He knew this was the big moment. Also, he knew God could not win, because both black pebbles were already in his mouth. His two fists held only the two jewels.

God pondered and gazed at the little fists, pretending to think deeply. He could see quite clearly that neither fist held a black pebble. He could see both black pebbles lying together in Frog's chin pouch, like eggs in a nest.

At last he said: 'I think I have it.'

Frog waited. His raised fists trembled slightly. What if God should see through his trick?

But God reached out his forefinger and touched Frog's left fist. 'That one,' he said. 'There's the black pebble.'

Frog opened his hand slowly and showed God the jewel. 'I'm afraid, God,' he said solemnly, 'you've lost.'

God sighed and slapped his knees. 'Your luck,' he said, 'is unbeatable. It's unbeatable.'

'And are all my winnings now truly mine?' cried Frog eagerly. 'That was the deal.'

'Yes, that was the deal,' said God. 'They're yours as if I'd given them to you when I made you. What a pity though. This will be terrible news for the rest of the animals.'

'They'll get used to it,' cried Frog. 'When I had nothing at all I nearly got used to it.' And he turned to go. He had scrambled and flopped down a step or two when God said:

'Wait a minute. Now you have to play my game.'

Frog stared.

'Come on,' said God. 'That was the deal. You can't possibly lose, you know that. You never lose.'

Frog wasn't so sure. He had never played anybody else's game. He heaved himself back up on to the veranda. He suddenly felt quite chilly.

God was holding out both his open hands, palm upwards. On his right palm sat a tiny ball of clay. Frog looked at the clay. 'Is that your black pebble?' he asked in a low voice. God chuckled.

'Yes,' he said. 'In a way. Actually, I was thinking I'd give this to Man, to make his new creature. You remember how he won the game against me? He won the power to make a crea-ture. I thought this might help him.' And he chuckled again.

What was God up to? Frog felt very uneasy. He licked his

lips with his long tongue. 'OK,' he said. 'Let's get it over. What do I win if I win?'

'Well,' said God. 'What would you like?'

Frog thought for a moment, and licked his lips again. 'If I win,' he said, 'you have to give me perfect luck. So that I never never never lose a game. No matter what. Ever ever.'

God raised his eyebrows. 'Very well. That will certainly be a huge prize. Why, you could gamble for the whole creation and everything in it.'

'And win it,' said Frog with a broad smile.

'OK,' said God. 'It's a deal. Now, which hand holds the clay?' And he simply turned his hands over, closing them as he did so.

Frog was secretly overjoyed. 'God doesn't know how to play the game,' he thought. 'He's forgotten to hide his hands behind his back while he juggles the clay about between them.' But he pretended to think hard.

'By the way,' said Frog. 'You've forgotten to say what I have to pay if I lose.' Frog was smiling to himself. He was so sure of winning. God really did seem not very clever.

'Oh goodness! How stupid I am!' cried God. 'Well, yes, now let's think. Well – I'll tell you what. Everything you've won off all the animals – if you lose you give it to me. That's not much to set against the whole creation, is it? I can't think of anything else.'

Frog frowned. For some reason he felt confused. His head was whirling. He stared at God's fists. At least, he knew which held the clay. So he didn't really have to bother about losing. How could he lose?

'It's a deal!' he croaked. 'And the clay is in your left hand.'

God turned his left fist over and slowly opened it. Frog stared at the empty palm. Empty? Empty? How could it be empty? 'Where's the clay?' he wailed. And his body seemed to freeze to a block of ice. Had he lost? Had he lost everything? All his winnings? No! No!

God shook his head gently. 'I'm afraid,' he said, 'you've lost. You've lost everything you ever won.' Opening his right hand, God showed Frog the ball of clay.

Frog's eyes had gone dry. He blinked them and licked them to wet them.

'Everything?' he whispered. And he drooped. He seemed to sink into a little heap, till his chin rested on the floor between his toes. His eyes were closed.

'I can't bear it,' he whispered. 'The animals will eat me alive.' He crouched there silent. But suddenly he moved.

'Give me another chance!' he cried. 'One chance. Oh, please, God. One little chance. One more round.'

'Very well,' said God. 'But it will have to be my game.'

Frog nodded weakly. 'Anything you say, God. But give me a chance.'

'OK,' said God, 'this time the ball of clay gives you power to change yourself, in a flash, to whatever you want to be. So if you choose the clay, that's what you win.'

Frog stared greedily at the little ball of clay. His hopes perked up a little.

'And this,' said God, 'is a hop.' And opening his left hand he showed him a tiny rose thorn.

'A hop?' asked Frog. 'What's a hop?'

'You know,' said God. 'Hop, hop, hop. Hippety hop. Pretty useful in a tight corner. So even if you don't get the clay, and the power to be anything you want – '

'I get the hop,' whispered Frog.

God nodded.

'Now choose,' he said. And he held out his two fists. Once again, he hadn't bothered to juggle the ball of clay and the rose thorn. Frog stared at the right fist – the one that had held the clay. But he wasn't going to be caught again this time.

'The clay is in the left,' he croaked.

God opened his left hand and showed him the rose thorn.

At that moment, a Lion's roar shook the air. Elephant was trumpeting through his trunk. Humming Bird whizzed among the jacaranda flowers. The plains and the forests shook with joy as all the animals found their losses suddenly restored.

Quickly, without another word, Frog hopped back towards the river.

And God sat smiling, watching him go, and listening to the joyful uproar of his creation. He tossed the two rose thorns on to the table, and carefully took the tiny ball of clay out of his ear.

'You can't beat God,' he chuckled.

The Screw

God looked up in dismay. What had happened to the Sun?
The light was failing.

There, in the middle of the sky, the Sun darkened. It wasn't
an eclipse or a cloud or a dust storm. Yet the Sun was glowing a weird red. Slowly, as God watched, it turned purple.
Then dark indigo. Then the Earth went dark.

All around him, with a roar, the cries of the creatures went
up. Panicky screeches of birds caught in the dark far from
their roosts. Wailing and hooting of the great herds of
Antelopes, only halfway through their eating. Shrieking of
the mice, dashing blindly into the wrong holes. Yelling of the
Owls in delight at the early start.

God climbed up the sky and began to inspect the dark Sun.
It was still very hot. His breath sent rainbow colours writhing
over it as he turned it on its axle and peered for faults. No
good. He would have to open it up and examine the works.

Chimpanzee, who had swung up behind him, clinging to
the string of his apron, reached out to touch the huge gloomy
globe.

'Watch it!' cried God, and slapped Chimp's hand away.
'Touch that with your fingernail,' he warned, 'and it will
frazzle you to the armpit. It's not as cool as it looks. The
black heat is fiercer than the white. What are you doing here
anyway? Get back to Earth.'

Then gently he began to unscrew one of the Sun's hidden
screws.

Dangling from the apron string, Chimpanzee watched.
And now God looked round for somewhere to put the screw.
Everywhere was sky. Finally, he nested the screw carefully on

the buckle of his sandal, and started on the next one. Soon he had four screws snuggling there, in the buckle of his sandal, while he began to ease open the trap door in the belly of the Sun.

At that moment, Chimpanzee reached out and with the tip of his finger and thumb took a screw.

His screech startled God so badly, he almost let go of the massive panel of the trap door, which would have banged down on his head. He only just saved it. He glared round in fury.

'Ape!' he roared. But he ignored Chimpanzee's flailing hand with its scorched finger and thumb. He was watching that screw falling through space. At the same time, he could not move to do anything about it. He held up the heavy trap-door panel of the Sun with one hand, while he reached cautiously down to rescue the three screws from his sandal buckle with the other, and put them between his lips. Then with his freed hand he cuffed Chimpanzee and sent him spinning down after the falling screw. Chimpanzee had not let go of the apron string. When the blow came, he clutched it even tighter. So he fell, still clinging to the apron, which had been torn off God's waist, and now fluttered above the falling Chimp like a half-open parachute.

'Find that screw!' God bellowed through his closed lips. 'When I've done this job I shall need it.'

When it reached Earth, the screw fell through branches and buried itself in dead leaves at the foot of a tree. Chimpanzee, falling the same way, crashed through the branches and bounced on the dead leaves. He lay there a moment, stunned. Then sniffed. A new smell!

He sniffed at his scorched hand in the darkness. Not quite that. Then he saw a glowing spiral of smoke rising from the dead leaves beside him. He parted the leaves and saw the screw, in a nest of smouldering leaves. Chimp was not brilliant, but he had his little flashes. And straightaway he knew what had happened. He knew what this was.

A baby Sun!

Poor old God was so dumb! Now Chimp knew why the Sun had gone dark. God simply hadn't understood. How could he know about babies?

Chimp was wildly excited. But as he peered into the glow, something came blundering out of the undergrowth behind him. Chimp was shouldered aside, and who stood there but Wild Boar, gazing joyfully into the pulsing den of little flames, where the screw was beginning to glow again.

'Come on! All of you!' squealed Wild Boar. 'A bit of the Sun's fallen off. We've got it to ourselves!'

Chimp could hear the whole family of Wild Boar storming through the forest. He had to move fast if he was going to save the Sun's child. These pigs had no idea. They would probably trample it out, or lie on it with their thick skins. He shook God's apron in front of Wild Boar's nose.

'This,' he announced in a loud voice, 'is God's apron. As you can see. And God said: "Wrap up the baby Sun, which you will find hidden in the dead leaves, and bring it to me." And he said: "Here, wrap it in my apron."'

Wild Boar stepped back and blinked. What was all this about God? Wild Boar was afraid of God.

Quickly, Chimpanzee folded the glowing screw and the smouldering mass of dead leaves into God's apron, wrapped it all up and, crying 'God is waiting', he set off at a run.

Fast as he ran, the rumour ran faster. The wild pigs were blabbermouths all right. Panting along, he heard Toucan shriek: 'Chimp's got a bit of the Sun! He's stolen it!' Then he heard Bongo bray: 'Chimp's stolen the Sun's heart!' Then he heard Anaconda howl: 'Chimp's pinched the Sun! No wonder it's dark. Chimp's got the Sun! Chimp's killed the Sun!'

And on all sides the creatures took it up: 'Chimp's pinched the daylight!' and 'Chimp's robbed God!' and 'Chimp's got the Sun in a bag!' and 'The Sun fell and Chimpanzee's eaten it!'

'Here he is,' screeched Fruit Bat. 'He's running away with the Sun. Catch him.'

And so, with Fruit Bat screeching above him, the running Chimp could hear all the creatures stumbling after him through the forest. 'Save the Sun!' they were screaming, and 'Chimp's got the Sun. Catch him!'

'Oh!' he cried. 'Foolish beasts! Brainless boobies!'

And still hugging his bundle he leapt into the cave of the chimpanzees.

'Who's that?' yelped his wife, from her cosy ledge.

Chimp didn't answer. Instead, he unrolled the apron. The glow of the screw in the smouldering leaves reflected from all the gems embedded in the cave walls and ceiling, and in the eyes of his wife.

'It's a bit of the Sun,' she cried.

'No,' he shouted. 'Don't you see? It's the Sun's baby. I saw it born. Look! I knew you'd love it.'

He had to shout. The din of all the creatures outside the cave was terrific, and growing louder. There were more every minute. And the floor of the cave shook with their commotion.

'What's going on out there?' his wife shouted. But Chimp couldn't hear her for the uproar, and he didn't see her lips move in the glow of the screw, because at that moment Buffalo bounded into the cave.

All the creatures outside fell silent.

'Where is the Sun you've stolen?' thundered Buffalo. 'You're under arrest.'

Chimp moved his mouth, but no words came out. The very sight of Buffalo, with his great eyes glowing red in the screw-light, and his black body glistening, had knocked all the words out of him.

But his wife had her brainwaves too. It came to her in a flash.

'Oh Buffalo,' she cried, 'thank goodness you've come. Quick, before it dies. Look, you can see it's dying. It's the newborn Sun. Oh! Oh! We have to save it. We have to keep it alive.'

And she pointed to the dim glow of the screw, in its leaves. Buffalo stared at the screw. Depending on how you thought, it could look to be growing slightly brighter, or fading slightly duller. It was very hard to be sure.

'Quick!' cried Chimp's wife. 'Bring in all the animals. I need them all. I know how to save its life. But I need their help.'

Buffalo was confused. But maybe she was right. If the Sun had shrivelled to that crumb of glow, it surely was in a poor way. It did make him think of a new-born calf, trembling there and not quite sure if it could ever get up. Yes, it certainly looked as if it needed help. It needed a nudge of some kind.

'Quick!' yelled Mrs Chimp, and she slapped his buttock. Then she turned and whispered to her husband.

Buffalo brought all the creatures crowding in.

'Keep to the walls,' he bellowed. 'Give it lots of air. It's only just born.'

Buffalo made a good policeman. Red eyes bobbed obedi-ently round the walls of the cave, under the sparkly gleam of the gemstones.

Chimp had gone out, but now came in again with God's

apron stuffed with dry dead leaves. He was doing exactly as his wife had told him to do. Then he came in again with twigs and sticks. Then again with lumps of broken dead branch. He made a gigantic heap of all these, while the creatures surrounded the glow in a circle of red eyes.

His wife was now explaining to all these creatures just what had to be done.

'This,' she said, 'is the newborn Sun. But, as you can see, he's very feeble. He needs strength. He needs help. He needs encouragement.'

The eyes glowed. Chimp was arranging more dead leaves over the screw and blowing on it softly. The whole lot suddenly flared. Little flames jumped and tossed up a few sparks.

'You see,' she cried. 'Even just looking at it you're giving it strength. But what it really needs is to feel at home.'

The eyes blinked, flickered and glowed again. There must have been fifty different animals in there, and over two hundred birds, with quite a few reptiles.

'What we need,' she went on, 'is to make this place like Heaven, where the Sun lives. Now you – 'And she pointed to Hare. 'You be the Moon. Come on.'

Hare tottered forward, uncertain. What did it mean, being Moon? 'How do I be Moon?' she muttered.

But Mrs Chimp was pointing at Anaconda. 'And you,' she said, 'you are the Planet Mercury.'

'The Planet Mercury?' boomed the great snake. 'Has it legs?'

'And you,' she pointed to Leopard. 'Be Venus.'

Leopard blinked, and twirled her tail tip.

So Mrs Chimp went on. And in no time she had them all ready. Wild Boar was the Planet Mars. Lion was Jupiter. Buffalo was Saturn. Horse was Neptune. Hyena was Uranus. Rat was Pluto. And Wolf was the One Without a Name.

All the rest she spaced around the walls in twelve groups. Each group had three or four animals, but mostly they were birds, no two the same, and all of them more and more excited.

'You,' she said to them all, 'are the Constellations. The fixed stars. You all stay where you are. But get ready to sing. When I start singing, all you – sing your heads off. Sing as if you were blazing stars.'

Then she turned to the nine chosen animals. 'And you,' she said, 'are the Planets. You can sing too, but mainly you have to dance. Now, Moon?'

Hare pricked up both ears, then flopped them again. She was wishing she had never come.

'Start dancing around the Sun,' ordered Mrs Chimp, 'just as the Moon in the real Heaven dances around the Sun in the real Heaven. Go on. Start. Close to the baby.'

Hare lifted her very big feet and hobbled a bit, feeling foolish.

'Dance,' yelled Mrs Chimp. And Hare leapt. Then, getting the hang of it, leaping and flinging her limbs, she capered around the bright fiery screw, where Chimp crouched feeding more dead leaves and now a few twigs into the merry little blaze.

'Now me,' sang Mrs Chimp. 'I'm Earth!'

And to the absolute amazement of all the beasts there, she began to twirl and leap around Hare, and Hare twirled around her, and they both twirled around the struggling little fire which the black hands fed with more and more sticks.

'Now, Mercury!' yelled Mrs Chimp. And Anaconda, keen to show off his magnificent curves, came writhing over the cave floor, and spun and knotted and unknotted the most stunning dance, around the blazing screw, outside the twirling Moon and Earth.

'Come on, Venus,' yelled Mrs Chimp.

Leopard leapt into the dance as if she'd practised for months. She seemed to be twisting through her own signature over and over in giant, ferocious flashing letters, with a whizzing flourish of tail. And she couldn't help it: as she spun and writhed and somersaulted around the others, she began to sing. It was if her wild contortions were squeezing the song out of her, like a mad and bounding concertina.

'Now, Mars,' yelled Mrs Chimp.

Wild Boar seemed to explode into dancing. He whirled like a top. He cartwheeled like a Catherine wheel, his tusks glittering in the throbbing flames of the screw, as Chimp fed in more leaves and bigger sticks. Sparks swarmed up, and the song coming out of Wild Boar resounded like a great iron bridge played by girders for drumsticks.

Soon, the whole lot were whirling there. On the outside, close to the Constellations, Wolf, a shaggy, raggy shape, danced on his hind legs with fiery eyes, his head flung back, letting a weird, wailing twist of song come straight up out of him, biting it off in lengths with savage clashings of his long jaws. Closer to the fire, Rat was going round and round, bouncing like a ball, singing in a deep, surprising bass voice, and each time he bounced was like the boom of a deep drum. And round and round, closer to the fire, Horse bucked and cavorted, like a rodeo jumper, all electrical flashings and shudderings, and seeming to shower off sparks, at the same time singing in a thrilling counter-tenor voice. Then next, closer to the fire, Buffalo. That was something. The dance of the Buffalo! And the song! Then Lion, who seemed to whirl in tatters of fiery air, like a dancer of seven burning veils. Then Wild Boar. Then Leopard. Then Anaconda. And on the inside, close to the blaze, Hare and Mrs Chimp, round and round and round.

And the Constellations, their eyes brighter than ever as the blaze grew and flung up its long orange tongues, they couldn't keep out of it. They began to jig where they stood. And all the birds sang as if every bird wanted to deafen the rest.

After a while, Chimp simply heaped all his branches and logs on to the fire, which now poured straight up like an upside-down waterfall of flame roaring into a cloud of smoky sparks. Then he sat back amazed, listening to that incredible noise, and watching the wild, whirling shapes of the animal Heaven, and the huger, wilder whirling shapes of their shadows on the glittering walls.

How long did it go on?

The animals didn't care. They no longer knew where they were, while their limbs flew and their song shook the mountain over the cave.

They never heard Chimp's shout. And they never noticed, as he dodged through the dancers, and stood in the cave mouth, waving his arms and shouting.

But then his wife did notice. She stopped dancing. Hare banged into her and went sprawling into the ashes of the fire, which were soft and warm. The fire was out! How long had the fire been out?

That broke the spell. The singing faltered. The dancers staggered to a panting stop. Then in silence they all stared at the cave mouth where Chimp's black shape was silhouetted against the bright sunlight.

Of course, they all rushed out under the recovered Sun.

'Success!' they sang. 'We got the Sun going!'

God was coming through the forest. He stopped, watching the creatures scattering joyfully. Chimp, standing in the mouth of the cave, saw God, and suddenly he felt horribly guilty. He'd forgotten something. What was it he'd forgotten?

'My screw,' said God. 'Have you got it?'

But that was the first Disco.

Camel

Camel was a mistake. He was simply made wrong. He stood in God's backyard, where the different kinds of clay and the fuel for the kilns lay in heaps, and he knew he was wrong.

And he felt wrong all over.

He opened his mouth, which was a bit like a horse's mouth, but longer, droopier, and somehow wrong. He opened it and strained. A groan came out. Then he strained again.

God could see that Camel was trying to speak.

Camel wanted to cry: 'Why have you made me like this? I'm all wrong. Take me back and remake me.' But nothing came out.

God did try to remake Camel. But it was no good. When the inside's wrong, the outside can never be right. He tried different tails. All seemed wrong on Camel.

He tried different feet. In the end he put back the first set – great, spreading, foolish feet that they were.

Camel's hump seemed badly wrong. But when God took it off, Camel fell on his nose. So he had to put that back too.

Finally God gave up, and Camel stood there with his head like a giant sheep, his neck like an old snake looking out of a tree, his back like a sand dune, and his long knock-kneed legs like a photographer's broken tripod.

He stretched out his neck and groaned. He wanted his groan to say: 'Remake me.'

But God shook his head. 'My first real failure!' he sighed. 'I'll have to scrap you, I'm afraid.'

Camel flung up his head. 'Scrap me?' He knew what that meant. It meant going on to the spare-parts heap.

He swung round and got his legs going. He went out through the yard gate in a cloud of dust. No matter how wrong and horrible he was, he didn't want to become nothing but spare parts for other creatures.

He loped into the middle of a valley full of dry thorn bushes, and stood there, hoping nobody could see him.

God would have chased Camel, but at that moment Man walked into his yard with a bleeding head. Woman was supporting him.

'The hair's not enough!' she wailed. 'It's no protection at all.'

'What's happened?' cried God. He was horrified to see that one of his best inventions had been damaged.

Man was so busy holding his head, and Woman was so busy comforting him, and God was so busy looking at the great scratches on Man's forehead, that none of them saw a dark shape leap up into the tree beside the gate. The boughs shook for a moment, then two green eyes peered out through the shadows of the leaves.

'Did you fall?' cried God.

'It was Monkeys,' Man gasped. 'A Monkey tried to claw all my hair off.'

God saw what was needed. He had just prepared the skin for a new kind of Pig. It hung on the line. Now he took it down and with a few skilful twists – there it was. A hat. A new protective hat. Almost a helmet.

He spat on Man's wounds, which healed instantly, and fitted on the helmet.

'Oh!' cried Woman. 'But it's so cute! Oh, please, God, me too. A Monkey could get me too. Oh, please, a hat for me too.'

'Quite easy,' murmured God. This time he took the skin of a big bushy sort of Weasel he'd been thinking about. The skin of a Fisher. With a few deft folds and tucks, there it was – finished. A pretty fur hat, with the tail dangling behind. Woman gave a squeal of pleasure as she fitted it on.

'Now you, God,' she cried. 'One for yourself. Let's all have hats.'

The green eyes in the dark tree jerked upwards a little, getting a better view, and blinked rapidly. Then they glowed, fiercer than before, watching the hats.

God smiled. These hats were a brilliant new idea. Man looked more powerful. Woman looked prettier. He scratched his beard and thought: 'Well, what about it? Why not a hat for me too?'

Suddenly, at that moment, he felt uneasy. He could feel something watching him. He turned. But he saw nothing, because the green eyes in the dark tree had closed tightly, just in time. They knew they glowed.

'This creature that attacked you,' said God. 'Are you sure it was a Monkey?'

'He thinks it was,' said Woman. 'But let me tell you, God, that was no Monkey. Monkeys don't have hooked claws. They have fingernails like me. Monkeys aren't bald.'

'Bald?' cried God. 'You say it was bald?'

The green eyes in the dark tree opened again and stared.

'Take no notice of her,' said Man. 'It was pitch black in the jungle.'

But God was frowning. 'Did you see footprints?' he asked.

'Like a Frog!' cried Woman. 'A Frog the size of a Gorilla.'

The green eyes blinked and became slits.

Man tried to change the subject. 'What about a hat for you, God,' he said. 'How about it? How about the whole sky? That would be some hat!'

'With the shooting stars!' cried Woman. 'And birds flying in it. And a thundercloud for a crest. And rain falling!'

Both God and Man laughed at that.

'A heavenly hat!' cried Woman.

That night when God went to sleep, he wasn't thinking about a hat. He was thinking about those footprints like a giant Frog's.

'So the Demon is back on Earth,' he whispered. 'And it sounds as though he's after Man.'

As he lay thinking in the dark, a small Bat came creeping down the wall, head downwards. It moved slowly. Its green eyes were tightly closed. Finally, it was hanging just above God's head.

It was the Demon! Sitting in the tree by the gate, it had heard and seen everything about the hats. And now, after making itself into this tiny Bat, it hung near God's head, trying to hear God's thoughts.

It was true, this Demon had grabbed at Man's head. But all he'd wanted was the hair. Actually, what he had really wanted was Woman's hair. But in the gloom of the forest he had grabbed at the wrong head. His wife had sent him to steal Woman's hair. And she wanted this thick mass of ringlets because she herself was as bald as the Demon himself.

The Demon didn't dare to go back to her without something. She was a terror. He was frightened of her. Sometimes, he thought he might just run away, and never go back to her at all. But he didn't even dare to run away. He always went creeping back, usually carrying whatever she wanted.

She always wanted something. She was so jealous of God's Creation that she wanted to make another exactly like it, but inside the Earth, under the Red Mountains. She sent the Demon out to steal God's creatures and plants. She now had a great many down there, though they had a poor time of it in the dark. But she was never satisfied. She always wanted more. And at the moment, her craze was to have the long thick hair of Woman.

But now the Demon had an idea. Instead of Woman's hair, he would get God's hat. He had seen how wonderful Man and Woman looked in their hats. And the hat hid the hair. Just as it would hide the baldness. Therefore a hat was better than hair. He could just hear himself saying to his wife: 'Here you are, my beauty, here is God's hat for you. I snatched it from God's own head for your sake.'

Then she would let out a shriek of delight that would probably shatter a big jug. 'God's own hat!' she would hiss. 'On my wicked little head!' Then she would laugh and give him a kiss that would tear half his moustaches out by the roots.

So the Demon listened deeply to God's thoughts. And after about an hour he could tell that God was no longer worrying about Demons. He had begun to think about hats. He was thinking: 'How about a hat with a crest like a Peacock? A hat made, say, of Leopard skin, with a ridge of Eagle tail feathers – as a high crest. And maybe a long flap behind, like a Peacock's tail, to keep the sun off the back of my neck?'

Then he thought: 'That was a funny idea of Man's – the whole sky for a hat! With shooting stars.'

He chuckled. But then, abruptly, he sat bolt upright in bed. A dazzling thought had just come to him. An inspiration!

He leapt out of bed. 'What a hat!' he cried. And he ran through into his workshop. 'Quick, quick,' he gasped, 'before you forget it. Oh what a hat!' And he set to, there and then, making the hat of his dreams.

He did not notice how a tiny Bat swooped from the wall over his bed and followed him, flitting low over the floor, and flew up to hang again, upside down, under his worktable.

Camel was tramping across the skyline. He had decided the

safest place for him was as far from God's scrapheap as he could get. As he ambled along the animals jeered at him:

'Hey, nose in the air, don't fall in a hole,' yelled a Coyote.

'Hey, galoshes, don't tread on your neck,' laughed the Gekko.

Camel just ambled on, pretending to watch the horizon. He had a funny walk. Each leg swung like a pendulum.

'Hey,' whistled a Canary. 'I need a bump on my back. Have you brought it?'

'Here he comes,' cheered the Baboon, 'with my new tail. Here comes the travelling heap of spare parts.'

'Have you brought my spare ribs?' asked the Leopard with a smile.

After a few hours of this, Camel thought of burying his head in the sand. The news had travelled fast and far. Even the Spiders in the thorn bushes knew what God thought of him.

'Maybe,' he was thinking, 'that is what it means, being a mistake. There's no place for a mistake. And I'm a mistake.'

So he walked all night. And as dawn lit the sky he found he had come in a wide circle. He recognized the hill and God's workshop. He was right back where he'd started.

Then he saw an amazing thing. It seemed the Sun was rising on God's hill. But at once he saw it was not the Sun. It was something altogether peculiar. It was God in a hat. But what a hat!

And as the real Sun rose in the east, God's hat blazed out in the west. The birds didn't know which way to turn. The animals ran in circles. But then they all started running towards God.

His hat was astounding.

It was a great pale blue dome of turquoise. And moving up

from the edge, from just above the middle of God's brow, was a huge, glowing ruby – like the red rising Sun.

The birds cried out, as if they could hardly bear it. The animals crowded to watch. As the real Sun rose in the east, and went behind a cloud, the dazzling ruby in God's hat rose higher, but instead of going behind a cloud it became brighter than ever, and golden. It had turned over. And now it was a huge round diamond, with gold behind it, so that it shone gold.

Man lowered his eyes and simply stood there trembling. Woman gazed and gazed, and her eyes filled with tears, as if to protect themselves from the dazzling fieriness of the hat.

And when all his creatures were gazing at him – and even Camel was gazing from behind a distant thorn bush – God took off his hat.

What he did then sent a cry of amazement through all his creatures. He turned the hat inside out!

And now that he put it back on his head, they could see that it was made of lapis lazuli, which is the rich, dark blue stone full of gold flecks like the night sky. And in this dark blue dome were studded all the Constellations of stars, as diamonds, emeralds and rubies, and a great Moon rose there made of tiny pearls.

Then God took the hat off again, punched it inside out, put it back on, and there was the blazing golden Sun again, climbing the turquoise dome.

'Which is best,' he asked Woman, 'to wear the day by day and the night by night? Or the day by night and the night by day? Which?'

But all she could say, in a trembling voice, was: 'Oh, God, what a hat! What a heavenly hat!'

At that moment a small black Bat appeared from nowhere. The Camel thought it was a big Bluefly. It landed on the hat and at the same moment became enormous. A Bat bigger than an Elephant wrenched off God's hat and flew upwards with it.

A roar of dismay went across the world.

God flailed his arms. Man and Woman stared up in terror.

'It's Frog-foot!' screamed Woman.

But God was quick. He hurled a thunderbolt. The Bat dodged in the air as the bolt went smoking past. Another followed and just scorched the claws of his left foot. He changed direction and flew at the sea. The next thunderbolt sizzled past his ear and went into a cloud.

Immediately the cloud seemed to explode. It started to stab downward lightnings at him. Terrible electric shocks ran along the tips of his moustache and stood crackling there. His eyes went orange, then red.

With a yell he dropped the hat.

All the creatures saw the glorious hat tumble from the sky, and the splash that went up as it hit the sea.

None saw what had become of the Demon Bat. He had become a tiny Kingfisher, the size of a Sparrow, and he was already scooting along within inches of the sea, in the hollows of the waves, where not even God could see him. And so he got to land and vanished into a clump of bamboo.

God sat on the dunes weeping. He simply could not believe it. The Demon! All the animals and the birds cried under the trees and in the trees. Woman rested her head on God's wrist, to console him. Man sat at his feet, his head bowed.

Camel watched it all. If only Woman would console him, as she consoled God! Then, heaving a deep breath, he groaned a long, soft groan.

Woman made God some hot supper. Outside, the Sun was sinking to the edge of the world as a fiery red ball.

'At this moment,' sighed God, 'somewhere in the depths of

the sea, the great diamond on my hat will have turned over, and the ruby will be glowing in its place, sinking towards the rim of the hat.' And he sighed again.

Then, a few minutes later, when the Sun had gone down and the full Moon was rising above the other side of the world, he said: 'And now my pearly Moon will be rising from the rim of the hat – but inside! All watched by the fishes. All in the bottom of the sea!' And he sighed again.

'What you need,' said Man, 'is some creature to go down there, and find it, and bring it back up.'

God looked at Man. Man had good ideas.

'Maybe some big fish could do it,' Man went on.

God shook his head.

'I didn't give them enough brains. If I had, they would have wanted to live on land. They'd have been unhappy in the sea. And I didn't want that.'

'Camel!' shouted Woman. She shouted in fright, because the Camel, still thinking about how Woman had comforted God, had just put his head in at the window.

God looked at Woman. What if she was right? Camel wasn't much good for anything else. But with a few slight changes he might be just the thing.

God leapt out through the door, and before Camel could get his long tangly legs swinging under him God had grabbed him.

'Not the scrapheap!' the Camel tried to groan. 'Please not the scrapheap!'

'You're the very thing we need,' said God.

The Demon raged in the bamboo thicket. He beat his own bald head.

'Idiot!' he snarled. 'Oh, idiot! You had it in your hands!'

But there was nothing he could do. He was a Fire Demon.

If he had tried plunging into the sea, he would have been extinguished. He was so furious with himself, he returned to his wife deep inside the Red Mountains and told her every-thing. He wouldn't have cared if she'd swallowed him. He felt he deserved it.

But when she heard about the hat, her reply was strange. She took a nugget of iron ore in each fist. Her face contorted. Her bald scalp knotted into lumps, her dreadful eyes bulged, her mouth opened slowly, as she stared at her husband. And in her clenching fists the iron ore crumbled, fumes rose between her fingers and molten iron splashed on to the floor.

'Get me that haaaaaaat!' she screamed.

By the time the Demon flew up into the world, God was lead-ing Camel to the sea's edge.

'Find my hat,' said God, 'and you will be first among animals. I will give you into Woman's care, and she will comb you and feed you. That is God's promise. Now go. And bring the hat into my hands.'

He slapped Camel's rump and the great beast set off, swinging his legs, towards the breakers of the sea.

God had made him able to walk under the sea. He had done this by making his hump hollow and filling it with com-pressed oxygen. At the same time, he had made Camel's bones very heavy, so he could not float. He could not even swim, with those bones. But he didn't need to. He now marched through the breakers and on down into the sea. As he marched across the sea bed it might have been dry land except for all the little fish that came to look at him.

God sat on the dunes, waiting. He watched a white sea bird, a Tern, circling and circling low over the sea. God smiled. 'That bird can't believe his eyes,' he thought. 'An animal walking across the sea bed. He simply can't believe it.'

God did not know that the Tern was the Demon.

And the Demon had a plan. He could see the Camel clearly, down through the green water. And the moment Camel found the hat, glowing on the bed of the sea, the Demon set off at top speed to Man's house. Man was out collecting food. The Demon worked fast. Woman sat in the garden, plaiting her hair so it could be tucked up under her hat. The Demon grabbed her, and when she opened her mouth to scream he jammed a big sponge into it. Then he tied her plait round her face like a gag and slinging her over his shoulder ran into the forest. But as he ran she kicked off one of her sandals.

Deep in the forest, he tied her wrists and ankles together with a creeper and pushed her down inside a hollow tree. He laid his ear to the tree trunk. 'Mmmmmmm,' it hummed, and 'Mmmmmmm,' like a hive of bees. Laughing, he ran back to Man's house, collecting her sandal on the way. He spilled water over a patch of the garden and trampled on it, leaving big froggy footprints. Then he flew up, as a Raven, carrying her sandal. Far below, he saw Man returning home. He dropped the sandal on to the path in front of him, then flew off, top speed, to the seaside, where he came down as a Tern, to sit bobbing on the waves, just beyond the breakers.

When Man saw the sandal, dropped by the bird, he feared the worst, and started to run. The froggy footprints were all he needed to see. He came howling to God at the seaside. God listened, jumped up, and the two ran off together.

A few minutes later, when Camel came marching up out of the sea with God's hat shining on his hump, he saw a figure waiting for him, on the dunes, where God had been.

'Where's God?' Camel tried to say. But the figure spoke:

'I am God's assistant. My name is Angel. Where have you been? God got tired of waiting. He's furious. I have to take you to him at once. Hurry!'

And he jumped on Camel's back and, sitting on top of the hat, directed him straight out into the desert towards the Red Mountains. Camel groaned and began to run.

All the rest of that day Camel went along at his best speed. After a few hours, they stopped at an oasis in the rocky desert. Camel was thirsty.

'Best be careful,' warned the Demon, who still had the shape of an Angel. 'The Demon lives in these water holes. He'll snatch the hat again if he finds us. We are carrying the Crown of Heaven, remember.'

And then, as Camel drank, the Demon snatched the hat off his hump and pushed him in. Camel sank straight to the bottom. It only took him half a minute to come walking out, but by that time, both Angel and hat had gone.

Camel ran round and round the water hole. He thought the Demon had pulled him in. 'And the Angel,' he thought, 'has gone to God to tell him that I have lost the hat.'

Inside the Red Mountains, the Demon's wife wears the hat. And the day of her kingdom is the day of the hat, when the diamond climbs over and down the dome of blue turquoise. And then she turns the hat inside out, and the night of the hat is the night of her kingdom. All her stolen plants and creatures are happier. But now that she has night and day, of a sort, she wants more and more of God's plants and creatures. So the Demon is busier than ever.

And out in the desert Camel wanders from oasis to oasis. He stares into the water holes. Sometimes he seems to see the hat on the bottom, with the moon and the stars. He can no longer walk down there under the water, because his compressed oxygen is long ago used up. Instead, he tries to drink the water hole dry. He fills the hump up with water. It's hopeless, of course. Then the hat seems to disappear, and he wanders along to the next water hole, groaning as he goes. And he stays out there, in the rocky desert, where he hopes, maybe, that he'll find the hat, in some small water hole, before God finds him.

The Grizzly Bear and the Human Child

When God created Woman he had to give her a toy. While Man was away in the forest, collecting food, she had to have something to play with.

God knew that she liked jewels. Jewels, gems and precious stones of all kinds. Man had found her a few of these and she would spend hours sorting them out, arranging them and simply gazing at them.

So God thought: 'A living jewel would be just the thing.'

That's when he invented Snake. How he made Snake is another story. But when Snake was finished, she was dazzling. Every scale was a different jewel. Best of all were her eyes. Her eyes were such powerful jewels they made God feel slightly funny when he looked at them.

'My word!' he whispered to himself. 'What have I done? I hope she's all right. But I must say, she's a beauty.'

Snake lay there, looking at God. She felt very dark and deep. She felt full of – full of – she wasn't quite sure what. But she knew she ought to keep it hidden from God, whatever it was. So she lay very still.

Woman was overjoyed with her new toy.

'You see,' God said, 'you hang it around your neck, and that's a necklace. Or she'll coil around your arm. And that's a bangle. Or around your waist, and that's a jewel belt. Or around your head, and she's a crown. Isn't she a beauty?

'And here's a little mirror to go with her. So you can see how beautiful she makes you look.'

Now Woman spent the whole day playing with her Snake. And Snake was very happy with their games. She would coil around Woman's neck, and rear up her neat little face beside

Woman's face, and the two of them would gaze at themselves in the hand mirror.

'Oh, my beauty!' Woman would say. And she would actually kiss Snake's cold little nose.

Snake liked this. But what she liked best was Woman's warmth.

Man wasn't so sure about Snake. Those eyes made him uneasy. So he built Snake a hutch, under the floorboards, out of sight. From there, Snake could slide out into the garden. Or she could come up through a hole under the bed, to play with Woman. But when Man was at home, Snake had to be out of sight.

As he came home in the evening, Man would whistle a tune, to warn Snake. Then Woman would say: 'Oh dear, here he comes. Away you go. Sorry, my little beauty.'

And she would kiss Snake's cold nose. And Snake would slide away down, under the floorboards. And there she would lie, in the dark, listening to Man and Woman and feeling left out.

One evening, Man brought home a Lamb. 'It's lost its mother,' he explained. 'Out there on the mountain, where life is tough. We shall have to look after it.'

So Woman looked after the Lamb. With Snake draped round her shoulders she would feed the Lamb milk from a bottle. And Snake would stare at the Lamb's furry little head, and its sleepy little eyes, as it drank.

Snake did not like this at all. Woman was too fond of this funny little thing. And once, when Woman suddenly snatched up the Lamb and kissed the top of its head, Snake went: 'Ksssssssssssssssssssssss!' And her forked tongue flickered in and out. She couldn't stop herself.

But the Lamb soon grew too big to cuddle. In fact, it very quickly turned into a Ram and galloped off to the mountain, where it looked for another Ram, so they could batter their heads together, which is what Rams love to do.

Snake felt happy again, coiled on Woman's warm stomach as she lay in the sun, or draped around her waist as she worked in the garden.

But then Man brought home a baby Rabbit – so tiny, it sat on his hand.

'Oh, he's lovely!' cried Woman.

And Snake, already under the floorboards, hissed: 'What now?' And she lifted her head so sharply she cracked it against the board above, and flopped flat for a moment, almost knocked out. That made her even angrier.

During the day, Woman played with the baby Rabbit and Snake had to pretend she liked it. Actually, she felt more like eating it.

'It would go down,' she thought, 'very smoothly. That would stop its idiotic little nose bobbing about.'

Instead, she did something amazing.

Woman was searching under her chest of drawers for the little Rabbit. She had left Snake coiled on her dressing table. Close to Snake's nose lay a comb. In the comb glistened two of Woman's hairs. A sudden thought came to Snake. She took the hairs between her lips and drew them out of the comb. Then, with a few twists, she coiled them around her head.

The next thing, Woman heard a strange voice – a woman's voice.

'Hi there!' it said.

Woman twisted around. There, leaning against her dressing table, was another Woman, almost exactly like herself and yet – different.

'Can I play too?' laughed the new one. And made three

wild leaps across the room, turning a somersault and landing on her knees beside Woman.

'Where's this diddly Bun?' she cried, and raked her arm under the chest of drawers. 'Hey, here he is. Well I never!'

And she dragged the Rabbit out by its ears, squirming and kicking.

Woman simply stared at her new playmate.

'Who are you?' she gasped. 'Where are you from?'

'I'm Snake,' laughed the new one. 'Don't I look good? Come on, let's go have some fun in the woods. Find some more Rabbits maybe.'

From that moment, every day, Snake turned into another Woman, exactly like Woman. And all day they played together.

'But how are you so like me?' Woman kept saying. And Snake would answer: 'I am another you.' So that's what Woman called her: 'Otherme'.

'I like that,' cried Otherme and, flinging her arms around Woman, jumped into the river with her.

But every evening, as soon as they heard Man's whistling tune, Otherme turned back into Snake, and slid down her hole into the dark. Woman never breathed a word about her to Man. Otherme was a very exciting person, even if she was a Snake. And if Man knew about her – well, he might spoil things. He didn't seem to like Snake at all. Anyway, Woman didn't want to share Otherme, even with her husband.

Now and again, though, Woman remembered the baby Lamb and the baby Rabbit. Even while she was out with her new playmate, maybe swimming in the river, she would suddenly remember the Lamb. She would lie there, floating on her back, thinking about the Lamb. Thinking about the Lamb always gave her the strangest feeling. A very sweet feeling. And she thought about it more and more.

One night, when the Moon had risen over the forest, Man and Woman lay in bed talking. And Snake lay under the floorboards, listening as usual.

'Aren't Lambs lovely,' Woman was saying. 'Isn't a Lamb the loveliest thing. Isn't it strange how it makes you want to cuddle it? I think it's the prettiest thing. It's just so pretty!'

'Very clever of God,' said Man, 'to think of the Lamb.'

'And the baby Rabbit,' said Woman. 'Why is it so pretty? Why does it make you want to cuddle it and kiss it?'

'Well,' said Man, 'it has a funny little round face. That's why. And funny little round ears. It's sweet, somehow.'

'Are all baby things like that?' Woman asked.

'Like what?' asked Man.

'Pretty,' said Woman. 'So you feel you want to cuddle them. And kiss them.'

Man was silent for a while. Under the floorboards Snake listened. At last Man said:

'Well, I suppose they are, come to think of it. Yes they are. Little birds. Even little pigs. Baby pigs are the sweetest things. Funny little faces.'

They were silent for a while. Snake listened to their thoughts working silently in the bed above.

Then Woman said: 'Would a baby of ours be like that?'

Another silence. But then Man said: 'I expect so. Yes, I suppose it would. In its way.'

After that, there was a long silence. Then Woman said: 'Will you ask God tomorrow?'

'What?' asked Man. 'Ask him what?'

'For one for us,' said Woman.

Snake slowly lifted her head. She listened hard. The house was so still she could almost hear the Moon. She thought Man had gone to sleep. But at last his voice came: 'OK, why not?'

Snake's eyes glared invisibly in the pitch black under the floorboards. They glared so hard they crackled. What was this? A baby Human Being? A new little playmate for Woman? First a Lamb. Then a Rabbit. And now this? Wasn't she, Snake, Woman's darling playmate? Wasn't she Woman's Otherme? Her living hoopla? Her adjustable jewel? So what was the need for a new little Human Being? With a funny round face and funny little ears?

Well, Snake would see about that! Snake would have something to say about that! Tense with cold fury, she slid along and out of her hole under the wall of the house, into the garden. Her eyes shone with dark power. A Frog's golden eyes were gazing at the Moon. Its body was wet with the dew. It did not know about Shake. But suddenly – it knew it could not move. An invisible power was gripping it. Then it was grabbed and swallowed. And it had no idea what had swallowed it. It simply went numb. Poor Frog!

Snake flicked her tongue. 'Tomorrow,' she hissed, 'we shall see. A baby Human? With a funny little face? A sweet little thing, with funny little ears? For Woman to play with and cuddle and kiss? Not if I can help it. Ksssssss! Ksssssssssss!'

Again she raised her head and looked towards the house, so silent in the moonlight. A brainwave swept from the tip of her tail to the tip of her forked tongue in one shiver. She slid back under the foundation of the house and up through her hole into the room. Man and Woman were asleep, noses in the air. By the light of the Moon that came in through the window, Snake reared up and looked on to Woman's dressing table. There it lay, the necklace of tiny red seashells, like red fingernails. She pushed her head through it and kinked her neck slightly so it hung there.

With the necklace swinging from her kinked neck, Snake poured herself back down through her hole, to her place

under the floorboards, and there she curled up, waiting
for day.

Next morning early Man kneeled in front of God, in God's
workshop. He had made his request. And now he waited.

'Well,' said God. 'I hope you are quite sure you know what
you're asking for.'

'Oh yes,' cried Man. 'We are, we certainly are. We've talked
it over.'

God gazed down at the top of Man's bowed head. Well, it
might be quite interesting, making a little Human. It would
be a change, anyway, from what he was doing.

In the middle of his workshop stood an immense Grizzly
Bear, on its hind legs like a Man. Its big round ears touched
the ceiling. Its paws were raised, and nearly touched the ceiling. On each paw were five claws, each claw about six inches
long and jet black. It was twice as tall as Man, with shaggy
dark brown and gingery fur. All it needed was the breath of
life. God was pleased with it. He didn't want to give it life
straightaway. Once alive, it would be gone – out into the dark
forest. No, he wanted to admire it for a while.

Just for a joke, he said to Man: 'You're sure your wife
wouldn't prefer this fellow? He's all ready to go. She could
have him now.' And he nodded towards the Grizzly Bear.

It was only now that Man saw what the huge dark shape
was. And his eyes bulged. The Bear was so huge Man hadn't
realized it was an animal. He had thought it might be a great
rug, God's giant bedspread maybe, hanging to air. But now
he looked at it –

'Ugh! Ugh! Ugh!'

Strange grunting noises came out of him and he began to
shuffle backwards on his knees. As if the Bear had stepped
towards him. He began to shake all over. He couldn't stop it.

'There,' said God, patting his head. 'Don't be scared. It's not alive. Here, take an apple. And tell your wife the baby's on its way. Off you go. Laugh. Be happy. Let me hear you laugh. How is your laugh these days?'

Man turned his bulging eyes and fixed them on God. His chin quivered.

'Go on,' cried God. 'Give us a good laugh. Come on, now – laugh!'

'Hahahahaha!' barked Man, and his eyes jerked sideways back to the Bear. He thought his laugh might make it attack him.

'Forget the Bear,' cried God. 'Come on, a good old belly laugh. Like this: HAHAHAHAHAHAHA!'

God roared with happy laughter. The whole workshop shook and the door banged open.

'Come on,' cried God. 'Now: HAHAHAHAHAHA!'

And: 'HAHAHAHAHA!' roared Man, imitating God and trying not to look at the Bear.

'That's it,' cried God. 'Again!'

'HAHAHAHAHA!' roared Man. 'HAHAHAHAHA-HAHAHA!'

It was actually a dreadful sound. And as he tried to laugh, Man's eyes switched to and fro between God and the Bear.

'Let's hear you laughing like that all the way home,' cried God. 'Let's hear how happy you are with your news. The baby's due tonight!'

'HAHAHAHAHA!' roared Man, as he backed out of the door. 'HAHAHAHA! HAHAHAHAHA!'

He backed down the ladder, fell the last few rungs, stumbled across God's garden, glancing wildly backwards, and plunged into the jungle. Every moment he expected to see the Grizzly Bear burst out after him.

'HAHAHAHAHA! HAHAHAHA!' Laughing in that horrible way, he stumbled and fell, got up and fell again.

Wrenching branches aside, falling over roots, he crashed through the undergrowth, laughing like a madman: 'HAHA-HAHAHA! HAHAHAHAHA!'

'Remember,' God shouted after him, 'tonight.' He shook his head, smiling, and turned to his bench. 'Now let's see,' he murmured. 'A Human baby. Shouldn't take too long.'

God had almost finished. He was just fixing the last of the tiny perfect fingernails when the room darkened slightly. Somebody stood in the doorway. He looked up.

'Hello, Woman!' God smiled a broad smile. He gazed at her. She really did look pretty good. The big red flower in her hair perfumed his whole workshop. Her red shell necklace gleamed. He had never made anything else quite like Woman. And today she looked extra special. She looked so gorgeous, in fact, he felt – just a touch of fear. That surprised him. His hair prickled slightly, looking at her.

'Almost finished,' he said. 'How do you like it?' He pointed to the baby and his eyes danced, expecting to see her stunned with the sheer joy.

Instead she burst into tears. She stayed there in the doorway, her face buried in her hands, her shoulders sobbing.

'What's this?' God was amazed. 'What's the matter? Isn't it what you wanted?'

She shook her head so hard her red shell necklace clashed to and fro and tears scattered from her face like jewels.

'No,' she sobbed. 'No, it isn't.'

'But,' said God. 'But – but – but – but what do you want? Man said – '

Woman lifted her face. Her great eyes shone, her eyelashes glistening with tears. She stared at him. He could feel the power of her eyes gripping his.

'The Bear!' she wailed. 'I want the Bear! I don't want the

baby I want the Bear! My husband didn't understand. The
Bear! The Bear! Oh! Oh! I want him! Oh just look at him. He's
all I want.'

'You want the Grizzly Bear?' God's voice squeaked. He
could not believe it.

'Oh please! Please, God! Please! Please! The moment my
husband told me about him I just knew. He's all I've ever
wanted. I'm sorry – I'm sorry – Oh, please!'

And with a sobbing wail she seemed to fling herself back
down the ladder, and lurched away over the garden, her arms
writhing like scarves.

'Ooooh!' she wailed. 'Ooooooh!'

God sat down. He truly was stunned. He shook his head
slowly. He could still hear her wailing sobs as she ran through
the forest. My, she was upset!

He looked at the baby on his bench. Then turned his head
and looked at the tower of shaggy terror – Grizzly Bear, his
great hooked paws lifted so high. He shook his head again,
slowly. And slowly, he shrugged.

Halfway to Man's house, Woman staggered to a halt, panting.
She leaned against a tree. She was still sobbing. But then – in
the strangest way – her sobs became chuckles. Then laughs.
She writhed her whole body and coiled into a loop, laughing.
She stuffed the red flower into her mouth to gag her laughter,
and the petals blew everywhere. She rolled full length among
the orchids. At last she lay there, panting, lengthening, growing thinner. She gleamed like a Snake, and – she was Snake.

Snake!

Smiling, her head lifted, she slid homewards, the necklace
swinging from a loop in the tip of her tail, and a petal
sticking out of the corner of her long, curved mouth.

*

Man had made a little cradle cot. Woman had made coloured blankets. They sat on their bed, knees up, waiting.

'Did God say he would bring it himself?' Woman asked.

'Hard to say,' said Man, 'how it will come. I expect he'll bring it.'

Man played a little tune on his conch harp, which was a big seashell strung with twisted horse hairs. It was his latest song:

> ' "Come into my kitchen," said
>   The Spider to the Fly.
> "Nine sour apples
>   Make a Sweety-pie." '

Woman gazed at the window, the tops of the trees, the Sun going down red and clear.

'Maybe we should meet it halfway,' she suddenly said.

'Let me,' said Man. 'You stay. I'll see if he's coming.'

Man went out through the open door. Woman lay back on her pillow. She was trying to imagine what a Human baby would be like. Well, she supposed this was what it was to be happy. She listened to Man's little conch harp, plinkety-plonk, and his voice, so soft and peaceful:

> 'Said the Fly to the Spider:
>   "Wrap me in a shawl.
> Oh I'll be the sweetest
>   Baby of them all." '

But then she almost jumped out of her skin. A horrible scream – 'Aaaaaaaghghgh!' – out there in the garden. So horrible, she thought it must be some horrible new animal. Some hideous new giant bird, just made by God, as a mistake.

Man appeared in the doorway. His face was all mouth, and

the scream came again – this time out of his face: 'Aaaaaaghghgh!'

He leapt on to the bed, grabbed Woman and fell with her over the other side of the bed. He rolled into the low space under the bed, bringing her with him, clinging to her tightly.

Now Woman heard a grunting roar. From under the bed, she could see something blocking the door-way of the house. Something was trying to get in, but was too big. It was jammed in the doorway, struggling to get through into the room. The house shook.

'It's the Bear,' gurgled Man. 'It's Grizzly Bear.'

She could see that its huge head, with its funny puffy cheeks and big round woolly-looking ears, was through the doorway. But its shoulders were too broad, its whole body was too massive to get in.

'Look at its ears!' she whispered.

'Ears?' cried Man. 'Never mind its ears. Look at its mouth! And listen to it. And wait till you see its claws. Don't you know what horrible is?'

Its roar was weird, like a vast iron barrel bouncing down a rocky ravine. And deafening inside that room. Everything in there danced and trembled.

But Woman only cried: 'What's it saying? It's saying something. Listen! Listen!'

They both tried to listen.

'Stop your teeth chattering,' cried Woman, 'so we can listen.'

Man clamped his mouth tight shut. Yes, they could hear words, quite clearly, in that vast, shaggy bellow coming from the Bear's throat: 'Mamma! Mamma!'

'Oh no!' whimpered Man. 'I thought God was joking. He meant it. Oh no! I can't believe it! He's sent the Bear as your baby.'

'Dadda!' roared the Bear, ripping great splinters off the threshold with its claws. The doorposts bent inwards and cracked loudly.

'Mamma! Mamma!'

'That thing my baby?' cried Woman. 'Oh, please, God, no!' Then she too started to scream. She banged the floor with her fists then put her hands over her eyes. So there they were, Woman screaming with her hands over her eyes and Man sweating with fear, holding her, both jammed under the bed. While the house shook and jolted and the great Bear's terrible face twisted and pushed, and gaped and roared, in the doorway, trying to get in.

And under the floorboards, under the screaming and crying couple, Snake lay in the pitch darkness, on wood shavings, in a great loose knot and smiled.

'How are things going?' said a big, familiar voice. At the same moment, the window was completely filled with a gigantic shining eye. It was God, peering in. 'Something wrong, eh?'

'Take him back!' screamed Woman. 'Take him back! He's too big! Take him back!'

God could see straightaway that things had gone awfully wrong. But what did they expect?

'Well,' he sighed, 'I really did think, you know, that Grizzly Bear might be a bit too much. But you would insist.'

His eye disappeared from the window and they heard his voice: 'Back there, Teddy! Come on, boy! Good boy! Come on, out of there.'

The doorway cracked again and the doorposts bent this time outwards as Grizzly Bear was pulled out backwards.

Woman crawled from under the bed and came to the door. She was fearless. Especially now God had arrived. She was also curious. God met her at the doorway. He handed her the

Human baby wrapped in a giant orchid of speckled purple. She gave a gasp and clasped it tightly.

'Oh, God!' was all she could say. And now she was crying, but this time with joy not fear.

God smiled and turned to Grizzly Bear who was sitting in the middle of the garden.

Man came from under the bed and looked out over Woman's shoulders. The Sun had just set over the forest, behind the Bear. The red-gold rays coming through the tree tops from behind made him seem fringed with fire. His round ears were fringed with fire.

Woman was happy. She smiled happily at the Bear. It looked like a big fat dog, quite friendly. 'Look at his lovely ears,' she said. 'Aren't they sweet! Isn't he sweet!'

Man pushed his brows up crookedly and pulled his mouth crookedly down. He thought Grizzly Bear was pretty scary in any light. He could not forget his big shock, and what he had gone through under the bed.

'His ears are all right,' he said. 'It's the rest of him I'm not so sure about.'

God led Grizzly Bear into the forest, and Man and Woman watched them go, fringed with fire.

'I want one,' Woman said suddenly.

'What?' cried Man. 'What now?'

'A Bear,' she said.

He was afraid that's what she meant.

'No!' he shouted. 'No. No. No. Anything you like – but not that. I draw the line at a Bear.'

'Only a little one,' she said. 'It needn't be alive. Just a little cuddly friend for this one.'

She laid her baby in the cradle so she could look at it there. Yes, there it actually was, moving its fingers.

Man did not want her going to ask God for a Bear. So he

made one. A very small Bear. Nothing like God's Grizzly, of course. Just a baby-size furry Bear. For eyes it had lumps of amber. And round, woolly-looking ears. Woman sat this little Bear at the foot of her baby's cradle, looking at the baby.

'Here's Teddy,' she said. Her baby screwed up its mouth and blew a bubble.

Snake under the floorboards had not moved. Only, it no longer smiled. Its eyebrows had come down over its eyes in a hard, cross frown.

The Last of the Dinosaurs

In the early days, God made some strange creatures. New ideas were quite hard to find. When he thought up a Clam, for instance, he went on for ages – simply making different kinds of Clams, or things very like Clams, such as Mussels, Oysters, Razor Shells, and so on. And when he suddenly got the idea for a Worm he went wild – filling up the rivers and lakes and seas and lands with different kinds of Worm. It seemed he might never make anything else except Worms. But in the end he got bored and suddenly thought of Spiders.

When he thought of Dinosaurs he said: 'This is it. This is perfection. I'll never get a better idea.'

He stuck to Dinosaurs for an incredible number of years. And every day he thought up a new one. Actually, each new one was quite like the old ones, but he'd give it more horns, or a longer neck, or twice as much armour-plating, or make it five times as big. As he finished these creations, they lumbered out from under his hands, and ran on to the plains, heads up, looking for trouble.

God's Dinosaurs were all the same in one thing – they were a very fierce lot. They spent their time attacking each other and eating each other. The big ones ate the little ones. The little ones ate the big ones. The whole world was a battle of Dinosaurs. Wherever a Dinosaur looked, he saw Dinosaurs fleeing from him with squawks, or Dinosaurs rushing towards him with snarls. They were tirelessly fierce. And the noise was terrific. Every kind of cry, from twitterings like Swallows to screechings like Elephants. Some Dinosaurs were smaller than Swallows, and some were bigger than Elephants – even though they looked more or less alike, with their steely claws, their strong hind legs, and their horrible Dinosaur eyes.

Those were early days, and God did not know the world had become such a shocking place. He was too busy making new Dinosaurs to think about what the old ones were getting up to. All that interested him was 'my next Dinosaur'.

But he was finding it harder and harder to think up new ones. And one day he was stuck. He was making his latest model – but somehow it wouldn't come out right. He rolled it into a ball and started again. It still wouldn't come out right. He pounded it into a lump with his fist and started again. It still wouldn't come out right. He slapped it flat with his hand, sighed, laid his arm on his workbench and his head on his arm, and fell asleep.

He woke up almost at once – with a start. What had wakened him? He blinked, and started to model the clay again. Then he stopped.

A strange brown creature sat up in the middle of the work-shop floor, licking its chest. It was quite small, the size of a thrush. It had a round face, round eyes, round ears, a round belly, a round bum, and funny little hands. God reached down and picked it up. It was soft. Furry. It was the first furry thing God had ever felt.

'What are you?' he asked, and he looked at the creature with eyes as round and wondering as its own.

It looked back at him and wriggled its whiskers. 'I'm a kind of Bushbaby,' it said.

'Bushbaby?' God was very puzzled. 'What is that?'

'A baby from under a bush,' the creature replied.

'You came from under a bush?' asked God. 'Now tell me. Where did you come from, truly.'

'You dreamed me,' said the Bushbaby. 'In your bushy head.'

God scratched his chin.

'I know I never entered your thoughts,' Bushbaby went on, 'because you were so busy trying to think up horrible Dinosaurs. But you did dream me. So here I am.'

Yes, God remembered now. He'd dreamed of a green bush. And something had shaken the leaves. And out of the bush had crept – this very creature. He was fascinated.

A totally new idea! Soft, furry beings!

In no time at all, he stopped making Dinosaurs. Now he was on to soft furry creatures. All his Dinosaurs suddenly looked old-fashioned and stupid.

'What a waste of time,' he thought. 'I've made far too many.'

But then he saw what happened to his new creatures, in the world of the Dinosaurs. They didn't stand a chance. Those terrible steely killers, with their terrible speed, and their terrible jaws full of fangs, tore the soft furry beings to bits, or simply swallowed them whole.

God heard his new inventions crying at night in the trees, where they huddled together. But they weren't safe even in the highest trees. Speedy, small Dinosaurs, nimbler than any squirrel, came ripping up through the leaves – and with stunning screams threw them down to earth, where other Dinosaurs waited. Or flying Dinosaurs came cruising up, and with a grab and a flap snatched them away, eating them as they flew, like sandwiches.

God felt pity for his little furry ones. 'I've filled the Earth,' he thought, 'with monsters. I simply have to get rid of them. They'll have to go. I want the Earth to be safe, for my furry beings.'

So he set about wiping out his Dinosaurs.

A Demon from under the earth heard what was going on. He rose like a puff from a volcano, and appeared before God as a creature from outer space. God was quite pleased to see him. He asked for cosmic news, and the Demon invented some. Then the Demon came to the point.

'Now you're scrapping your Dinosaurs,' he said, 'we thought you might sell a few cheap. On our planet we have only fungus.'

'Too late,' said God. 'I doubt if there's one left. When I do a job, I'm thorough. Sorry about that.'

'If I find one, can I have it?' asked the Demon. 'There might be just the odd one left.'

'So long as I never see it again, it's yours,' said God. 'But you won't find one. I made my gaze deadly, and I let it rest on the valleys and the plains, and – poufff! – Nothing but fossils.'

'I'll just have a look round,' said the Demon, 'if that's all right.'

'Look in the caves,' shouted God after him.

The Demon was already speeding to the caves. And there in a deep tunnel, protected from God's deadly gaze, he found a Pterodactyl, still alive.

This Dinosaur had immense wings, a crocodile head, and terrible Dinosaur eyes that were mad with hunger.

'Is it safe yet up there?' asked the Dinosaur.

The Demon had brought him a Bushbaby. And as the Dinosaur gulped and swallowed, he told him that the happy days on Earth were finished. 'The moment God sees you,' he said, 'you are extinct. I'm afraid your day's past. But I can help you. I have a job for you.'

And so the Demon housed the Pterodactyl in a great cave, under a mountain. Each day he brought him a furry being, or a Snake, or a Lizard, to eat. And the Pterodactyl's job was to guard the Demon's gems. These gems were the Demon's only food.

The Demon was gathering all the gems in the world, and all the precious metal – the gold, the silver. He worked night and day, till the sweat trickled down his back and dripped off his stumpy tail.

He leaned against the wall. 'I have to get it all,' he explained to the Pterodactyl, 'before Man comes. Man will want it all, when he comes I shall have to fight him for every jewel. And, now that God's invented the Bushbaby, Man won't be long a-coming. Oh no, he's on his way right now. And when he comes – I shall need a guardian. I shall need you.'

'This Man you speak about,' said the Pterodactyl, 'will he be a sort of Bushbaby?'

'Bigger,' said the Demon. 'Meatier. And Woman, his mate, meatier still.'

The Pterodactyl's eyes did not change, as he smiled with his four-foot-long row of fangs. 'This,' he thought, 'is better than lying flat among the fossils.'

And pretty soon, Man arrived. And soon after him, Woman. On the third day, Man found a jewel. And when he gave it to Woman, she jerked her head back, and her mouth opened like a baby bird's: 'More,' she cried. 'More.'

A week later she found a little nugget of gold in a stream, where she was searching for pretty pebbles. She came to Man. 'This stuff,' she said, 'it's magic. Look at it.'

And when Man looked at the nugget of gold he felt the weirdest sensation. His palms were suddenly wet with sweat, a shiver crept up his back, his teeth ground together, and he gripped her wrist. He gripped it so tight that her fingertips swelled red as cherries. Then, very gently, with the finger and thumb of his other hand, he took the little lump of gold from her. And he gazed at it. It was shaped like a popcorn. And as he gazed, his brow tightened its wrinkles till it resembled a clenched fist, pressing down over his eyes, and his chin trembled.

'Where did you find this?' he whispered.

'It's mine,' she cried. 'Finders keepers.' And she snatched it back.

So they had their first fight. And when Man had won and had hidden the gold he told her: 'I only want to make it safe. Now let's find more, together.'

'Jewels too,' she said. 'You have the gold and I'll be quite happy with just the jewels. How about that?'

The Demon, sitting in a bush, smiled. He had worked hard and well. He knew the earth was almost empty of gold and gems. They were all in his cave, under the Pterodactyl.

He then slipped across to the hiding place, took the lump of gold, and ate it.

'Another puzzle for Man,' he laughed, and as he soared back to his cave he snatched a snake off a rock for his pet.

Man came to God and complained. There was no gold. There were no jewels. Or so little, it was making his wife sick. He needed the gold and jewels, yes and silver too, for her health. And what bit of gold he had found had vanished.

God couldn't understand it. 'The earth should be full of those things,' he said. 'What's happened to them?'

When God asks a question, something has to answer. And now it was a snake, that stuck its head out of a hole in a tree and cried: 'The Demon collected the whole lot. The Demon's plundered the earth. It's all in his cave. Under the mountain. And he guards it with that horrible Pterodactyl that ate my mother and father.'

God's eyebrows rose. He had to laugh. So that's what the creature from outer space had been! And out of his laugh came a brainwave. He frowned, raised his right hand, and snapped his fingers.

In that second, all the gems, all the lumps of gold and silver in the Demon's cave, melted. Like a colossal heap of snow.

And they flowed out into the rivers of the world as streams of fishes. Every kind of fish was created there, in that flashing snap of the fingers. The Pterodactyl floundered and screeched, then flapped up on to a cave ledge. The Demon stared. Then he understood.

His cry shattered that mountain. And out of his cry came a burst of magic power. He changed the Pterodactyl into a bird no bigger than a Goose. The long neck was still there, and the long mouth. But the bird had feathers, and strange long legs.

'Go wade in the rivers,' the Demon shouted. 'Save my treasures. Find my treasures. Go, go.'

The Pterodactyl bird flapped up out of the cave and sailed over the rivers of the Earth. Everywhere under the windy ripples he saw the glimmerings of the fish, the glints and flashings as they turned.

'Gather them,' yelled the Demon, flying above him. 'You stay as you are till you've gathered them all.'

So there he is. But how can he gather them all? He wades along the edges of rivers, peering down. Now and again he jabs. And now and again he does come up with something. But it's never a jewel, never a lump of gold or silver. It is bright, maybe. But it is never anything but a fish. So he swallows it.

And sometimes, remembering his happier days, he grabs a Lizard. Or a Snake. Or even a Water Rat. And he swallows it. Man has called him Heron.

And when he flies up, with his broken-looking, ponderous wings, and lets out his cry, his awful scrarking gark, he reminds you of a Pterodactyl. And when you see him close up, and get a good look at his terrible little eye, you know, for certain, he is one.

The Secret of Man's Wife

Once again, God had dreamed a startling dream. And once again, when he woke, he'd forgotten it. What was it? He sat at his workbench, staring at a knot in one of his floorboards. Something dazzling had appeared in his sleep. Something to do with Man.

He was still puzzling, trying to coax his dream back, when he realized that somebody was standing in the open doorway of his workshop. He looked up and saw Man, wearing the most woebegone expression.

God took a deep breath. Another complaint! When would Man come to him without a complaint? But he shot up his eyebrows, smiled with delight, and cried: 'Man! How are the carrots coming on?'

Man licked his lips. He lifted his face for a second and God felt a little pang of pity as he glimpsed the awful toiling difficulties behind the brown eyes. Then Man's gaze sank again to the floor, as if the weight of his troubles were too great to hold up.

'What's the matter?' cried God. 'Has something been digging them out?'

'It's not the carrots,' said Man. 'They're fine. It's my wife again.'

God nodded. 'Hmm!' and waited. Now, he thought, here comes the complaint.

'She's restless,' said Man.

God waited.

'In fact,' Man went on, 'she's become altogether – peculiar.'

God raised his eyebrows. He was always interested to hear about his creations. They were full of surprises.

'So what's new?' he asked, in an easy voice, reaching for a bit of clay. 'How is she peculiar?'

'Can you explain,' asked Man, 'why she is always looking past me?'

God frowned, and rolled the clay between his thumb and forefinger.

'She's always looking towards the forest,' said Man, 'as if she were expecting – somebody. She leans on the doorpost and stares – at the forest. She's always sort of – waiting.'

God waited.

'Then,' said Man, 'when I'm doing something, repairing my sandals or carving a new paddle, I feel this weird, chilly feeling, and I look up and – she's watching me. She's not looking at me in a normal way. She's watching me, out of her eye-corners, with a look that –. A very strange look. As if I were – I can't explain it. And the moment I see it and ask her what's the matter she gets up and goes out. She goes off somewhere. Into the forest.'

God stroked his beard.

'What does she do there?' he wondered aloud.

'I think,' said Man, 'she meets somebody. And she laughs – she has this laugh. It's not a happy laugh. A completely peculiar laugh. She laughs, showing all her teeth – then starts somersaulting all over the garden. Then she starts crying. She sits there sobbing.'

God frowned. This certainly was pretty strange.

'Who do you think she meets in the forest?' he asked.

Man stared at him. 'I think,' he said, 'I think she meets your wolf.'

God stood up and slapped his hands together, flattening the clay into a leaf.

'What an idea!' he cried. 'What makes you think that? That's a crazy idea.'

312

But Man went on, still staring at God, so that God did just wonder, for a second, whether Man had gone a wee bit crazy.

'I keep getting this feeling,' he said, that my wife wants to be a Wolf.'

Now it was God's turn to stare. He was stuck for words. 'Wants to be a Wolf?' It did sound crazy.

'Nearly every night,' cried Man, 'I dream she's a Wolf running in the forest. Or she's a Wolf with its forepaws on my bed, staring down at me. And I wake up, and do you know what?'

God was almost afraid of what he was going to hear.

'She's pacing up and down the room panting. And I'll swear, in the dark, her tongue's hanging out.'

'No!' shouted God. 'You're dreaming it.'

Man paused for a while, his lips clamped.

'And then,' he added, 'there's a smell.'

God's brows twisted two or three different ways at once. What now?

'It's actually quite an exciting smell,' Man went on. 'But it's – not exactly doggy, not exactly – '

They both became silent, staring at each other. God sat down.

'Well, what can we do about it?' said God at last. 'What do you want?'

'I've thought about it,' said Man.

'What have you thought?'

'If you,' said Man, 'can extract from her whatever it is, whatever this wolfy thing is, that makes her so peculiar, maybe we could have that as a whole separate – animal. A sort of pet, maybe. Or maybe just let it run wild. And that would leave my wife as she used to be. As you made her. Nice and normal.'

'Ha!' God laughed and slapped his knee. 'Well,' he thought,

313

'who knows? Who knows what peculiar sort of creature will come out of her, if what Man says is true?'

'Maybe I'll watch her awhile for myself,' said God. 'Then decide.'

So God began to watch Woman. And it was just as Man had said. She had become peculiar. Locking herself in Man's cupboard, laughing and weeping. And at the full Moon she did more than pace the floor, she ran out into the forest – letting out short, awful laughs, more like shrieks than laughs. She would come home next morning worn out, scratched, muddy, and sleep for a whole day.

At other times, especially at the new Moon, she would pace about Man's house, almost running, occasionally turning a few somersaults, or breaking into a wild whirling dance, where she seemed to have several extra legs and arms, doing the most amazing tricks – like dancing for minutes on end, her arms and legs spinning round in one blur, on top of a tiny stool, or bounding round the room from wall to wall without touching the floor, or scampering about the garden arched backwards with her face between her thighs at fantastic speed.

God shook his head. He was baffled. Maybe Man's idea was the solution. But whatever the crazy thing inside Woman was, how was he going to get it out?

He went to ask his old mother's advice. As he told her about Woman she seemed almost to go to sleep. She sat in her corner, her funny long hands folded over her head and her head bowed. When he'd finished, he thought she really had dozed off. But suddenly she said: 'It sounds like a Demon.'

God gave a start. A Demon? He was always forgetting about the Demons.

'A Demon's got into her,' his mother said again. 'Or, if not a Demon, something very like a Demon.'

'So what's to be done?' asked God. He felt quite helpless. 'Can't we get it out, whatever it is?' And he sat there wondering just what kind of Demon. Some sort of fly? Or worm? Demons can take any form.

Then, speaking very slowly, his mother explained what had to be done . . .

'. . . and that's your only hope,' she said when she'd finished. 'And it might go wrong.'

God went to find Woman. Instead, he found Man, stretched out on his bed, looking pale and ill. Man stared dully at God. 'She's gone off again,' he said.

'What happened this time?' asked God.

'Nothing,' said Man. 'I only said: "I love the black hairs on your legs." You know, you gave her a few sort of wispy dark hairs on her legs.'

God nodded.

'And she let out a terrible wail,' said Man. 'As if I'd reminded her of something dreadful. And she ran off into the forest. It's getting me down, God.'

'Today,' said God, 'we're going to fix this.' And he set off into the forest.

He followed her deep tracks in the soft jungle soil. She'd been running, her heels had made deep holes. Soon they came to harder ground and God had to use his sharp eyes. Suddenly he knew he was being followed. He slipped behind a great clump of lilies. And who should come along, bent double, inspecting his tracks, but Woman.

'What a nice surprise!' he cried, stepping out in front of her – but she had already fainted.

He carried her to his workshop and sat her in a chair. Her

head lolled, her limbs flopped. 'Wake up,' he whispered, patting her cheeks. But she was still out cold.

He stood scratching his head. What could he do if she wouldn't wake up? He felt painfully sorry for her as she slumped there, with her long eyelashes closed, her plump little mouth slightly open. Could his mother be right about her? Could she really be possessed by a Demon? His favourite among all his creations? She looked so delicate and pretty.

Just then his mother came in.

'Well,' she cried, 'aren't you getting on with it?'

God pointed at Woman. 'Shhh!' he whispered. 'She fainted. I scared her.'

'Ha!' crowed his mother. 'Fainted? A likely tale! You don't know the tricks of these Demons. Anyway, that's good. It makes it easier. Tie her to the chair.'

Woman stirred and moaned softly.

'Quick!' his mother almost screeched. 'Before she wakes up.'

God tied Woman's limp arms and legs to the chair.

'And a rope tight round her waist, tight to the chair,' cried his mother.

God did that too.

'And a gag,' cried his mother, and she gave him her own scarf. God tied the scarf round Woman's mouth, gagging her.

'Now where's the clay?' asked his mother. 'We've got to have the clay.'

God brought out a lump of clay, nicely soft, about the size of a pillow. He thumped it and kneaded it and shaped it roughly into a ball.

'Put that on the floor in front of her,' ordered his mother. God did as he was told.

Woman had opened her eyes. She stared wildly at God's mother. She knew about God – but God's mother – Man

316

had never mentioned God's mother. She tried to cry out: 'What are you going to do to me?' but only managed to gurgle. When she realized she couldn't speak, she was more frightened than ever.

'Stoke up the furnace,' cried God's mother. God began to shove logs into the great glowing doorway of the furnace at the back of his workshop. Woman rolled her eyes towards the jumping flames.

'Build up a good big blaze,' shouted his mother as the flames crackled into a roar. 'We want to get her red-hot through and through. The heat can't be too fierce. White-hot would be best.'

Woman now rolled her eyes towards God's mother, trying to make them scream for help. But God's mother bent over her only to say: 'Are you wearing any jewels, my dear? If you are, we might as well have them. The flames will ruin them and that would be a pity.'

Woman's eyes went dry with horror. She stared again at the flames, then at God's mother, and gurgled. She twisted in the ropes. Her toes and fingers writhed. But God's knots were good.

'Bring out the anvil,' cried God's mother, 'so we've lots of room to swing the hammers.'

God lifted the massive iron anvil out into the middle of the room, and leaned the two long-handled smith's hammers against it. His mother took hold of one of them and made a practice swing. She was immensely old, but that didn't make any difference to her power. As she whirled the hammer everything in the workshop seemed to flinch. When the hammer hit the anvil, Woman's head bounced as her chair jolted, and a spark stung her knee.

Woman had now closed her eyes and tears poured over her cheeks into her gag. Were these two actually going to shove her into the furnace and make her red-hot and then pound her with those hammers, as if she were a horseshoe? She tried to faint again but she couldn't.

God and his mother were inspecting the ball of clay.

'It should do,' his mother said, poking it. 'You see, there has to be somewhere, some bolt hole, for her good Angel to go. We don't want to hurt that, do we? So we make a hole in the clay, here, then her good Angel can dive into it out of harm's way.'

God made a hole in the clay, pushing his fist into the middle of the ball.

'That's enough,' said his mother. 'I've done this before. As we slide her head-first into the furnace, and as the flames get a really good grip on her, her good Angel will come whizzing out. You won't see it. But it will dive into that clay. There it will be absolutely safe. Then we'll simply roast her old body to a crusty crisp in the flames and pound it to dust with our hammers. And that will be the end of the mischief. It's quite easy. You can wet the dust and make fresh clay for something else afterwards.'

Woman's eyes seemed to want to leap out of her head and through the window. Her hair stuck out on end all round her face. Then she stared at the clay ball. At the dark hole in the clay ball. Then at the raging and throbbing glare of the furnace's open door. Then at the anvil. Then back at the lump of clay and the dark hole in it.

God was saying: 'And I suppose I can just remake Woman out of this ball of clay, with her good Angel inside it.'

'Clever boy!' crowed his mother. 'You've got it. It's all quite simple. Right. Now. Are you ready?'

And she fixed her great round hungry eyes on Woman with a savage glare, like a frightful Eagle. 'Into the flames with her!' she screeched, and God picked up the chair with Woman tied to it. He raised it over his head and took a step towards the furnace.

At that moment the ball of clay gave a thump and wobbled. God paused and looked at it. His mother looked at it.

Sure enough, it was squirming, like a sack with somebody inside.

In one great leap, God's mother pounced on the clay and with one smack of her hand closed the hole.

'Now,' she cried, 'quick. Get a shape on to this.'

God set down the chair, hoisted the clay on to his work-bench and began pummelling at it, pulling at it, tweaking it, pressing it, gouging it with his thumbs. He went at it non-stop, as if he were battling in a dark room with an invisible assailant. And at last he had it. And there it was. He held it up in his two hands, at arm's length, and laughed as it bunched and kicked and twisted.

It was a strange beast. And, true enough, it looked quite wolfish. But it was red – nearly the colour of the furnace flames. And its throat, and its belly, were white – even whiter than Woman's face, who lay there in her gag and her ropes, her eyes closed, once again in a dead faint.

Its slender legs were black, black as the wispy hair on Woman's shins. Its eyes were amber. And as it writhed, it seemed to laugh, and its fangs were white and curved like tiny new moons.

Suddenly it twisted right out of God's hands, hit the floor, bounced in one streak out through the door and was gone.

God's mother laughed a cackling sort of laugh, wiping her hands on her apron. Then she gently undid the gag from Woman's mouth and untied the ropes.

'Take her home,' she said. 'She'll need a good sleep now. We scared it right out of her.'

319

'So that was the Demon?' asked God, as he picked up Woman in his arms.

'That,' said his mother, 'was not quite a Demon. I'm not sure what it was. But it was very pretty.'

'Well,' said God, 'it looked to me like what I'd call a Fox.'

After that, Woman was a new person. A few days later, Man came to her very excited. 'I've seen a new beast,' he told her. 'A dazzling new beast. God really is getting better all the time. I met it on the path. It was so gorgeous I asked it to come home and live with us and be a pet.'

Woman pretended to be surprised as he described its red fur, its amber eyes, its slender, jet-black legs, its blazing white chest and chin and its miraculous lovely tail.

'And wouldn't it come?' she asked. 'Did it reply?'

She really did feel quite curious to know the answer.

'It replied,' said Man. 'It was very polite. It said: "O Man, O husband of glorious and beautiful Woman, it is the fear of being anyone's pet that has turned the tip of my tail quite white." And it showed me the tip of its tail. And, do you know, it was perfectly white.'

'What a pity!' said Woman, but she smiled to herself.

She never told Man what she had gone through in God's workshop. And God never told him either. So Man never knew the Fox had ever had anything to do with her.

But one day in his orchard he heard a soft clapping, behind his raspberry canes. Creeping close, he saw an incredible sight. His wife sat there, clapping her hands lightly, while the Fox danced round her on its hind legs, leaping and twirling, its wonderful tail floating round it like a veil, its silvery tongue hanging and its teeth flashing in its long smile. He was so astounded he simply walked right up to them crying: 'Wonderful!' But before he had finished the word, the Fox had vanished. In a flash, it was nowhere to be seen. Where had it gone? How could it disappear so completely, so quickly? Man blinked. Had he been seeing and hearing things? Woman stood up and yawned. She came towards him, smiling sleepily as if he'd wakened her up from a nap.

And Man felt so mystified that he said nothing. All he did was gaze at her, smiling slightly, frowning slightly. He simply did not know what to make of it.